MAD SCIENTIST JOURNAL

PRESENTS

THAT AIN'T RIGHT

Historical Accounts of the
Miskatonic Valley

EDITED BY
JEREMY ZIMMERMAN
AND DAWN VOGEL

Dn V
4/16/17

TABLE OF CONTENTS

FOREWORD

The first Lovecraft story I ever read was "The Music of Erich Zahn." It was collected into an otherwise forgettable anthology of "spooky stories" targeted at teen readers. I didn't have any idea who Lovecraft was at the time. But the story stuck with me. I would later be introduced more formally to the works of H.P. Lovecraft in high school, when a guy named Chad loaned me a bunch of Lovecraft collections in addition to a bunch of *Advanced Dungeons & Dragons* books. (I returned the Lovecraft. I still have his *AD&D* books. Sorry, Chad.)

But "The Music of Erich Zahn" has continued to stand out for me. It fostered a love of not only the strange but also a strange fascination with fictional locations. What started with Lovecraft's Rue d'Auseil expanded to include such locales as David Lynch's Twin Peaks, Sue Grafton's Santa Teresa, *Bioshock*'s Rapture, and the sleepy desert town of Night Vale. Places that seem larger than the stories they live in.

But Lovecraft's Miskatonic Valley has always held a warm place in the cockles of my heart. It somehow feels more tangible than many other fictional burgs. A horrible place that you might end up coming across on a dark and foggy night. Seeing it through the eyes of so many authors was a treat, and one I hope you will also enjoy.

This book would not be possible if not for the generosity of our Kickstarter backers. In particular, we would like to recognize the contributions of Stephen Acton, Don Ankney, Matthew Carpenter, Andrew Cherry, Terence Chua, Eric Cook, Bob Desinger, Zedd & BJ Epstein, Chris Gates, Darin Kerr, K. Kitts, Brendan "HollyKing" Leber, Marlo M., Jamie Manley, Steven Mentzel, John Nienart, Katherine Nyborg, Diane Osborne, eric priehs, Alx Sanchez, Deb "Seattlejo" Schumacher, Wendy Wallace, Catherine Warren, and You Know Who.

Yours,

Jeremy Zimmerman
Co-Editor

A MATTER OF SCALE

AN ACCOUNT BY DR. RILEY LOVEGOOD
as provided by Emily C. Skaftun

You know that thing where you become aware of something, then suddenly you see it everywhere? Like, maybe a year ago I saw cavatappi on a menu, and I had to ask the waitress what it was. The day after that, I was at the grocer and the only pasta on the shelves was *cavatappi*. Or anyway they had more than one brand of the curly noodles in stock, when I only just learned that they existed. It must have been there all along, right? Because the other alternative is that cavatappi was in the store *because* I was now aware of it, and that model of the universe is one I simply cannot live in. If that's the kind of universe we live in… well, I'm getting ahead of myself.

Let's assume these things have been around since the beginning.

I want to go back to the beginning. And that is my family crest.

Many of the older families of the Miskatonic Valley have shields with lions or gryphons or other beasts. Ours—it's sort of a symbol. It has a few sharp lines that seem familiar, like a rune or Cyrillic or Chinese character (but it's not—trust me, I've looked). It's bulbous and symmetrical and yet deeply *wrong*. It resembles an animal if you squint a certain way. If you ignore biology and allow for tentacles to replace most other body parts. If you accept that eyes are windows to the bottomless, meaningless, dark, soul-devouring depths of space.

But that's only if you accept that those things on the crest are eyes.

The symbol is like a Rorschach test, telling more about the beholder than itself. Furthermore, it's like cavatappi. Once you see it, you can't stop seeing it everywhere. Come to think of it, it even *looks* a bit like cavatappi.

Father saw it in the ocean. He thought a beast slumbered below, trapped on an undersea island. Actually, he thought it was a god, and that it was his destiny to find and awaken the god, who would then go on a rampage and destroy the fragile sanity (and home planet) of insignificant humans. I don't know why Father thought this was a good idea.

He sold the scheme to Miskatonic University as a scientific survey to discover what creatures live in the ocean's depths. Giant squid, perhaps. Not the Kraken, or Leviathan. Certainly not Cthulhu.

He didn't find it there, and returned a broken man.

It was Mother who identified the god Father sought as Cthulhu. She introduced him to a cult worshipping this and other demon gods, where his family crest was sensibly taken as proof that he was a chosen one.

I dismissed their obsessions. If I'd believed in their apocalyptic gods, I suppose I'd have feared them—I certainly fear the other cult members, with their worship of gibbering madness.

But I had more important things to worry about than sunken continents and mythical monsters. Rural New England escapes the scrutiny of, say, Appalachia, but a real problem of poverty surrounded us. Nutrition was an issue, as was hygiene, safe drinking water, and disease. So rather than devote my life to the search for ineffable evil, I became a doctor.

I kept a small office at the MU teaching hospital—mostly so I'd have an excuse to "run into" Gina, in Research—but most of my work involved visiting patients in their far-flung homes, bringing basic medicine to folks who really needed it.

༃

There is a lake just outside our town where children swim and old men fish. Nestled between craggy hills choked with mouldering pines, Needle Lake was shady all hot summer long, and frozen solid all winter. I always hated it. It was one of those lakes where one step off the bank puts you knee-deep in frigid water, a second step gets you waist deep, and by the third step you're swimming. The water was murky and, to my mind, menacing.

Who knew what was down there?

Legend said Needle Lake had no bottom, but I always knew it did. A lake that had no bottom would pass right through the Earth, and you couldn't just have a hole in the planet like that. Magma and other stuff would bubble up and fill it, and certainly water wouldn't stay in it. The truth was that no one knew how deep the lake was, until a few months ago. A team of cartographers from old MU finally surveyed it and came to the shocking conclusion that it was 1,666 meters deep, or 5,466 less evil-sounding feet deep. It was the deepest lake in the world.

Considering the lake's small size, this was even more shocking. Its sides must truly drop straight down, as though a giant bored a hole in the Earth. MU was determined to (literally and figuratively) get to the bottom of this mystery.

Of course, Father and his cult of lunatics were even more excited. This explained why he hadn't found slumbering Cthulhu in the ocean! All this time the god had been in our own backyard! His eyes lit up with manic fire when he heard the news.

Miskatonic still had Father's equipment from his failed oceanographic voyage, so they enlisted him to guide the deep-diving submersible, nicknamed DeeDi, into the bottomless pit, cataloguing what they found there. We were alone on the boat when he winched her aboard—none of the undergrads MU had assigned could stand to work with Father, so he'd roped me in as an assistant.

DeeDi swung to the deck with a gentle scrape, dripping mud and an ichorous green slime like putrid seaweed. Nevertheless, Father ran to it like a long-lost lover, hugging and nuzzling it like a kitten. "What eldritch secrets have you brought with you?" he whispered.

I turned my head away in revulsion, as he smeared lake-gunk all over himself. The trees on the nearest shoreline shook in a breeze. To me they looked like multi-limbed figures crossing themselves against a great evil. For the barest of moments, I glimpsed the symbol from my family crest among them, before flexible branches bent another way and the mirage passed.

ᚱ

I'd been watching the video feed as DeeDi explored the lake, so I knew no colossal monster slumbered there. There were barely any fish either, though they may simply have been nimble enough to stay out of DeeDi's headlights. The deeper she went, the less we were able to see through the stagnant murky water.

But that very murkiness told us that *something* was down there. When we putted into the dock, the first thing the undergrads did was hose DeeDi off with a high-pressure hose and decontaminants and collect the sealed samples she'd collected. They hosed Father off too, eyes darting askance at each other as they did.

I never knew for sure what DeeDi dredged up, as the University never released that information. I cannot actually prove that what came next came from Needle Lake.

But it did.

It took a while to notice the change in Father. He'd been nuts for years, maybe always, and he surrounded himself with people who supported and reinforced his insanity. When he started speaking in tongues, *Ph'nglui mglw'nafh Cthulhu R'lyeh wgah'nagl fhtagn*, and so on, he was at a cult meeting. The others simply joined in.

Soon, though, he became ill. He couldn't eat, and when he did he could keep nothing down. He spiked a high fever and shook with the chills it wrought. I carted him in to the MU teaching hospital after a day of this, but we couldn't save him.

Mother buried him in an ornate coffin, carved with the family crest. The day was drizzly and flat gray. And when I looked at the crest in the cemetery, clods of dirt raining upon it and turning to thick, dark mud, it looked like a virus.

Oh no, I thought. *What have we unleashed?*

Father wasn't the only one it was too late for. By the time he died, the hospital was full of people like him, ranting in a consonant-heavy babble and vomiting up their lives.

℔

After Father's funeral I went straight to the lab at the hospital. I didn't even change out of my black dress, just threw a lab coat over it, swapped heels for sneakers, and knocked on Gina's window. She looked up from a microscope, frowned, and then waved to me with gloved hands. She stood and stripped them off, opening the door with a geeky smile on her face. People were dying, but she had a mystery to solve, and her enthusiasm for her work couldn't be hidden.

I smiled back at her, despite a growing cold fear in my stomach.

"Riley," she said. "You've got to look at this." She stood behind the wheeled stool she'd just vacated, gesturing to the microscope's eyepiece.

I was terribly afraid I'd see a familiar shape. "Dammit Gina," I tried to joke, "I'm a doctor, not a microbiologist."

She didn't laugh. She just grabbed me by the shoulders and gently pressed me onto the stool. I bent my head to the microscope and saw—I really couldn't say. It didn't look like anything I'd seen before and, to my immense relief, it didn't resemble my family crest.

My relief was so immense I almost laughed. To think I'd almost believed in Father's end-of-the-world nonsense!

As I watched, one of the little blobs shivered and stretched and split into two. It seemed to happen very fast, but what did I know?

Gina explained to me, very impatiently, that this microbe behaved unusually. It seemed able to manipulate the host's DNA, yet it replicated using mitosis and a lot of other highly technical stuff that I mostly failed to follow. The kind of doctoring I did largely comprised prescribing antibiotics and ointments and referring patients to specialists. Joking aside, I was rusty on the biological basics.

I tuned back in when she said she could develop a vaccine. And then it was all I could do not to kiss her like that soldier in Times Square. Maybe for lots of reasons.

ɤ

Gina delivered the vaccine in less than a week. Many people died in that week, and MU was losing control of their carefully tended secrecy. Rumor had it the CDC was on its way to take over if we didn't clamp down on our disease STAT.

Gina tested it on herself, because she is a real-life hero. It worked, so we gave it to everyone. It even worked, in slightly modified form, as a treatment for people who'd already been infected. Overnight the death rate from the new disease dropped to zero, and everyone in the Miskatonic Valley sighed with relief.

I did a round to all of my rural patients, vaccinating all of them. The county made the vaccine mandatory in schools and offered it for free at the library and post office and all the chemists.

With the danger behind us, I took a break to mourn my father.

We hadn't exactly seen eye to crazy eye in life, but I found I missed him. Insane or not, it was nice to be around someone with that kind of certainty. Without him, life seemed ordinary. I often found myself drifting off, eyes locked on the crest above our fireplace.

A phone call snapped me out of distressing thoughts. "Help, Dr. Riley," the voice said. My phone's caller ID said Mike Maguerrin, but it didn't sound like his voice—it was discordant, almost inhuman in its depth, like there was a growl underlying it.

I asked a few follow-up questions, but he was unresponsive. I suspected tonsillitis or strep throat, made sure I had tongue depressors and flashlight, and set out to help poor Mr. Maguerrin.

ɤ

It was dark when I got to the Maguerrins' house, and quiet as a grave.

I rapped on the screen door, and for a long moment heard nothing. When sound came, it was in the form of an otherworldly wail that loosened my bowels. I admit that I almost dropped my medicine bag and ran like a ninny back to my car. But I'd taken an oath, and furthermore curiosity compelled me to see what was inside the house, even if it was some form of monster. I felt my father with me, his apocalyptic curiosity tugging me forward.

The screen door creaked open, and behind it I found the door unlocked. I pushed inward very slowly, calling out for Mike, or Clara, little Belle and even baby Billy. All I heard was a sort of whimpering from down the hall. I fumbled on the wall for a lightswitch, finally flicking on the porch light. It did little to illuminate the house, and much to lengthen all the shadows into eerie monstrous forms. But it was light enough for me to pick my way across the living room floor toward the hall.

The living room looked like it had seen a fight. A shoddy armchair had been overturned, and books and other detritus littered the floor. A lamp lay broken on the floor, still plugged in. "Mike!" I called again. "It's Dr. Riley. I'm coming toward your bedroom."

A grunting murmur was my only answer, and a scuffling that got louder as I approached the door. And then a little girl's voice from behind me nearly scared me out of my skin. "Dr. Riley," it said, and of course it was only Belle. I turned and saw her in the low light, a silhouette of a little girl clutching a baby doll in one hand. And yet something about it seemed off. I groped again at the wall for a lightswitch, and this time when I found it the light was almost blinding.

And what I saw... Words fail me. Belle was a little girl still, but she was also... not. Her skin was a bilious shade of green somewhere between mucus and seaweed, and her once-long hair was gone. In its place—and, indeed, in many places on her naked body—tendrils sprouted that waved and groped in the air with unspeakable intelligence. I could swear that some of them were eyelessly watching me. Her eyes were not a child's any longer. They were black pits deeper than the murk of bottomless Needle Lake. They were abominable eyes.

I recoiled, and stumbled backward right into Mike and Clara's room. In here, too, the light was off, but what spilled in from the hall was more than enough to reveal the unutterable horror that lay within. It was a monster. The very monster I'd feared through childhood, the very monster from my Father's fevered dreams. It writhed like a mass of snakes, shifting like a mirage of hot pavement. Its skin looked similar to Belle's, but with more maggoty limbs and more of the... tentacles... that sprouted from its head and torso and other parts I could not name.

Worse still, this creature that writhed and moaned and seemed unable to right itself—it had two heads.

"Doctor," Belle said, now quite near to my side, and her voice sounded rough and low, as though she were coming down with strep throat. "What's wrong with Mom and Dad?"

"Where are they?" I started to ask, but then I looked to Belle, festering and slimy-looking. I looked back at the two-headed thing in the room. As I watched, the heads grew closer together, like mitosis running in reverse. Ripples spread through the palsied, tentacular body, as mass shifted. And just then, one appendage flailed toward me, and as it did a glint of gold caught the light.

Against all sense I stepped toward the hideous limb and grabbed it, feeling my way toward what passed for fingers, where I'd spotted the gold. I had an icy weight in my stomach, already sure I knew what it was.

It was a wedding ring.

I threw the limb away from me, shrieking incoherently. If poor Belle was looking to me for help, she would be severely disappointed, for I could think of nothing but escape. The heads of the figure in the room shifted even closer to each other, blobbing into one. And for a moment, before the terrible heads resolved into one, I saw in the figure a shape so burned into my brain that I could never stop seeing it. But it was really there this time, big as life: two-headed Cthulhu, the Lovegood family crest.

But the horror didn't stop there. When I finally found my quivering legs under me and turned to run, for the first time I clearly saw the doll that Belle was holding. It wasn't a doll at all; it was baby Billy, his skin as leprous as the rest of theirs, but his head bashed in on one side. And she wasn't holding him by the hand either; their hands had grown together into one deformed appendage, linking them like paper dolls.

I drove without knowing where. But I wasn't surprised to end up at the hospital, rapping on the window of Gina's lab. I *was* surprised to find her there, it being late evening, and the crisis, as far as anyone knew, solved.

"I need to see it," I said by way of greeting. When her only response was a puzzled look, I continued, gesturing to her microscope. "The vaccine. Show it to me."

She nodded. "We've had some very... weird... reports of side effects. Rashes and such. Psychological effects. It's like nothing I've seen before."

I couldn't respond. On the one hand, to call what I'd witnessed *side effects* was the most enormous understatement ever. But on the other hand, I'd expected her to disbelieve me. I'd *wanted* her to disbelieve me, because I wanted to be wrong. Here in the hospital, under the harsh fluorescent lights, none of it seemed possible.

It took Gina a few minutes to prepare a slide, and in that time I doubted myself. Surely I'd imagined the whole thing. After all, madness ran in my family. I had seen a thing because I was looking for it, was always looking for it, thankyousomuch Father. I scratched absently at an itch on the inside of my leg.

When the slide was ready I leaned toward the microscope, prepared to laugh at my foolishness. I closed my left eye and squinted into the eyepiece with the right.

And there it was.

It wasn't exactly the same as the family crest, or the monster I'd seen at the Maguerrins' house. Not at first. But watch these wee beasties long enough and they'll show their fanciest trick. One of the cells in the slide stretched, parted, and slowly cleaved in two, replicating. And as it did, for a two-headed moment, it was the symbol from my crest, the missing puzzle piece in my descent into madness.

I stared long enough to watch it happen again and again. And more. The monstrous cells divided, but then they converged, and just as Mike and Clara had, they merged into one. The resulting cell was the same as the others, only larger and growing larger still the more of its neighbors it consumed.

An itch on the back of my hand brought me back to the present. I scratched it with my other hand and felt skin peeling off in thin strips under my nails. My eyes snapped down and, to my horror, I saw three perfect strips of scaly reptilian skin beneath what remained of my own flesh.

ಠ

I knew immediately how the story would play out. Mike and Clara Maguerrin had already become one, and Belle and Billy were well on their way. I had no doubt that it was happening in all the houses of town, in each one where people had been inoculated against Father's disease.

The cure was much, much worse than the disease.

They'd rise from their various homes and wander out, and when they met one another, they'd merge like mercury beads coming together. They'd merge and merge until—*Ph'nglui mglw'nafh Cthulhu R'lyeh wgah'nagl fhtagn*—until Father's vision, his—*my*—destiny was fulfilled, and Cthulhu rose.

Logic told me that Father would want to be a part of it, so there was only one sensible thing to do. It wasn't easy with my skin flaking away, but I enlisted Mother and the surviving members of the cult, and they helped me dig. I injected his body with the vaccine, hoping it would take hold despite the formaldehyde in his dead veins. The cult members took it from there. They chanted and held each other as their flesh putrified and they became one.

But I had other plans. Oh sure, I knew we'd all be together in the end, serving the Great One. But before that happened I figured I had one last human choice to make, the most human of all choices, really: I could pick who to be nearest to.

I chose Gina. I ran to the hospital, and this time I was not surprised to find her in her lab, her skin like a puddle of quavering jelly. It was hard to tell, with her face transformed into a blasphemous, throbbing mass framing eyes like infinite malevolence, but I swear she opened her tentacles to me.

DR. RILEY LOVEGOOD, daughter of esteemed astrophysicist Corina Elderbaum and marine researcher Thomas Lovegood, earned her M.D. from Miskatonic University and went into private practice. She's run several marathons and charity races, including a few zombie runs. These days, Riley spends most of her time with partner Gina as part of the ineffable evil overtaking New England.

EMILY C. SKAFTUN is a graduate of the Clarion West Writers Workshop, and holds an MFA in Creative Writing. If she could zap things out of this dimension there'd be a lot less traffic, chewing gum, and rain. Despite the inability (yet!) to vanquish rain, Emily lives in Seattle with her husband the mad scientist and a cat who thinks he's a tiger. She dabbles in roller derby and other absurd opportunities as they come along, while writing about fate, flying tigers, and strange fish. Emily is the Managing Editor of the *Norwegian American Weekly*. *Hun lærer norsk, men sakte.*

GOAT

AN ACCOUNT BY MIKE LE CLAIR
as provided by Nathan Crowder

In Archer Hills, the dusty little town in Texas where I grew up, football is king. Hell, it's damn near our God. Everyone remembers Troy Waubach, who went on to play wide receiver for the Denver Broncos fifteen years ago. Boys like me wanted to grow up to be lords of the gridiron. It gives us power, control, a way out. Then my dad got kicked to death by a horse, and Mom had to take a job in Danvers, Massachusetts, my junior year just to put food on the table. I begged for her to let me stay with Billy's family to finish out high school, but she wouldn't hear none of it.

I hated Massachusetts. It was cold. The locals were pale and quiet. And the Danvers High School football team sucked. And I mean sucked. I made varsity quarterback for the Danvers Falcons without hardly trying. The only other decent players on the team were Steve Lewis, who transferred in from Pittsburgh three years ago, and our star running back, Jimmy Dales. First game of the season we got beat 42-3. Second we lost 28-7.

We weren't kings. We were losers. Game coverage in the school paper got buried on page three. We needed a win, and we weren't going to get it against Arkham, who had won the state championship the year before. Our Homecoming game was coming the week after the Arkham game. Longtime rivals, the Dunwich High Black Goats, I hated them without knowing anything about them. Because that's how football rivalries worked. And if you couldn't win the Homecoming game, why bother?

So we got together behind the big, abandoned hospital outside of town, me, Steve, Jimmy, and a sixer of cold Sam Adams Jimmy lifted from his daddy's fridge. I had a plan. "We need to go send a message to Dunwich High. Something to let them know we mean business. Something to get up in their head."

"This is a bad idea, Mike," Jimmy told me. "We usually beat Dunwich. Why mess with them?"

"I don't know," Steve said as he intently peeled the label from his beer bottle. He was a defensive tackle, a big slab of meat with a crew cut and a 3.8 GPA. "Dunwich looks tough. They beat Arkham in their first game this season. I'm with Mike. Maybe we should do something. The three of us can't win the game by ourselves."

Jimmy drained the last of his beer, stared at us from under his mop of shaggy brown hair. He was a townie, grew up in the county, the last several years in Danvers itself. He always got skittish about driving on the back roads late at night. Full of superstitions about the outlying towns, like Innsmouth, Haverhill, Dunwich. Jimmy was one hell of a running back. But damned if he weren't jumpy about the craziest bullshit.

I leaned in. "You told me they had a bonfire the night before the game, right? Big pep rally bonfire to get the team whipped up?"

Jimmy nodded. "My cousin graduated from Dunwich. He told me about the bonfires."

"So maybe we get there early. Shake them up. No one will even know it was us."

Steve opened another bottle. His attention was off, away from us, down the covered stairs that led to the small cemetery behind the hospital. "Danvers is a small town, Mike. They might suck at football, but they're not idiots. When our team hears about it, they'll figure out it was us."

"We tell everyone we went to Boston," I told them. "Heck. We start telling people we're going to Boston and build up an alibi now. Then day before the game, we take my mom's car, race down to Boston and take a few pictures of us there, then race back to Dunwich and hit 'em. We post up our pictures from Boston and no one will know any better."

Jimmy took a long pull on his beer, a crooked smile around the lip of the bottle. "Shit, Mike. That could work."

"Goddamned right that could work."

"Ok, I'm in," Steve said.

"Yeah," Jimmy agreed reluctantly. "You're our quarterback. You call the play."

"Good. A week from Thursday, we hit Dunwich where they hurt."

Steve narrowed his big brown eyes. "How we going to do that?"

"We kill their mascot and string it up over the bonfire."

They paled, looked at each other, back at me, made ready with their objections. Pair of pussies like that, probably didn't want to get blood on their Chuck Taylors. But I grew up on a working farm and went hunting since I could carry a rifle. This wouldn't be the first animal I killed and gutted.

"I'll do the deed," I told them. "But you have to help with the ropes."

"I thought you meant spray painting something, or maybe cutting the tires on the team bus," Steve said. "We can't kill a mascot, even if it's just a goat."

"You won't have to kill anything," I said, my voice hard, like a general on the field, the quarterback. "I told you. I'll do it. That a problem for you, Jimmy?"

Jimmy's jaw was tight, his back straight. "I told you I was in. I'm in."

Steve didn't say anything. I tried to stare him down, but he kept his eyes turned away. To the ground, to the cemetery grounds off through the trees down the slope—anywhere but at me.

He'd come around.

That weekend, we lost to Arkham 37-13 and Dunwich won their game against Haverhill by an even wider margin thanks to the Haverhill star wide receiver missing the game with a broken arm. Dunwich was having a blessed season.

I didn't see Steve anywhere except practice. He started avoiding me like he owed me money. Saw me coming and ducked out the other way. I didn't try sending him texts to talk him into it. Shit like that was how people slipped up all the time. Leave no trail. That was the trick. Jimmy said he'd talk to him, that he'd turn him. I don't know if they talked or not, but Steve didn't show up to school on Thursday.

Fucking coward.

Jimmy was solid, though. He was waiting next to my mom's Saturn, his blue and white letter jacket next to the red car looked like a goddamned American flag. I felt a swelling in my heart at the sight. For a second there, it felt like I was home, like everything made sense. God, football, apple pie, the way it was supposed to be.

Me and Jimmy shot down to Boston like a goddamned Roman candle. Got a bowl of chowder, snapped a few pictures on our phones, hopped back on the road towards Dunwich. I could barely contain myself. This was what I had been missing. Not just football, but the understanding that football was more than just eleven guys fighting for every inch of the gridiron against another eleven guys. It was war. It was life. It was religion.

The dark, gnarled branches over the Miskatonic Valley road swallowed the sun. Shortly before we plunged into full twilight, our headlights lit the sign, "Welcome to Dunwich," on the narrow road into town. Barely dinnertime, and the place was a ghost town of old houses and scrabbly trees in rocky yards. Dunwich was a shit town. The tallest building was a pale church that scratched the night sky like a skeleton's hand. Dunwich didn't even have a McDonald's, and the only person I saw on the streets was a tall, thin figure walking a sickly dog in an under-lit park. This was the town that was kicking so much ass? It seemed hard to believe.

Jimmy must have figured I was nervous. I hadn't said a word since we drove into town. I had even turned off the mix CD I burned for road trips. "Everyone is probably having dinner," he told me.

"Whatever. Creepy goddamned town."

I made my way to the high school. Town this size, it wasn't that far. The place was old, brick, a three floor center section and three, shorter wings off the sides and back. Auditorium was on the left, the gym off to the right, with the dark athletic fields behind and to the side. We got there early enough to beat the pep rally, and there were only three cars in the lot with faculty stickers in the back window. Jimmy instructed me to pull around to the right, where there was a narrow dirt road back to the school groundskeeper shed.

Wasn't nothing but a steel garage back there—one of those pop-up buildings that you could buy at the feed lot or hardware store back home. It was big enough for a riding mower and the heavy training equipment for the football team. It was locked up tight from the outside, no lights on, no cars. We parked alongside, far enough to be out of sight should someone walk back that way.

"Now, where's that bonfire?"

"In the woods a bit," Jimmy said, taking a flashlight out of his pocket. "Never been there, but my cousin told me how to find it."

"And the goat?"

"The goat will be there." Jimmy's voice was quiet. I didn't question it. I reached under my car seat and pulled out the bundle I had tucked there first thing in the morning. A pair of knives and a cleaver, wrapped up in a sturdy apron. They had a familiar weight. It had been months since I'd gotten to kill something, and the anticipation was a knot in my chest. I tried to keep from smiling.

"You sure take football seriously," Jimmy said from ahead of me.

"What else is there? School sucks. The girls in Danvers are either ugly or don't care that I'm a quarterback. I used to think I might be good enough to get noticed, get a scholarship to a decent college to play ball. I figured if I can shine enough playing for the Danvers Falcons maybe I could get seen, but if we can't win games it's never going to happen. Back home, football was everything. We had faith in the Hail Mary. Worshiped at the fifty-yard line. Game night was a Friday night prayer meeting and the whole town was there. Here... it's like... hell, I feel like a missionary among the pagans."

Jimmy laughed. He ducked beneath the black twist of a lightning-blasted tree, turned back to smile at me. "Must be a Texas thing. This part of the country, Mike... I don't know. We can be a little old fashioned. Up here, church is church, religion is religion, and football is just football."

I hurried to keep up. I didn't like the woods. We didn't have woods like this back in Archer Hills. This was no sparse scattering of pines and cottonwoods. This was hardwood. Oaks and maples and hickory that might have been here for a hundred years. Their branches knit together, choked out the starlight. Their roots interwove, rippled beneath the dirt like black varicose veins. Everything was quieter here under the trees, made me want to whisper. The air didn't move.

"We almost there?"

Jimmy said nothing.

I raised my voice a bit, not realizing I had whispered my question the first time. "I said..."

"I heard you. It's not too late to turn back, you know." Jimmy stopped walking, turned off his flashlight.

I fought back my immediate panic over the plunge into darkness.

Up ahead, I saw a slight glow through the trees. A few electric bulbs, I figured, strung up to light the area around the goat pen. I didn't need Jimmy anymore. I could finish alone from here if I had to. The bundle in my left hand had the weight of grim intent. "Why would I do that?"

Against the distant glow, I could see the silhouette of Jimmy shrugging his shoulders.

To hell with this. To hell with him. I forged past, lured on by the glow of the lights. I had to walk slowly to keep from tripping over the uneven ground, but it wasn't far. It wasn't long before I saw the small pen with the attached shack next to a good-sized clearing. Wood had been stacked up around a wooden post in the center. The bonfire all set up, just waiting for the torch to set it ablaze. I could smell gasoline from the edge of the clearing. Gasoline and goat shit. Not a soul in sight.

After the cover of the woods, I felt exposed crossing the clearing to the goat pen. I kept low, scurried across the gap as quickly as I could. My mouth was dry. Heart racing. I pictured the hot, coppery gush of blood as I severed the goat's throat and my cock pressed against the zipper of my jeans. I missed this almost more than I missed winning.

The goat wasn't in the pen, so I figured he was in the attached shed, which suited me just fine. Less chance of someone seeing me in the act. I reached the door to the shed. Paused in the shadows to catch my breath while I checked the door. Just a simple hinge clasp. It wasn't even locked. Idiots. It was like they had never had a football rivalry before!

I twisted the hasp, opened the door, and slipped into the darkened interior.

Even in the total darkness, I could tell immediately that something was off. It felt too close. Too quiet. I couldn't even hear the goat bleat in fear, and I wondered if Dunwich might have already taken him out of his enclosure entirely. I fumbled for a light switch on the wall, found nothing. Reached out for a light cord, muttering, "Where's the goddamned goat?"

My hand touched a man's face. Doughy, brushed with stubble. From either side of me, a handful of people chuckled. The guy whose face I touched had a voice like molasses. Dark, sweet, devoid of mirth. "Goat's right here, boy."

I got tapped, a hard, crisp blow to the back of my head. The knives and apron hit the ground about a second before I did.

I don't know how long I was out. I woke up on my feet to more pain than I've ever experienced in my life. My shoulders were ablaze, and it took me a few seconds to realize that they were dislocated, the shoulder muscles torn. Through the pain, I realized the back of my hands were touching each other, tied behind me to a post. In my panic, I didn't immediately realize where I was. It was the overwhelming smell of gasoline that reminded me.

The bonfire. I was tied to the post in the middle of the goddamned bonfire. A line of figures dressed in hooded brown robes came out of the woods. They kept coming, joining in a wide circle around me. Could have been a hundred. Maybe more.

"I'm not afraid of you!" I lied, shouting myself hoarse. "You can't do this! This ain't right!"

Nothing. No mercy, no reaction. Just still figures, waiting, watching.

"It's just a goddamned football game, you bastards!"

I heard Jimmy's voice behind me. "So quick to give up your faith now that your God has abandoned you?"

I craned my neck to see him. Twisted left and right, even though the daggers of pain in my shoulders threatened to make me black out again. All I saw were the shadows of a few robed figures. My attackers, I figured. My attackers and Jimmy, my Judas. "Jimmy. You gotta let me go."

"I don't have to do anything," Jimmy said. "I'm not even here. I'm in Boston right now, texting a few friends about how Mike Le Clair dragged me to Boston, got pissed off, and ditched me. As far as they know, my cousin is on his way to pick me up and drive me back to Danvers."

I heard the sound of flames, saw the glow from a torch being lit behind me. The crowd that was gathered around us started chanting something. Dunwich had the worst cheerleaders I've ever heard. I couldn't understand a word of it.

"Jimmy, come on. This isn't funny anymore. You don't even play for Dunwich."

"Don't get me wrong, Mike," he said, lowering the torch to the gasoline-soaked wood. It erupted in a whoosh of flame. He practically had to shout to be heard over the sound of fire and me screaming. "I like the game. But it's not my religion. It isn't Steve's either, but he's lived up here long enough to know when to stay on the sidelines. Knows better than to be the goat. We have older ways in the Miskatonic, Mike. Much. Older. Ways."

MIKE LE CLAIR is a Texas-born high school football quarterback, recently relocated to Danvers, Massachusetts. A below average student, he was raised on a working ranch and has the drive of a natural-born leader. Anyone with information to his whereabouts should contact the Arkham County Sheriff's Department.

NATHAN CROWDER is a product of the great American southwest infused with enough pop culture to power a small city. Despite writing in a variety of mediums and genres, he is never far removed from a touch of horror. His works have appeared in the anthologies *Coins of Chaos*, *Blood Rites: An Introduction to Horror*, and *Cthulhurotica*. Online he can be found at Nathancrowder.com where he blogs about writing, media, and fringe candy.

THE CRUMBLING OF OLD WALLS

AN ACCOUNT BY NEIL GRAYSON
as provided by Craig D. B. Patton

'm not ashamed to admit that I'm writing this because I'm scared. More scared than I've ever been. I don't understand what's happened here since the storm. And if things get worse… well, there should be some sort of record. Something that maybe someone can use to figure out what took place. It'd probably help to include some context, so I think I should start by going back a bit.

God. I feel like I'm in high school again, splashing the hot mess of my emotions onto the pages of a journal. But this is not about me at all. And it's definitely not all in my head.

Karen and I met at a Halloween party in Boston. One of those corporate affairs with smoke machines turned up too high and too many people dressed as zombies. I went as Dr. Venkman from *Ghostbusters* because people tell me I look like Bill Murray anyway. Karen went in a black cocktail dress and had this bulbous, swamp green head piece with yellow eyes and tentacles. She looked amazing. Bizarre and unique and sexy all at once. So I walked up and asked her if she knew she had a squid on her head. She told me it was a Great Old One. I asked if she'd explain what that meant if I got her a drink.

She said yes and that was how it started.

Two years later we were married. Started out in my apartment, but she had always talked about wanting to live in Aylesbury where she grew up. Aylesbury was where she learned about the Great Old Ones. They were these monsters with complicated names in dark folklore tales. The sort of stories eccentric people tell kids to give them nightmares.

Anyway, at first I wasn't crazy about the idea. Aylesbury was a tiny town out in the woods in the north central part of the state. I'd grown up in Cambridge. I was used to the crowds and the energy of the city. I liked riding the T and going to the Museum of Science and spending 4th of July on a blanket on the Esplanade for the Pops concert. Karen liked it too, but not as much and it wasn't *home*.

In the end, I changed jobs to work at a company on 495 and started commuting on Route 2 so we could live in her childhood town. Lots of people live their whole lives here, I learned. It's not much more than a Colonial-era village with streets and buildings and businesses named after families who have been here for generations. Honestly, it's a bit rough around the edges. There are potholes in all the roads and some abandoned buildings, but Karen says it's much better than it used to be. Things are supposedly much worse across the Miskatonic River in Dunwich. Never been.

Aylesbury does have a strange sort of charm. I had never expected to fill out a rural mail delivery form with the postal service. Cell phone reception is spotty at best. But all in all, it's nice enough. I've enjoyed living among these rugged, thickly forested hills.

But all the trees brought trouble this October. A freak early winter storm dumped heavy snow and then ice overnight. I lay awake for hours listening to the sound of limbs snapping and trees tumbling down the ridge. By morning, we had no power and the roads were blocked by downed trees, downed poles, and dangling wires.

Five days later was Halloween. We still had no power, no cell coverage, and nobody seemed to know when we would have either. On the bright side, I was feeling good about storing up so much potable water, batteries, and propane before the storm hit. But I was getting stir crazy and told Karen I was going for a walk. She tried to stop me. Sort of. But after a couple of assurances that I would be careful, I set out.

Outside the full moon hung in a clear sky. The snowpack was splashing the moonlight everywhere. The world was aglow with it. I didn't even need the flashlight I'd brought. But the air was frigid. I was glad I had taken my winter coat.

The darkened streetlights were like fists raised by the utility poles in fury. The houses were as dark as the lamps. Not a single light or candle glowed in the windows. People were hunkered down, burying their bones beneath sedimentary layers of blankets.

It was the most boring Halloween night walk ever. There were no Jack-o-Lanterns shining on the steps. No motion-activated monsters lurching and wailing. No backlit faces leering out of windows. The neighborhood looked abandoned, like the world had ended and someone had forgotten to tell me.

I wound my way around the debris that had made the road impassable for cars. After a while I glanced up and stopped in my tracks. I had never seen such a sky. The lack of artificial light for miles around had unveiled an uncountable number of dim, distant stars.

A few houses further along I came to the first spectacular example of the storm's power. A massive limb had snapped off a maple tree and landed with the leaf-covered twigs down and the jagged, twelve-inch thick end bowing the utility lines. The next house had a birch tree leaning on the roof. The lines to the next house on the opposite side of the street angled sharply down from the pole and vanished into a thicket of fallen branches.

I came to a small clearing. At the back was an old stone gate framing the access road that climbed the trap rock ridge behind the neighborhood. The snow between the gate and the road looked pockmarked. I switched on my flashlight and shone the beam across it. There were dozens and dozens of footprints.

We had hiked the access road a few times. There was a cell tower anchored to an enormous exposed shelf of basalt at the top. I thought about how extraordinary the view from there would be. But I hesitated. It would take longer. Karen might wonder where I was and worry. I decided it would be alright. I'd be back soon enough. I stepped into a track of boot prints and followed them.

The access road arced in a lazy curve upward. I followed the prints as they twisted around or under the downed limbs and trees. It was an easy climb, popular with families, and I could see the tiny prints left by children's boots mingled with the others.

I was almost to the top when the tracks abruptly merged and turned left. A featureless muddy streak dipped off the side of the road, crossed the drainage ditch, and disappeared between the trees.

I shone my flashlight into the woods, puzzled. I hadn't known there was a trail there. It didn't look like much. There were no blazes marking it. But there are probably hundreds of unofficial trails in these woods. I had explored a few of them, but preferred to stick to the clearly identified ones. Karen teases me sometimes about being "a city mouse." As if wanting to avoid getting lost in the woods is silly. But I couldn't get lost if I just followed the tracks. Something the natives thought was more interesting than the view from the cell tower was out there.

Wary of slipping on the icy mud, I picked my way down off the road and followed the prints. After a short distance the path opened up, following a six-foot wide slot between two stone walls that angled sharply uphill. The seemingly endless series of crumbling, moss-covered walls in these woods amazes me. All of that work, hauling stone after stone to mark boundaries that no longer matter.

I kept the light trained close to my feet. The path was more rugged than the access road and I stumbled over rocks and tree roots. After several minutes of climbing, the rock walls ended where the ridge became almost vertical. I shone the flashlight up and saw that the path continued through a series of switchbacks to reach the top. Beyond the pillars of the trees at the crest there was open sky.

I started up, panting and puffing great clouds as I went. I was looking forward to teasing Karen. At least I had gotten my exercise. She had stopped doing yoga when the furnace went out.

There was a figure atop the ridge. I had thought I might find someone up there but it startled me anyway. I pointed the flashlight beam toward the stranger, keeping it low to avoid shining it in their eyes. But it wasn't a person. It was a statue.

It stood at the center of a clearing that ended at a cliff, the land plunging away to the rounded hills beyond. The statue was maybe nine feet tall and constructed entirely of branches and sticks. The head was like a giant bird cage made from slender branches. Thicker pieces framed the torso, thin sticks forming a dense weave between them. Beneath, branches as thick as my arm flared out and down to support it. I had the impression the statue was facing away from me, looking out across the Miskatonic River Valley to the north.

I walked closer, studying it. The branches and sticks were bound together with jute. Dozens, hundreds of tiny lashings and knots worth of it. An enormous amount of time and effort had clearly gone into creating the statue. It belonged in a museum or an art gallery somewhere, not hidden up here.

There was something inside the torso. At first I thought maybe a squirrel had built a nest. I shone the light on it. It was a jumble of narrow, folded pieces of paper. One was flared open and I saw elegant loops of blue ink. A line, flowing into a cursive "e" and "m".

It was a note.

I had a sudden memory of my semester in Japan as an exchange student. Our group had visited dozens of Buddhist and Shinto temples. At many of them, there were stations where visitors wrote prayers on strips of paper and then tied them to structures. Had it been the Buddhist temples or the Shinto ones? I couldn't remember. Neither made sense for the homogenous, white population of Aylesbury. People here think Olive Garden is exotic dining.

I walked around the statue. On the side facing the cliff the notes were bunched much closer to the surface. One was sticking a half-inch out. It would be easy to pull it loose. A stiff breeze might have done it.

I stood there looking at that note for what felt like a long time, resisting what I wanted to do. Finally I swept the flashlight in a slow arc around the clearing. I half expected to see a crowd standing there, arms folded, glaring at me. But I was alone. Satisfied, I looked at the note again.

I memorized the spot where it stuck out. It felt important that I put it back in the same spot afterwards. Respectful. Then I took gentle hold of the note and gave it an exploratory tug. A moment later it was in my palm.

The paper itself wasn't anything special. Standard, white office grade stock. I tucked the flashlight under my arm and unfolded the note. The rustling and crackling of the paper seemed impossibly loud and I glanced around. I was still alone, but my heart pounded faster anyway.

It skipped a beat when I saw the writing.

Black ballpoint pen strokes, squat lettering, the capital letters barely taller than the rest. It read:

I don't love him anymore. Release him, and a complicated name I can't remember the spelling of. Narlatotep. Something like that. It reminded me of the names in the folktales Karen had told me about. The stories of the Great Old Ones.

But it was the writing itself that bothered me more. It reminded me of Karen's. I tried to picture her cursive, how she formed each letter. But she hardly ever handwrites me anything besides signing a birthday card.

I read it several times. I licked my lips and tried to read it aloud, but had no voice. I could not speak those first four devastating words.

I shivered. I suddenly wanted very much to be home with Karen. Not out there alone in the dark.

I folded the paper back up with trembling hands and ran my fingers along it twice to crease it. I would put it back and then I would go home.

Taking the flashlight in my hand again, I shone it on the statue. I found the spot where I had removed the note—a narrow opening beside a stick shaped like a femur. But the note shook in my hand. It wavered past the opening.

I tried and missed again.

And again.

The fog of my breath had thickened. It was colder than when I had left home. Much colder. That was what was wrong, I realized. I shifted my grip on the note so that I had more control over the end. I just needed to concentrate.

I shifted my feet and that's when it happened. My foot struck something and I lost my balance. I lurched down and sideways. My knee drove into one of the statue's legs. There was a loud *snap* as it gave way beneath me. I tumbled backward to the ground, flailing at the statue to try and catch myself.

For a dizzy moment, I thought it would topple onto me. But it fell away from me instead, sticks snapping and cracking within it all the way down before it landed with a splintering crash. Then there was utter silence.

I got up slowly and shone the flashlight on the fallen statue. It was just a pile of brush now. Branches and sticks jutted out at all angles. Bits of jute dangled from some of them and hung in tangled clumps from others. Any resemblance to a figure was gone.

The notes had spilled across the ground beside it. I walked over and looked down at them. Many of them were open. I started reading one after another. I couldn't help myself. I'd already violated that place. What did reading a few of the notes matter?

Some, like the one that might have been Karen's, bore neat and precise handwriting:

My Mother is in so much pain. She's ready to die. Release her,

I don't know how to reach my son anymore. Release him,

I can't stop drinking. I've tried. Release me,

But on one, the letters were slashed in an angry scrawl:

I will no longer live in fear. Release me,

Another was stained with tears, the letters blurred:

I'm ashamed of what he did to me. But I'm more ashamed of what I did about it. Release us,

Still another bore the sloppy printing of a child in green crayon:

Plese make Daddy come back. I miss him. I love him. Relees him,

And every one of them ended with that strange name. Narlatotep or whatever. They were addressed to him. Or her. Or it. I don't know the stories well enough to guess.

All at once a wind rose from the valley behind me. The strips of paper fluttered and danced up into it, sailing in all directions and none. I turned and looked out past the cliff, out at the enormous night sky, out at the great and terrible canopy looming over us all.

What had I done?

I felt a rising buzz of unease, that primal itch along the back and scalp you get when you sense you're no longer alone.

That was enough for me. I hurried back down the path as fast as I could safely go. The beam of my flashlight danced wildly as I went. I saw jagged branches against the night sky, stark white skeletal shrubs, stones like misshapen skulls with recessed shadows for eyes. I only fell once, when I thought I heard something crashing through the trees in pursuit and looked over my shoulder. But there was nothing there and I scampered back to my feet and ran the rest of the way.

Karen wasn't home. I thought at first she must have gone out looking for me. But then I noticed her boots and coat still by the door. Even if she had just gone to a neighbor's home she would have taken them. I must have panicked then because I don't remember going back outside. I just know I wound up in the street calling her name over and over. There was no answer except for the rattle of branches and the rising howl of the wind.

It's been two days now. No sign of Karen. No sign of anyone. I've knocked at a dozen houses and no one is home at any of them. The doors are all unlocked, but that doesn't mean anything. People trust each other here, Karen always tells me. It's like a family.

But every family has its secrets. And I think maybe I stumbled into some of this one's on the ridge that night. I just don't know what any of it means. Tomorrow I'll pack food and other supplies into the car. I borrowed a chainsaw from Charles Blount's garage, since we're like a family. I'm going to try and drive out. I don't know how long it will take to find someone, but I can't just stay here. The wind has stopped and the silence is crushing. Even the birds are gone.

Guess that's it.

NEIL GRAYSON grew up in Framingham, Massachusetts. After earning a degree in advertising from Syracuse University he settled in Cambridge, Massachusetts, and worked for marketing agencies for several years, eventually transitioning into the region's booming biotech industry. He met his wife, Karen Davis, at a corporate party. The couple married two years later and moved to the north-central Massachusetts town of Aylesbury, where Karen grew up. Neil is currently an Art Director for Wargo Designs in Boxborough. He is a lifelong Red Sox fan who never believed in the Curse of the Bambino. His current whereabouts are unknown.

CRAIG D. B. PATTON writes stories, poems, flash fiction, drabbles, and other things made out of words. Some of his work has been published in *Supernatural Tales*, *Illumen*, *Wily Writers*, and other markets. He has a triptych of poems forthcoming in the Lovecraft inspired anthology *The Terror of Miskatonic Falls* (Shroud Publishing). He lives and writes in New England. You can learn more at flawedcreations. wordpress.com and follow him on Twitter at @craigdbpatton.

THE LAUGHING BOOK

AN ACCOUNT BY DR. ABIGAIL Z. PHILLIPS
as provided by Cliff Winnig

The Special Collections department at Miskatonic U lives in the basement, below the foundations of the old library. I've seen photos of that pseudo-colonial structure, all red brick and white columns. Its architecture evoked neither the purity of Grecian lines nor the principles of New England design. Rather, it recalled the temple of some antediluvian cult. Nobody but a few troubled and peculiar classics majors cried when it burned to the ground, its brick façade caving in from the heat. The new Whateley Library rose in brutalist glory, all concrete and glass, and loomed over an entire quadrangle, but no one who'd seen the old building ever complained.

Yet the subterranean vaults holding Special Collections predate even the old library. Following old Barnabas Elmsley, I descended the clean, modern stairs toward a thick, lead-lined door. Rumor had it they'd installed it to block trace amounts of isotope decay, which had interfered with the ethernet cables enmeshing the new building. Elmsley unlocked the deadbolt and heaved the door open with a grunt. Briefly, I wondered what a Geiger counter would show, and then I stepped through into the gloomy stone stairwell beyond.

There, I saw no trace of the vanished red brick. Instead, huge cyclopean stones lined the walls. As a Massachusetts native, I could tell the pale, fossil-filled blocks had not been quarried locally.

Elmsley flipped a switch on the wall. Ancient fluorescents flickered to life and bathed the giant bricks in their harsh light. The shadows cast by the fossils and other imperfections formed sharply delineated pools of black. Still, I could tell the upper stones had melted, their uneven edges full of troughs and crests. The latter seemed to reach for the door like petrified pseudopods. I saw a few red bricks had survived after all. They'd been shoved into place to help square these blocks with the wall, a final reminder of the old library. That meant that whatever flames had touched the ancient stones had predated the library fire. No sign of soot covered the blocks. Perhaps they'd been sandblasted clean at some point.

Elmsley turned to look up at me. "Mind the steps, Abigail. They're slippery."

He might also have laughed. I barely heard the papery sound above the buzz from the lights, but I smiled as if we'd shared a joke. "I'll be careful."

"A good attitude, miss." He turned away from me and gingerly made his way down the stairs. "Yes, a good attitude for life."

One might expect the stairs to be damp, but moisture vanished on this side of the door, replaced by a crisp chill. I understood now why it was worth the bother to put the university's most precious books down here. The river runs close enough to campus to make the air humid, especially now in the autumn. Books can decay if one doesn't take precautions.

Though dry, the stone stairs were smooth with the characteristic groove from the tread of many feet. As I carefully descended, I wondered whose feet had worn those grooves, and when, since almost nobody came down here now. If I hadn't been doing a special reading course with Dr. Hite, I wouldn't have permission to be here myself.

I'd picked him precisely because he could and would give me that permission, let me work with texts even the other faculty members weren't allowed to access themselves.

The stairs turned sharply to the right, and then again. Presently they opened into a narrow room with wooden desks against the side walls. All but the far wall showed bare pale blocks. Elmsley squeezed between the desks to the wooden door set into that wall, which was itself frosted glass. He pulled out his key ring and unlocked it, then turned to me where I stood a few paces behind.

"Your slip, please."

"What? Oh, sorry." I reached into my jeans pocket and fished out the paper Dr. Hite had signed, with the catalogue number of the *Codex Hedersleben*. Its official name bore the small German town of its discovery, but unofficially those who knew of it called it the "Laughing Book," due to the disturbing illustration that appeared on its frontispiece. Like most scholars, I'd only heard of the drawing. The university had never permitted it to be published.

Elmsley took it and frowned, as if he disapproved of my research materials. Finally he nodded once, frowned more deeply, and told me to wait at one of the desks. He stepped through the door in the back wall, and I caught a glimpse of the stacks: metal shelves with glass doors, each one locked. A variety of books lined the cases, some oddly shaped, and others bound in bizarre materials. Then he shut the door and locked it behind him, and all that remained was a vague sense of movement through the frosted glass wall.

I turned and surveyed the room. The desks were all plain, worn, and old. The wooden chairs pushed under them looked equally uncomfortable. At the far side of the room, near the entrance, stood a small round table holding a cup of pencils and a stack of note pads, all that was allowed in Special Collections. I'd had to leave my purse, my phone, even my jacket back at circulation. I was glad for the sweater I'd thought to wear, at least. The place was freezing.

And something about the bricks bugged me. I leaned over a desk to examine one closely. I'd taken common core biology, but I didn't recognize any of the tiny fossils, spiraling shells and bodies with spines of unknown function. They might date back to the Cambrian for all I could tell. But that wasn't what bugged me. It was the color of the rock itself.

"Like it's familiar," I told the empty room. "Even though it's totally alien."

I heard the door in the back being unlocked, then opened. "What's alien, Abigail?" Elmsley emerged, carrying a thick book bound in grey. He placed it gently on the desk I'd been leaning over.

"Oh, the bricks they used down here."

"You'll get used to them. Special Collections closes at five. Ring when you're ready to go, and I'll come to put the book back."

For some reason, I found the thought of his leaving me alone disturbing, even though it made sense. Elmsley did more than just run Special Collections. Dr. Hite had vouched for me, so I could be trusted to be on my own.

"Ring?"

He nodded towards a rope I hadn't noticed that hung behind the round table. "Just pull." Without a farewell he made his cautious way back up the stairs.

I watched him go till he vanished around the turn. I suddenly realized that without my phone, I'd have no idea of the time. Next time I'd bring an old-fashioned watch, but for today I'd just have to guess. I'd come to the library at ten, so as long as I didn't get lost in my research…

I looked down at the book. The leather binding was white at the corners, as if perhaps that had been the original color. No writing adorned the cover. "Well, you'd better not be *too* interesting, or the next thing you know—"

A loud clang echoed from above, followed by the unmistakable sound of a key turning in the deadbolt. Elmsley had locked me in.

I grabbed the back of the chair and tried not to hyperventilate. *He's just taking precautions*, I told myself. *Standard procedure. He's not going to entomb me down here. I can always call for help, at least if I can get a signal.* I rolled my eyes. "If I had my phone."

My rational brain knew that whatever happened, he'd be back before five. So even if for some reason the bell didn't work, or nobody heard it, the worst that would happen is I'd miss lunch. I was a grad student, so that was nothing I hadn't survived before.

Besides—look around, Abigail. See any other students with access to Special Collections? Summoning the gumption that had gotten me here in the first place, I crossed to the table, picked out a pencil and pad, and returned to my desk. I resisted the urge to yank on the bell rope while I did these things. I pulled out my chair, sat down, and slowed my breathing. *Now this book...*

This book, I hoped, would be the keystone for my dissertation. Like several other medieval texts, it purported to detail travels to distant lands. According to summaries I'd read, it described the many unlikely peoples and animals its author had encountered along the way. It also contained highly detailed drawings of them. I expected some crazy adventures by mariners who'd probably eaten too much ergot-ridden bread before landing. It would have fit neatly into a dissertation on the fantastic in medieval travel literature, had I been writing one.

But no, my dissertation was on actual European travels to North America. Leif the Lucky was all very good, if well-trodden, scholarly ground, but this book predated him by a century. What had sparked my interest was a footnote to an article by Blackwood and Smith in *Massachusetts Botanical Review* of all places, to which Dr. Hite had called my attention. They asserted the leaves and roots painstakingly described and illustrated in the codex matched flora native to New England. In other words, the Laughing Book's author had been here a hundred years before Leif Ericson discovered Vinland and, having written down what he'd found, returned to Germany.

I hoped. If—after a year cramming as much Old High German into my brain as I could—I could read the darn thing. And if Blackwood and Smith had been correct. And if I could tell truth from fancy when I looked at the manuscript.

I opened the book. The endpapers were newer, added by an eighteenth century binder, and depicted a vaguely floral pattern in faded black. I turned quickly to the first page, and to its left I saw the frontispiece.

How to describe the creature? It might have been meant as a cockatrice. Its scaled bird body had a long, snakelike tail that wound between three stalks on top of its bearded human head. At the top of each stalk was another head, but not at all animalistic, or even human. The first seemed to be some sort of astronomical symbol, though with a face of sorts drawn between its lines and curves. The second held a sun, and the third a moon. Both had faces as well. The tail wove between the three stalks and ended in yet another face, this time a bird's. The bird looked down at the bearded human face, which looked back at it. All five faces were laughing, as if sharing a joke. From their look, though, the jape must have been barbed, maybe full of what the Germans call *schadenfreude*, delight in the suffering of others.

Someone chuckled behind me.

I leapt up, knocking down the chair, which banged into the chair behind it, then thudded onto the floor. No one was there, of course. I closed my eyes and breathed until I felt my pulse begin to slow, then opened them again. Still no one but me, the book, and the fossils in the walls.

"Well, Abigail, we're off to a good start," I told myself. "Let's see if we can *read* some of this book before Elmsley comes down with a butterfly net to cart us off, eh?"

I righted my chair, sat down, and turned the page.

ᚱ

That first day the work went slowly. The German proved thorny, and the handwriting took some getting used to. Plus the fear of being locked up and forgotten built until I finally did pull the bell rope. I didn't hear a sound, but maybe ten minutes later—it felt like years—Barnabas Elmsley returned to fetch me. Turns out it was just past one.

So I grabbed a late lunch of pizza and a latte at the Div School coffee shop and read over my notes. Though I'd translated only the first two pages, I'd also copied one of the illustrations as best I could. It was of a conical helm. I'd have to compare it later to my Dover book on medieval armor, but I was pretty sure I'd never seen anything like it.

I went home, brushed up on Old High German declensions, and fell asleep. When I woke the next morning, I knew where I'd seen blocks like the reading room's: in my dreams, dreams I'd been having for some time, only to forget each morning. But now, having seen the ancient bricks, I could pin those phantasms in my memory like insects in a display case.

I'd been a warrior, a regular Joan of Arc, fighting monsters through a medieval version of Arkham. Only this town, in addition to being all thatched roofs and wooden walls, boasted a castle that looked suspiciously like the Misk U campus, but made out of the strange pale stone. I fought creatures that screamed with mouths within mouths, creatures whose voices buzzed inside my head, and silent, deadly fungoid assassins. Always I gritted my teeth and fought bravely until I heard the laughter. It seemed to come from the cloud-shrouded sky above, but no—it was the cockatrice thing from the frontispiece, a hundred feet tall, all five heads watching me, laughing.

I wanted to ask Dr. Hite about the drawing, but he taught all morning on Fridays. Instead I headed back to the library, determined to spend a few more hours with the book before I saw him.

As before, Elmsley led me downstairs in his slow, deliberate way and fetched me the book. This time before he left he squinted at it and grinned. At least, I think he grinned. On him it came out like a rictus. "You like the pictures?"

"Oh you've seen them?"

"You see a lot of things down here."

I waited for him to finish the thought and grew impatient when he didn't. "In the books, you mean."

"Eh? Oh yes. I've been working here a long time, you know. A long time. Since before the old library burned down."

I resisted the urge to ask him the story behind that fire, telling myself with Elmsley I'd lose the whole morning to it. This time when I heard him shut and lock the lead-lined door, I felt only a sense of missed opportunity. *Oh well, I'm sure I'll get it from him one of these days. It's not like I won't be here a lot with this book.*

I turned back to the page I'd been working on, but then on a whim I started skimming, flipping through the book and looking at all the pictures. I found more examples of ancient pieces of armor and weaponry, again nothing that quite looked familiar, and detailed drawings of plants. I imagined the author had started his trip on the coast, doing botanical drawings and finding the odd rusted helm or dagger from some ancient skirmish. Traces of other explorers, even earlier? Perhaps.

Then pictures of animals appeared. I saw a raccoon and grinned. Yes, the author had reached North America. In the late ninth century. I leaned back in my chair, savoring my moment of triumph.

I must have laughed. At least chuckled. In any case, the sound echoed strangely in the room and the stairwell beyond. I thought I heard other voices, deeper, harsher, laughing along. This time I didn't leap up. Instead I froze. When the last echo died, I lowered my chair and waited. Nothing. No laughter, no monsters coming out of my dreams to fight me.

Maybe I'll just copy some of these drawings, especially the raccoon, to show Dr. Hite this afternoon.

I stood and padded over to the table with the pencils and pads. As I reached for a stubby #2, I heard another laugh behind me, from the direction of the book.

I didn't turn. I just pulled the bell rope and waited.

The laughter continued.

Great. I'm going crazy. This book is everything I hoped it would be, proof of the earliest visit from Europe to North America, all I need for my dissertation to be wonderful. Except that I can't actually read the book, because the only room in which I'm allowed to read it is so weird, I start to hallucinate.

Still the laughter continued. Then came a scratching sound, like a dog pawing at a door, followed by a series of clicks. I squeezed my eyes shut.

At last I heard Elmsley turning the key in the deadbolt and the door swinging open.

I felt a rush of air, so strong and sudden it nearly knocked me forward onto the table. Pounding sounds came from behind me, as if broom handles were banging on the tops of the desks at my back.

The laughter, at least, had stopped. I opened my eyes to the empty room. *Of course it's empty. I knew it would be empty.* Nonetheless, I wanted to leave, and right now. I took a step towards the exit and froze again.

The scream barely sounded human, but I recognized Elmsley's voice just the same.

ᚱ

I'm not really sure how long I stood there at the bottom of the stairs. I kept thinking someone else would come. Someone else had heard him scream, hadn't they?

I dismissed the idea of its being another hallucination. My imagination could not have come up with that sound. Surely not. I've taken first aid and CPR courses, but this hadn't sounded like a fall or a sudden heart attack. It had been a scream of terror, and it had been cut off.

Alone in the reading room, I strained my ears for something else, even the sound of Elmsley breathing, but I heard nothing. Eventually, I knew I'd have to see what had happened. There was no retreating. I could hide under a desk, or I go look.

I checked my watch. It was now almost noon. Time to go find Dr. Hite. I covered my mouth to stifle a giggle, not so much for fear of being heard by whatever might have attacked Elmsley—and was still lurking on the stairs above me?—but for fear of never being able to stop.

I crept silently past the first bend, then the second. I saw the blood pooling in the grooves of the stairs before I saw the body. Blood silently filled the depression until it spilled over the side, formed a tiny waterfall, and began to fill the next stair down. It had trickled its way down five stairs by the time I arrived.

Above the blood, just outside the open door, lay Elmsley's body. At least I thought it was Elmsley's body. It was dressed like him, in his conservative suit, cut as if for a younger, healthier version of himself. It clutched Elmsley's key ring in its pale, bloodless hand. Only I couldn't truly be sure, since his head had been bitten off.

This time I didn't bother trying to slow down my breathing. I just kept climbing the stairs, keeping to the side of the blood-filled depressions, until I reached the door. Then I stepped carefully over the body to stand on the landing.

I heard a scraping sound behind me, coming from below. Without thinking I grabbed the keys and tried to shove the door closed. The body was in the way of course, and in my panic I couldn't bring myself to drag it away.

There wasn't really time, anyway. A second or two later a figure stepped into view around the bend in the stairs, and I looked into my own eyes.

Well, my eyes as they'd be if they were a pale, pale grey. But the face was my own, if you allowed milk-white hair and ivory skin. Oh, and armor that looked like it stepped right out of the Laughing Book, which now that I thought about it, might have. She held a longsword in her right hand and a wickedly serrated dagger in her left.

My doppelgänger's eyes widened as she glanced at me, the body, and me again. No, not me again. Past me.

"Get behind me!" she hissed. "Now!"

I leapt poor Elmsley's body, slipped in a puddle of blood, and slid down to the next landing, where I banged my knee on the far wall. The armored girl ran past me and, with a wordless cry, attacked whatever she'd seen behind me.

What the hell. I looked.

The creature might be something from the Laughing Book. Maybe I'd find its illustration if I went down and checked. A dozen segmented legs supported a bloated, tubular body. On each end of the body was a head. I couldn't see much of the far one, but the near one sported a circular mouth with multiple rows of teeth, surrounded by six or seven eyes somewhat evenly spaced. The eyes appeared totally human, which leant a strange air of pathos to the beast. It seemed to be pleading with me. At its far end, the other head turned. I watched it chew and swallow.

Then the girl stood between us. She hacked at one of the eyes with her sword, but apparently just to distract it. As it wailed, she dove below and used the serrated dagger to open its belly. Viscera burst from the thing's gut, poured over my savior, and flowed down the stairs. As the bowels came apart, Barnabas's gnawed and blood-covered head popped out. It began to roll towards me.

That got me moving. I retreated to the reading room, which

thankfully contained only the furniture and the still-open book. I slammed the book closed, then realized I was still clutching the keys. *The stacks!* I could hide there for days, I was sure of it.

I tried the first one I grabbed, but it didn't even fit in the lock. I tried the next, and the next, and...

The sound of boots coming from the stairs made me spin around. My gore-covered savior slipped past the desks—getting slime all over the backs of chairs—and grabbed me by the wrist, though not ungently.

"We have to go."

I nodded. "I know." I held up the keys.

She grinned, then noticed the book and frowned. "I might have known. Take that."

I grabbed the book and tried to hand her the keys, but she'd already opened the door.

"It was unlocked?"

She nodded. "The *vrak-larunn.*" She must have seen my blank look. "One of its heads can pick locks." She took my wrist again, dragging me into the stacks. We rushed past volumes I'd have gladly taught freshman history for a year to peruse for a single minute. Yet given what I'd just witnessed, I had no trouble keeping up.

An ancient-looking iron door was set into the back wall of the stacks. My guide pulled out a key of her own, unlocked it, and ducked inside. It led to a narrow, low-ceilinged tunnel of bare stone, one step up from a natural cave. And it was dark.

Not wanting to touch her gore-covered armor, I followed the sound of her footsteps. She led us down, then up, then finally out onto a hillside in another world.

ࢗ

The landscape, while alien, reminded me of my native Miskatonic Valley. Rolling hills stood in the same basic configuration, covered in the elms, willows, and pines of home, but the stone had the pale shade of the blocks back in Special Collections. And the sky...

Though cloudless, it stretched chalk white from horizon to horizon. The sun, if that's what it truly was, could barely be distinguished—a bright sphere of white surrounded by the dead-white sky. I tore my gaze away. It felt as if that star might seep into my soul and drain my life and energy as it had the sky's.

Naturally, I recognized it all from my dreams.

"Where are we? And, if I may ask, who are you?" Not to seem rude, I added, "I'm Abigail Phillips."

My guide turned and, to my relief, smiled. Despite the gore and the ivory skin, I recognized that grin from the mirror. Genuine happiness. "I'm Avigraal d'Arrukam. We should be safe now for a while."

I returned the grin. "I, uh, want to thank you for saving my life."

Avigraal shrugged, as if she did this sort of thing every day. Maybe she did. "My pleasure. It's not often I get to rescue myself, or at least my analogue." She cocked her head sideways, looking at me. "You are from the other Arrukam."

"Arkham, you mean?"

She nodded. "That's how you say it in your world, I suppose. Come. It looks like rain."

She led me downhill into a stand of dogwood. Just beyond we came upon her horse, or what passed for one. Pale, like his rider, with a zebra-striped mane. He had claws instead of hooves and the sharp teeth of a carnivore. Avigraal patted his neck and swung herself into the saddle. She held out a hand to help me, and I climbed up easily enough. I had no choice but to put my arms around her as we rode, though at least the coating of viscera seemed to be drying. A bit. I tried to ignore the smell.

Despite his feet, Avigraal's beast felt like a real horse, even after she urged him into a canter. He moved in near silence on the wooded path.

For the first time since I heard the phantom laughter, I felt safe. Perhaps that's why I started crying. Huge sobs shook my body, one after another. Avigraal said nothing, offered no comfort beyond her presence, but that was enough. I clung to my pale double until the tears dried and the rain began. At first, the rain seemed a comforting thing, the patter of water on leaves reminding me of my own Miskatonic Valley, of my home. Then we broke from the cover and began to get drenched. I had nothing more protective than jeans and my sweater, but Avigraal reached into a saddle bag and pulled out a wool cloak.

"Put this on."

"What about you?"

"My armor's Arrukamish. It won't rust from this rain. Besides, you need to protect the book."

I threw the cloak over myself and the Laughing Book, pulled the hood over my head, then watched the rain slowly rinse viscera off Avigraal's armor. The drops were not clear, but a milky white, as if they'd picked up chalk dust on the way down. Maybe that's what made the sky white, I thought, but the rain didn't smell of chalk. Now that Avigraal was being washed clean, everything smelled of home. Even her mount smelled like the horses of my childhood.

In the distance, our destination sat at the valley's base: the medieval Arkham of my dreams, bright castle where the university stood in my world.

"Arrukam, I presume? It's beautiful."

"Heh. From a distance, for certain. You did well back there."

I chuckled ruefully. "Sure I did. I slipped in a puddle of blood, fell down the stairs, and ran away." My knee still ached a bit, a silent accuser of my cowardice.

"You knew enough not to get between a *vrak-larunn* and its prey. You had no armor, no weapons, no training I imagine, not in your world."

"I've had a few years of aikido."

She turned and gave me a quizzical look.

"A martial art. It involves throws and rolling out of falls. Not that you'd know it based on today."

Avigraal laughed. "I'm sure they don't teach you to fight on wet stairs."

"Well, that's true."

"They should."

"I'll mention it to my sensei next time I'm in class, assuming I ever get home."

"I think you might. We'll ask the duke. He can help you. Just don't lose the book."

"The man who wrote it. He visited Arrukam, didn't he?"

"Yes. From across the sea."

"And from my world."

"Might be. Ragnol the Lost."

"The lost?"

"You'll see."

"Wait, are you saying the author of this book is still alive? It's over a thousand years old!"

"Time between your world and mine flows strangely."

"So years could pass back home while I'm here?"

"Or less than an hour. I could not say. You will see, if you make it back."

I stayed silent for the rest of the ride, rolling that thought over and over in my mind. I'd make it back, I resolved at last. I couldn't afford to act like I had on the stairs, or even before then when Elmsley had locked me in. I'd push back the fear and keep my center, as my sensei would say. And I'd be clever.

We passed farms and a few desultory herds of sheep before we crossed into the town proper. There, everyone had pale skin and white hair, like Avigraal. Their clothes were a bit more colorful, if worn and faded. They looked like a mime troupe from a Renaissance faire, albeit a dolorous one. No, not dolorous—hostile.

"Why are they staring at us?" I whispered.

"Hush. Keep the cloak tight about you. They see your skin and hair and do not trust your humanity. They are peasants. They know nothing of Arkham."

I did as she said, yanking the hood as far forward as it would go and burying my face in her back. Still, I heard the angry whispers, saw their glares from the corner of my eye.

We rode past the castle gates into a courtyard that looked like Misk U's humanities quad. She reined in her beast on the far side, in front of the administration building, only here it was the main keep. We dismounted and, as the rain had stopped, left the cloak with the groom who took her beast. I followed her inside.

We passed through an atrium. Armored guards opened thick bronze doors, and we entered the great hall. Compared to everywhere else I'd seen in this world, the room held a riot of color. Above a gallery, high stained glass windows lined the walls, painting that white sky a dozen bright shades. I quickly turned from them, though, with their graphic scenes of knights and monsters killing and dismembering one another.

We passed a few dozen courtiers, dressed in elaborate finery of many fabrics and textures, all white but bathed in the many colors cast by the windows. Though dazzling, they didn't compare to the figures at the dais on the far side of the room.

One looked like me, in that he had Caucasian skin, brown hair, and deep blue eyes. After our ride through Arrukam, the colors seemed strangely demonic even to me. The man wore motley of jet and gold, though with an air of long-suffering dignity. An iron chain ran from his neck to a bolt at the foot of a throne carved from a single block of that fossil-filled stone.

On it sat the being who must be the duke: a hooded and robed figure whose body appeared made out of shifting, shimmering sand. It rippled across his featureless face to breezes I could not feel, and it glittered like mica.

Avigraal crossed to the edge of the dais and dropped to one knee. "Your Grace."

The sand under the hood shifted to the face of a grinning man. It stayed that way, unmoving, even as words issued from it. "Rise, brave Avigraal." He spoke in Modern English, as she had with me on the ride. "Have you news of the castellan?"

Avigraal stood but kept her eyes down. "Aye. Sad news, Your Grace. The *vrak-larunn* reached him before I did."

"Elmsley?" I asked, too incredulous to keep silent. Avigraal shot me a sharp look. I ignored it. "He was your castellan? Here?"

She glowered at me. "No, you fool. His analogue."

The duke took in the exchange in silence, but the sands shifted his face to stern disapproval. "Let your analogue speak. You brought her here for a reason."

"Only to save her from the nightgaunts. When they smelled the blood of the *vrak-larunn*..."

"Of course." The duke turned to me. "It will not be safe in your world for a while yet. They will come and take away any who saw."

"Elmsley?"

"Only if he saw the body of the *vrak-larunn*."

No way to know until I returned, I supposed. If I returned. "I'm sorry about your castellan."

The duke inclined his head, faceless again. "He traveled between realms, knowing he risked the beasts of the threshold."

The fool cackled, a strangely melodic sound. "Oh my liege, oh my liege, give Ragnol leave. I would take this pretty thing back to my king, far across the sea, the sea, the heaving sea." He stepped toward me till his chain grew taut, his smile widening. "You see, you see, the book is with me. She holds it in her hand, the book I penned, before ever I lay eyes on the Laughing Beast."

The duke's face shifted to a mask of mirth. He reached down and pulled at the chain, jerking Ragnol back. "That isn't your book. That's your analogue's book."

The fool frowned in puzzlement.

The duke's face vanished, replaced once more by the shifting sands. "You remember Ragnarrl the Sad, my old fool. He found you across the sea and a world away, brought you here to show me the miracle. You killed and ate him for his troubles."

The fool clapped his hands. "He spun on a spit. His jester suit fit! How could I have not made him die, when his clothing did fit? I ate, I ate, and the meat tasted great!"

"And now you wear a chain, my pet. But you rhyme like old Ragnarrl and tell queer stories."

Ragnol hopped up and down. "I do! I do! I'll tell you one too, if you give me the girl as meat for the stew!" He winked at me, and I stepped back. He didn't wait for his duke's reply, but started singing at the top of his lungs. "Oh I knew a thief, a jolly old thief, who had a daughter fair—"

Throughout this exchange, Avigraal stood silent and stoic, but I feared Ragnol's bargain, even if the duke hadn't really agreed to it.

"Wait!" I held up the Laughing Book, certain now that here in the castle lay the real *Codex Hedersleben*, the one written in my world that described my version of North America. "I'll gladly exchange this for Ragnol's book."

The duke's face returned, this time looking thoughtful. At its appearance, Ragnol's voice faded to sullen silence.

"Show it to me," said the duke.

As I stepped forward, I grew aware of a commotion behind me.

I turned to see the bronze doors open with such force they banged against the wall. A soldier entered, visibly terrified. "My liege! The children! The piper's returned them."

The duke rose. "No!" He moved towards the soldier and fell apart. Glittering sand cascaded from his cloak. It splattered on the dais and flowed toward the door, reaching it in seconds. Avigraal drew her sword and strode after him. I stood gaping, unsure what to think. Outside came the laughter of many children, yet it had an edge to it. Animalistic. Red in tooth and claw.

I moved to follow Avigraal, when a hand grabbed my shoulder.

"And where would you be going this bright, bright day, stew meat?" The courtiers had fled, I noticed. Ragnol and I were alone.

That's when I discovered that, faced with the right situation, my aikido training kicked in after all. I grabbed Ragnol's fingers in a *sankyo* hold, squeezed them painfully, and spiraled his elbow toward the ceiling. Shifting my weight, I moved smoothly into the *omote* form of the move, which easily left slack for his chain. I pinned him to the ground, his elbow locked and his fingers still in my grip. That particular hold was technically not aikido, but an older and nastier variant.

"Now, Ragnol. Is that any way to speak to a guest?"

"Not my court! Not my home! Taken was I, over the sea!" He craned his neck to look at me, as I'd pressed his face to the floor.

"Yes, yes, I heard all that. But you're the court jester, and I'm a guest of the court. Oh, and in case you were wondering, I'm in a bad mood. Just today I've run from a *vrak-larunn*, slipped on human blood, got smeared with gore, and threatened with being added to a stew. And I haven't even had lunch yet."

"Please don't break your arm!" he cried.

"What?"

"I said please don't break my arm!"

He had, actually. Twice Only he'd switched to Old High German, and I'd needed two tries to understand his pronouns. I could read the language, but I'd never heard it spoken aloud. Nor could I respond in kind. *Just keep speaking English and hope for the best.*

"Take me to your book. The one you wrote."

"Don't ask me that, good woman. It's all I have of home."

"Think how happy you'll be when someone actually reads the damned thing. Hell, I'll write my dissertation on it."

Ragnol glowered at me but held his tongue.

Meanwhile, the laughter swelled outside the room. Adults were joining in, merging with the children's voices. I hadn't seen any children when we'd ridden through town, I realized. What had the soldier said? The piper had returned them. As in Hamelin? I wondered what he'd done to them in the meantime.

I put a bit more torque on Ragnol's arm. "Time's up. Will you take me to your book, or do I break your elbow?"

"Please!" the fool cried. "Set Ragnol free. He'll be loyal to thee!" Back to the singsong, but at least he did it in English.

I smiled wryly. "Truly, your loyalty is worth so much, the duke had you in chains."

"I swear it, my sweet, by the boat and sea that bore me to thee. To the book, to the book! You'll see, you'll see!"

"Swear by something you care about." *But what? Ah yes...* "Swear by your Laughing Beast."

Ragnol screwed up his face. "No! Not fair! You can't! I wanted stew!"

I twisted his fingers.

"I swear by the Beast, the Laughing Beast, I shall be true, as the old sea shone blue."

Probably the best I'd get. Oh, the things I do for my dissertation...

I let him go. He rose to his knees, crawled to me, and kissed my sneakers.

"Stop that!" I pulled out the keys I'd gotten from the castellan. "If you get my shoes wet, I'll hack off your balls." Despite the fact that I clearly had no knife on my person, he scooted back and sat rocking till I found the right key.

His grin was so wide when the chain fell away I regretted my decision, but he didn't attack, just stood and motioned me forward. "This way, this way. Old Ragnol will lead you away, away."

While that didn't exactly fill me with confidence, I followed him. I could tell this would be like the stairwell. I'd fall apart later. I hoped. If there were a later.

Ragnol's book lay closed on a reading stand in the duke's study. This one had been bound in a skin of oily black scales. I opened it to the first page. Relief flooded me as I recognized the hand: Ragnol's handwriting was a dead ringer for Ragnarrl's. Even better, the frontispiece showed nothing worse than a Passenger Pigeon. Yes, this was a book I could use.

I quickly closed it, put down Ragnarrl's book, and picked up Ragnol's. "Come on. Let's go home."

"Really? You'd take old Ragnol home, cross the wide, wide sea?"

"We'll see about that. I'll take you to our world, though. But let me warn you, you'll find things have changed."

He didn't seem worried by that. In fact, he clapped, jumped up and down, and did a cartwheel or two while I crossed the room. "Well," I called from the doorway. "Are you coming?"

One more cartwheel, and he stood beside me. "I'm yours to command. How do we return?"

"On the edge of the valley there's a door in the hill. We go through it to a tunnel..." His face fell so thoroughly I couldn't continue. "What?"

He took my sleeve and led me back to the empty great hall. From there we crossed to the bronze doors, then past the atrium to the front doors.

At first they seemed like the sea, so thoroughly did they cover the courtyard. A sea of flesh. Thousands of children filled the grounds and the streets beyond, having their fun with the adults. Some they pulled apart. Others they impaled with sharpened straws, through which they drank their blood. Still others they simply trampled to death. All the while, everyone laughed, assailants and victims alike. We'd never cross that throng. We wouldn't even get ten feet.

I backed toward the bronze doors, fearing they'd already seen us. When we reached the great hall, Ragnol plopped onto the floor and silently moped. I plopped down next to him.

How long we sat that way, I couldn't say. I didn't check my watch. The laughter continued unabated, but slowly I grew aware of another sound: the tread of some giant beast as it approached the town, then entered it, no doubt crushing people with every step.

Someone appeared in silhouette by the outside doors and ran towards us. We scrambled to our feet, but it was Avigraal, weapons and armor once more covered in gore. She grinned. "Arrukam is doomed. You must flee before you see it." A chuckle escaped her lips. Then she tittered.

"The duke?"

"He tried to fight them, to stem the tide, but they were so many. We had to retreat." She turned. "He was right behind me. Ah, there…"

Sand the color of blood poured through the atrium and into the great hall. It rose in two columns, which met and branched, forming the rough outline of a man. Though silent, his face bore a mask of mad laughter. He shambled past us, returning to his throne.

Avigraal snickered as she turned back to me. "It's too late for us, I fear." She pointed to Ragnol. "And him. You can only look upon the Laughing Beast for so long. Even its image—"

"Causes madness," I said. *That's why Misk U never reproduced the illustration.*

Avigraal covered her mouth, but she couldn't hold back the hearty laugh that rose from her throat. Clearly unable to speak, she nodded. Tears streamed down her face.

She's right. I must go. But where? I couldn't think of a damned thing. So I put down the book, reached over, and gently removed her helm, letting it clatter to the floor. I stroked her hair and, as her laughter turned to sobs, embraced her, my long-lost twin.

Ragnol started tugging on my sleeve.

"What?" I snarled.

"Home! Home! You have to go home! It's here."

And he was right. With a huge crash, the Laughing Beast arrived, crushing an outbuilding. I glimpsed a giant avian foot. The hall darkened. Looking up, I caught the beast's silhouette in the stained glass.

"Here!" Ragnol still pulled on me. I let go of Avigraal, and he handed me the book. I took it without thinking. "It's here!"

"Yes, damn it! I know the Beast is here!"

"Not the Beast—home!"

"But it's…" And then I knew. I grinned at him, careful to contain the laugh it threatened to become. "Thank you, Ragnol. Thank you." I ran back toward the study. Behind me, Ragnol and Avigraal fell to the floor in helpless spasms of mirth.

ᚱ

I used a side door to cross into the next building, then the next, taking the route I used around the quadrangles in winter, when I wanted to stay indoors. The castle wasn't identical, but it was close enough. I reached the main quad, where I'd have to go outside, but here the crowd barely existed. Across the square I saw something like the old library at Misk U, and I ran for it. It didn't take long for a group of giggling children to pursue me, but I had longer legs and a good lead. Besides, I was running for my life. I crashed open the door, then ran towards the back of the main room. The trouble was, I had no idea how this building was laid out. It too was a library, but where had they hidden the stairs to Special Collections?

Behind me came the laughter of children. Many children.

I threw open a door in the far wall and found myself in a hallway that went left and right. I turned left. I've often wondered what would have happened if I'd gone right, but I try not to dwell on it.

The branch I took led to a stairwell. I raced down it, taking two at a time, till I came to a lead-lined door. Frantically, I searched through my keys till I found one that looked about right. I tried the lock, and it turned. Laughing kids appeared at the top of the stair, but by then I'd forced the door open wide enough to squeeze through. I slammed it immediately. They reached it and pushed from the other side, but I managed to hold them back till I could lock it. That left me alone in total darkness.

I waited futilely for my eyes to adjust, then gave up and felt my way down the stairs. These turned to the left, but I followed them anyway into a narrow room full of crates. I passed through without banging into too many of them and found the door at the far side.

When I came out on the hillside, the sun had just begun to set. I saw the river, the trees, and the familiar buildings of modern Arkham. I'd never been so happy to see the Miskatonic Valley. Clutching the book, I carefully made my way back to town.

I stopped at home for food and a shower. My laptop told me it was still the same day, though after five. I decided to go to the library anyway and try to get my purse and coat back.

Elmsley met me at circulation.

"You're late, Abigail. And coming from the wrong direction."

I chuckled. "Got lost in my book, and speaking of which…" I dropped Ragnol's book onto the table, watching Elmsley's face. His eyebrows rose slightly, but he gave no other sign of surprise. His analogue had come down from the main library, I recalled, not from the door below that had admitted my own.

"I see I've underestimated your research abilities."

Elmsley made as if to grab the book, but I snatched it back. "I'm going to read this at home."

"It belongs to the library."

I held it up so he could see the spine. "Do you see a catalogue number?"

He pursed his lips but didn't contradict me.

"My dear Mr. Elmsley, here's what's going to happen. You'll return my purse and my coat. I'll take them and this book back to my apartment, where I shall translate the text into English and copy the illustrations. Then it's yours. I love the university and see no reason why I shouldn't donate this book. But I'll be damned if I'll read it downstairs."

He considered me for a moment. "You're a scion of one of Arkham's founding families, are you not, Abigail? A Phillips…"

"Yes."

He nodded, as if that explained everything. "Very well. Let me go get your things."

A Massachusetts native, **DR. ABIGAIL Z. PHILLIPS** completed her undergraduate degree in history at Harvard, followed by a doctorate at Miskatonic University. Her dissertation—*Towards an Architectonics of Early European Exploration: The New World Travels of Ragnol the Bold*—assured her a return to Harvard as a professor of European history, followed by early tenure. She is the author of the popular history book *Before Columbus: Ragnol and Leif's America*. She remains an in-demand speaker at academic events, including this year's graduation ceremony at Miskatonic. Able to present even the driest of historical facts with flair and humor, Dr. Phillips has enlivened many a university event. Her colleagues have remarked on how she can find the humorous side of anything, able to laugh at even the oddest of times.

CLIFF WINNIG's short fiction appears in many anthologies, including *When the Hero Comes Home: 2, Gears and Levers 3, The Aether Age: Helios, Footprints,* and *Retro Spec.* The twitterzines *Outshine* and *Thaumatrope* have published his very short fiction. Cliff is a graduate of the Clarion Science Fiction and Fantasy Writers' Workshop and a three-time finalist in the Writers of the Future Contest. When not writing, he plays sitar, studies martial arts, and does social dance. He lives in the San Francisco Bay Area with his wife Debby and their children, who always seem to be laughing. In 1990, he drove with three friends to Providence, Rhode Island, to attend the H. P. Lovecraft Centennial Conference at Brown University, where he saw many cool things in glass cases. He can be found online at http://cliffwinnig.com.

PASSENGER

AN ACCOUNT BY REBECCA BROWNING
as provided by Evan Purcell

My husband and I drove in silence. I think he was still shaken from the sanitarium. I tried to talk to him, to get his mind off that horrible place with its gray walls and bandage smell… But he wouldn't say anything. His jaw was clenched and his knuckles were white against the steering wheel.

Drew was always like that after a visit with his father.

"Honey," I said, because I always call him honey whenever he's on edge. "Honey, please. You know, we've never stayed in Massachusetts long enough for me to see… well, anything, really."

He unclenched his jaw long enough to say, "We've seen enough."

"I mean," I said, "it would be wonderful to visit the town where you grew up. You never talk about it, and I just…"

He looked at me then, and his gray eyes were ringed with red. I'd say he looked unhinged, but after seeing what his father had turned into, I knew that was an exaggeration. I couldn't read his expression, except to say that it was cold and perhaps a little panicked, too.

Stop me if I'm giving away too many details, of course. I want this matter resolved as quickly as possible, and I certainly don't want to blather on about… I would like this all to be over.

I'm sorry.

So we were about twenty minutes outside of Arkham, which as you know meant that we were deep into the woods. And with just the one road… Well, I could understand why Drew was on edge.

The trees, oh God, all around us, they were just so… Well, you know. You're from around here. You know what it's like, at night. Everything is twisted. Nothing seems alive.

"Honey," I said again, because he kept looking at me. And the roads had so many turns. I was afraid he would…

"Do you think he'll ever get better?" Drew asked. He was talking about his father, of course. I'm sure you have those medical reports. Or at the very least, you can get them. I don't want to waste your time with my father-in-law's diagnosis, except to say that he'd been put away for most of his adult life. I'd never seen him outside of these yearly visits. And every time, he seemed worse.

Please stop me if I ramble. I want to help as much as I can. It's difficult, you know.

I didn't want to lie to Drew and tell him everything would be okay. He would be able to tell that I was patronizing him, and that, well, that might get him in one of his moods. He was already half way there.

So I just mumbled, "I don't know," and waited for him to calm down.

The trees, they were darker now. Bigger. They seemed to reach toward us from all directions. The road seemed to be shrinking. I stopped breathing without realizing, and only started again when Drew scared the breath back into me.

He shouted, "Christ!" and I jumped.

"What's wrong?"

But he didn't answer. At least not with words. Instead, he just pointed toward the edge of the road. He pointed toward the shadows, toward nothing, as if that answered my questions.

"Honey, I don't…"

He said, "What's he doing out in the middle of the woods like that? Doesn't he know it's not safe?"

"Who, dear?"

He pointed again, toward that same spot at the edge of nothing.

"Drew, do you want me to drive?"

The car was beginning to slow.

For a dark moment, I worried that we were suddenly out of gas. But the fuel gauge said that we were just over a half tank, so that wasn't the problem.

Drew had just decided to pull over. He pulled over exactly where he had pointed. There was nothing here, except for those twisted trees and the darkness beyond.

"Don't get upset," Drew told me.

I was already upset. My breathing was ragged. I almost asked him if he wanted me to drive again, but somehow I knew that would set him off. The rings around his eyes were a darker red now. I knew he'd be… affected after seeing his father, but he'd never acted like this before. The night air was cold, but his forehead glistened with sweat. Small beads of it pebbled along his hairline.

"Now, I know you don't believe in picking up hitchhikers…" Drew said.

Hitchhikers? I looked around the car. There was no one nearby. Not in any direction. Even the darkness seemed unusually still, like there was no life in the woods. It was a windy night, but nothing moved.

"Honey," I said.

"Don't worry," Drew said. "He seems trustworthy."

"Who?"

Drew glanced toward the seat behind mine, as if there were somebody standing directly outside the window. He nodded in that direction. "Well?" he said.

"What?" I asked.

"You know the door handle doesn't work from the outside. Let him in. You can reach." He stared at me. He waited. He wanted me to open the door behind me, even though there was nobody there.

"I'm sorry, Drew, but I don't…"

"It's okay!" he said. He was trying too hard to sound soothing. He smiled at me, but his eyes didn't crinkle.

"I don't…"

"Open the damned door!" he screamed. He slammed both his palms against the steering wheel.

Now, I know how this sounds, but Drew never treated me that way before. He never yelled at me, not even during his angry spells. Whatever he was feeling, he would always direct it toward something inanimate, like a wall or a plate. But tonight, the way he looked at me and screamed… I don't know. And he was just covered with sweat.

I had to humor him.

So before he could scream again, I reached over the seat and pushed open the back door. It opened a crack, letting in more of the restless night air. The door didn't move. I figured that now Drew would realize no one was out there.

But then the wind shifted and the door swung wide open.

Nothing happened. No one entered the car, of course, because no one was there. We waited, night spilling in through the open door. Everything was motionless, in limbo.

I looked at Drew for answers. I dared not speak. I dared not move. Drew ignored my presence, and instead smiled politely toward the backseat, as if we had a new passenger sitting comfortably behind me.

BAM!

The wind shifted and the open door swung shut. It rattled me.

The car felt colder now. I couldn't see my breath, but my fingertips were growing numb.

Drew continued driving. I looked down at my watch, but it was too dark to make out the time. And I didn't want to turn on the over-head light. That would distract him.

So instead, I stared at the dark road ahead, at the twisted branches that formed the edges around us. My neck hairs prickled. I knew there wasn't anyone behind me, but I couldn't help myself. I felt watched. I felt as if that man, that nonexistent man, was smiling in the backseat and admiring my hair.

"That's a nice hat," Drew said. With horror, I realized that he wasn't talking to me. He was complimenting the passenger. "It seems a bit old fashioned. I like that. You don't see that kind of hat anymore."

Drew paused. Then he laughed and said "Of course. Thank you."

He was having a conversation with that man. And from the look on his face, it was a pleasant conversation.

"Five years now," Drew said.

That was how long we'd been married.

"So where are you headed?" he asked. "I can take you as far as… Oh, okay. That's perfectly fine."

I tried desperately to tune out his voice. If I could just pretend that I couldn't hear him…

"I know," he continued. "It's a difficult situation."

It was no use. No matter what I did, I couldn't block Drew's voice from my ears. Have you ever heard just one half of a conversation? It's hard to follow along sometimes, but you can always tell when the conversation turns awkward.

It was turning awkward.

Drew's voice got louder. He didn't seem angry, but he did seem upset, off his game. His eyes glanced in my direction, but only for a second. He said something about the woods, about how safe the woods were at night.

I still don't know what he meant by that.

We drove on, and Drew laughed nervously at some unheard joke.

Then he stopped talking. He waited. It was like a switch had been turned off.

A long moment later, he turned toward me. "Well?" he asked.

"Um… what's going on?" I said.

"Aren't you going to answer him?" Drew asked.

Apparently, the passenger had asked me a question. I knew I couldn't bluff my way out of this one, because he would know right away that I had no idea what was happening. So I slowly reached out and placed my hand on his knee. "Honey," I said. "There's no one there."

He pushed my hand away. I expected him to say something now, to start arguing with me, but he didn't. He didn't even look at me. He just stared at the road with a blankness in his eyes that could've meant a million different things.

In this new silence, my sense of uneasiness grew tenfold. Even though I knew it was irrational, I felt eyes looking at me from the backseat. Then—and please don't judge me for what I'm about to say—I felt a gentle pressure on my shoulder. My left shoulder. It felt, for all the world, like a hand pressing down.

I even looked at my shoulder, expecting to see a hand-shaped imprint on my loose-fitting shirt… But of course I saw nothing. I simply felt the grip. It was definite and cold.

"Sorry about my wife," Drew said. He continued talking with the man, laughing and pausing and talking in a steady rhythm. He asked the man questions. He talked about our trip to Arkham. He didn't mention the sanitarium, of course. I was grateful for that.

And then he stopped. I caught his eyes in the rear view mirror, and they were staring in horror at the man in the backseat.

I cannot describe to you the look of terror on Drew's face. It was more than just a reaction to something that the passenger had said. No matter how off-color or threatening, no human words could illicit such a reaction from Drew. No. He was reacting to something else entirely.

It was as if some great, horrible thing was changing before his eyes. As if the passenger himself had stripped off whatever appearance he once had and revealed something underneath. It was... I thank God now that I did not see what my husband saw.

That was when he started screaming. At first, it started as a scream of horror, one that rang throughout the car and seemed to explode out of his throat. One, uninterrupted scream. And then it changed. He regained some of his composure and began to form words. "Out!" he screamed. "Get out! Stay away from her!"

He was screaming about me. He was protecting me.

Drew once again fell silent, allowing the passenger to respond. I got the feeling, and I don't know why, that the passenger was bargaining with Drew. It was as if he was offering Drew some deal, some ungodly deal.

"Never!" my husband screamed.

He flinched. The passenger must've shushed him with a finger. If he even had fingers. For the next moment, Drew leaned toward the passenger and nodded, trying to keep his composure and listen rationally.

At that moment, I realized that the car was parked on the side of the road. I'm not sure when Drew stopped driving, but I must not have noticed.

"Yes, I understand," Drew said.

"Honey," I whispered. I needed this to stop. I couldn't allow my husband to just sit there and talk like that. It was... wrong.

Drew dove toward the passenger.

My husband is a large man. I was not expecting to see him maneuver his entire body over the car seat and fling himself into the back.

He balled up his fist and punched at the passenger. Then he reeled backwards, as if the passenger had punched him back.

They fought. Wildly. Fiercely. It was almost comical, seeing my dear husband thrash about like that. He grunted. I'm not positive, but

I believe his shoulder popped out of place. There was a snap.

In the struggle—while the car rocked back and forth, while I screamed Drew's name over and over—the door swung open. A blast of night air shot inside. Drew has long hair, and his hair went wild. I couldn't see his face, but I could tell it was bloodied and bruised.

Drew thrashed around, faster and faster, as if something was holding him down and tearing him open. His arm swung around and accidentally bashed against my face.

I blinked, just for a second. And in that moment, he broke free of whatever was holding him down. He dove out the car door.

He stood at the edge of the woods, screaming nonsense. "It's me you want!" he screamed. "Stay away from her!" This was when I finally saw his face, and it was much worse than I'd thought. One eye had already swollen shut. A solid line of blood ran from the corner of his eye to the corner of his mouth. His nose looked broken. Of course, all these wounds could've been self-inflicted. You didn't see how wildly he thrashed about in the backseat. I wouldn't have been surprised if he broke his own nose in the struggle. But then again…

"Come and get me!" he screamed, but he couldn't even finish the sentence before he toppled backward onto the gravel. It was as if the passenger dove at him with such strength. Such ungodly strength.

Drew punched and kicked at the air above him. He scrambled to his feet and disappeared into the night.

I waited such a long time, afraid to move, afraid to even breathe. I heard Drew scream once more. He was deep in the forest now, and his voice seemed weak, but I understood the word, and I knew that it was directed toward me. "Go!" he screamed. And with that single word, his voice cracked.

So I slid across the front seat and drove away. I turned around, because I remembered passing this station as we drove through Arkham. It was probably closer to just go straight, but… I don't know. I came here instead.

And that's why I'm here now talking to you. I know I sound crazy, but… please find him. I'm so very worried right now.

It's just… I know he's out there in the woods. I just don't know if he's alone.

REBECCA BROWNING (née Harrison) is a housewife from Baltimore. She briefly attended McDaniel College, before meeting her future husband Drew Browning in a physics class. The couple has no children. If you have any information regarding the whereabouts of her husband, please contact the Arkham Police Department.

EVAN PURCELL is a writer and teacher. He loves to travel the world, and is currently living and working in central China. Wherever he goes, he tries to collect as many stories as he can. For information on his writing and travels, you can visit EvanPurcell.blogspot.com.

THE HILL

AN ACCOUNT BY PAUL C. BOWEN
as provided by Damir Salkovic

"But you must have some idea of where they come from." The
young man in the suit sitting across from me smiled, but the
smile failed to register in his eyes. "A theory, or an educated guess at
the very least."

"I'm no biologist," I said, arranging the pens so that they touched
the corners of the notepad, forming obtuse angles with the sides. It's
a recent compulsion I've picked up—the strangest thing, but sharp
angles and certain surfaces evoke funny images in my mind. The kind
of funny that makes you laugh all the way into a rubber room and a
jacket that ties in the back. "But I've seen the pictures and read the
reports. Whatever these things are, they defy all categorization. They
conform to no known taxonomy."

"In what sense?"

"In every sense." A man passed in front of the glass door, glanc-
ing in with exaggerated indifference. The circus show goes on—the
resident nutcase interviewed by yet another faceless government suit.
"The best scientific minds in the nation have tried to make sense of
them and failed. Part of this failure—a big part, if you ask me—is the

staunch refusal to accept that this may be a form of life evolved under conditions utterly different from those prevalent on Earth." How else to explain the impossible coupling of crustacean and fungoid features, the sacs and chambers and brightly colored glands, the ciliated head-like organ slung on the end of a long, rubber-fleshed neck, the large, leathery wings whose structure suggests a purpose other than flight? But to propose such a theory—to merely hint at it, even as a joke—is to commit instant career suicide.

"Aliens." There was disappointment under his sarcasm. Every suit hopes to extract some crucial missing piece that all the others have overlooked, something that'll help them unravel the unsolvable mystery. "You think they landed here from another planet."

"Not quite." I took a deep breath. This was the hardest part: I wasn't sure what I believed myself. "There was no spaceship, or little green men. Their arrival here could have been an accident—a rift, or a hole in reality, made by something else…"

But the suit was rapidly losing interest. He picked up the pens and notepad and brought the conversation to a polite close. I didn't offer to escort him to the elevators. There's a sculpture in the center of the landing—a piece of modernist junk, if you care for my humble opinion—with a few too many sharp angles for my taste.

It was a bunch of kids in Arkham who found the first of the things, bobbing in the murky water of the River Street canal. They'd broken into one of the abandoned warehouses to smoke dope or scrawl obscenities on the rotting walls or grope and mess around in the dark, empty corners. Scared the hell out of them—seen from a dusty window above, raw and pink in the last rays of the sun, the thing looked like the naked head and torso of a drowning victim. I'd never have the guts to do what they did, hook it out of the water with a length of rusty pipe, but kids these days are something else. Then the researchers from Miskatonic University's environmental center got their hands on it and contacted the Massachusetts Department of Environmental Protection. The good folks at MassDEP took one look at the contamination reports and lost no time in dialing our number.

By the time this specimen, safely encased in a biohazard box, arrived at the EPA headquarters in Washington, D.C., four others had been discovered: one in the town of Bolton, in a small brook tributary to the Still River, and three by fishermen off the coast of Kingsport—but these three so decayed that they couldn't be dissected or analyzed. All save the one near Bolton had floated down the Miskatonic, and that one could have crawled up one of the drainage ditches that fed into the river. I wasn't present at any of the autopsies—if you can call them that—but we were shown images and a heavily edited video. I tried to put them out of my mind. You couldn't let yourself think about them too much. That way lay insanity.

But the profoundly alien anatomy of the thing found in Arkham was the least of our concerns at the time. Some thought it to be a rare mutation, others dismissed it as an elaborate hoax. The real problem—the one that rang the alarm bells in the DEP and EPA offices in Boston and got Headquarters involved—was something unseen and deadly, but all too familiar: the tests had revealed high levels of chemical and organic contamination in the tissues of the specimen. The findings were puzzling at first, but it didn't take us long to identify a probable source.

For over three centuries, the Miskatonic Valley had been a wild, dreary place defined by the brooding river, which powered the pulp and textile mills and irrigated the farms along its banks. Over the past century, the demise of local industries and a steady trickling away of old families had spelled a slow, lingering death for the valley. Tracts of ancient forest and abandoned farmland west of the river could be bought for next to nothing. Throughout the eighties and nineties, soaring land prices and the expansion of cities had made this bleak wilderness attractive to big agriculture; stockyards, feedlots, and meat processing plants now dotted the gloomy landscape.

The revival had come too late to breathe life into the ghost towns along the river, old ramshackle places with rustic names—Dunwich, Aylesbury, Arkham—and interstate highway development had cut the valley off from urban centers like Boston and Lowell. But the environmental spillover was another matter. Tissue analyses from the Arkham specimen pointed to the illegal dumping of large quantities of organic and chemical waste into the ground waters that fed the Miskatonic. The poisoned waters of the river posed a threat to the inhabitants and ecosystems of the valley and the fishing communities near its estuary. There was no predicting the full impact of the disaster; the contamination could spread toward the south and east, into the endless network of underground waterways, leaking into the water supply of millions.

The EPA decided there was no time to waste and dispatched a team to collect water samples along the river. There were four of us: Bentham, Nielsen, and I from the Washington, D.C., office and Yeung from Boston. Our job was to determine the sources and extent of the contamination and come up with a stabilization plan for the affected area. It wouldn't stop there; the Agency was out for blood, and already there were rumors of criminal charges for noncompliance and neglect.

Of the four who left, I'm the only one who made it back alive—if you can call this living. Sleep brings nightmares of howling winds and dim, mountainous shapes treading the chasms between the stars. Reality feels thin and worn, a frayed fabric through which terrible sights can be glimpsed; the whisper in my mind grows louder, taunting me with oblivion. My mind feels infected. Madness stalks the shadows, and the drugs keep it at bay for now—antipsychotics, barbiturates, a bunch of other pills with names I can't pronounce. A dubious haven at best; once that's gone, I know what to do. Better to die than to gaze upon the visage of that horror again.

When the time comes, I'll be ready.

The plan was to spend two days collecting samples and analyzing them in the mobile laboratory in the rear of the van. If our assumptions were correct, we'd be able to trace contaminant movement patterns back to the source of the Miskatonic, located in the hills near the town of Dunwich. On the other side of the hills lay the gray wasteland of slaughterhouses and meat packing plants from which the contamination was thought to originate. If the data checked out, the rest would be in the hands of the Agency's Office of General Counsel.

We set off for New England in the early hours of a cold spring day, the bleak dawn sky heavy with promises of freezing rain. The deluge let up by the time we turned off the highway near Lawrence and ventured into a labyrinth of winding country lanes. A silence fell upon us as our surroundings emerged from the rainy haze. Gone was the flat, drab expanse of the highway; around us rose a forest of tall white pines and oak that seemed to swallow the cracked road. In the shadows past the first line of trees, the fallen leaves and deadfall arranged and rearranged themselves into eerie shapes with each flicker of transient light. Farther into the woods, the tangled shrubs grew taller than a man and warped trees stood by the roadside, their roots sticking out of the earth like claws. It was as if we'd crossed some invisible border into a weird, unfamiliar world.

The ominous foliage gradually thinned out to reveal a wavy horizon of low hills and the banks of a river wreathed in white mist. Far ahead, the hills gradually gave way to a range of mountains, looming blue mirages over a boundless expanse of forest and marshland. A sense of vague unease stirred in me as we drove along the wide, silent river, the hills towering above us like dark sentinels at the entrance to the valley. But any doubts and fears I had were quickly forgotten in work. We found rooms in a small but clean motor inn near the quiet old town of Arkham and spent the first two days driving out to the sampling sites and analyzing the water, looking for changes in contaminant concentration. The initial findings confirmed the Agency's suspicions; all we needed now were samples from the source of the river, and the lawyers in gray suits could take it from there.

According to our GPS, Dunwich was an hour's drive from the motel, but the road the device indicated either did not exist or had vanished under the encroaching growth. At Dean's Corners, a sleepy backwater dominated by the black bulk of a pulp and paper mill, we asked for directions and ended up following an eroded dirt track that wound up the steep hillside and back into the valley. It was past noon when we rounded a narrow curve and saw a covered bridge across a stream in the valley below, and beyond the bridge a huddle of gambrel roofs in the shadow of a soaring mountain.

The houses across the bridge lined up on either side of a wide, unpaved street. They bore the marks of great age and neglect: collapsed roofs, rotting outer walls, moldy clapboards. Many doors and windows were boarded shut. But there were signs of life: shadows darted into doorways and figures moved behind dusty panes as we drove through what passed for the center of the village, past the sprawling ruin of a church whose fallen steeple jutted into the sky like the broken horn of a mythical beast. The ground floor of the church had been converted into a sort of general store: sacks of flour or feed and shelves stocked with canned goods could be glimpsed in the darkness within. A group of men, dour-faced and unkempt, sat on the steps and wooden boxes passing around a bottle. They fell silent at the sight of the van, their lined faces blank and unreadable.

The county registry showed the land behind which the spring was located to be the property of a Harlan Whateley of Dunwich,

Massachusetts. But our attempts to determine the whereabouts of the Whateley farm were met with averted gazes and terrified silence. It was clear that the village folk didn't trust us and that they wanted us gone, clearer still that Whateley's name evoked in them a mix of hatred and superstitious fear. Finally an old drunk we'd bribed with a bottle of liquor pointed us to a logging track that led into the hills on the other side of Dunwich.

The van struggled up the rutted path, gears straining and engine whining. Harlan Whateley's place, an ancient farmhouse falling apart at the corners, sat in the middle of a clearing beneath the dark, steep rise of Sentinel Hill. Save for an old truck parked by the crooked timber porch, there were no signs of human presence about the place. Farther up the incline, an immense building of stone and wood leaned against a rocky outcrop—a vast barn-like structure with no visible windows or doors, its foundations elevated on pillars. A small stream flowed beneath it and trickled into a muddy ditch at the side of the road. The sight of that monolithic hulk in the silent wilderness filled me with foreboding; it evoked the grim image of a temple of some dark deity, waiting for a sacrifice to approach the long-abandoned altar. By the look on the others' faces, I could see that they shared my sentiment. None of us spoke much—the unnatural silence of the place grated on the nerves, and the shadows that grew longer as the day waned played strange tricks on the eyes.

The logging track weaved along a precarious ledge, then ended abruptly at the edge of a forest. We parked the van and hiked the rest of the way, carrying our equipment with us. The spring was a pool of dark, still water, cupped between rocky knolls; by the time we climbed down and got what we came for, the sun was already sinking behind the hills. Nielsen was at the wheel as we made our way down, eager to be far from Dunwich by nightfall.

I never saw what flitted across our path from the gathering shadows—there was a vague impression of something large and flesh-colored, moving with a sort of leaping gait, flailing its membranous appendages in the lights of the van. Nielsen swore and swerved to avoid it; the van veered to the side, narrowly missing a huge pine tree. The wheels struck a rut and for a terrifying moment the heavy vehicle threatened to roll. It came down with a crash that drove the breath from my lungs and careened down a slope, branches and small trees scouring its sides. My head slammed into something hard; stars exploded in my vision. Then all was darkness.

ᚱᛟ

By some miracle, none of us was seriously hurt—I had a nasty gash above my temple and Nielsen a broken nose, but Yeung and Bentham had gotten away with no more than bruises and scratches. Luck was on our side—a gnarled bole had stopped the van's progress at the edge of a yawning precipice. Apart from a litter of broken glass and a shattered monitor screen, the lab equipment seemed to have survived the crash; most importantly, the vials with the samples were intact.

We climbed up to the road and tried our phones, but there was no reception. Dusk was falling fast, the horizon outlined in a red glow. In the failing light I saw something I hadn't noticed before: patches of bare grass on the forested hilltops, with strange stone formations perched in their midst. One such formation crowned the hill above the Whateley farm. For no apparent reason, the sight sent a chill up my spine.

There was no chance of us making it back to Dunwich before dark, and the thought of spending the night in these hills was too terrifying to contemplate. No one had gotten a good look at the thing that had leapt in front of the van—Nielsen turned very pale at the question and shook his head insistently—but the images from the autopsy of the Arkham specimen were fresh in our minds. Bentham suggested that we go down to the Whateley farm and ask for help—whoever lived there had to have a landline, or could give us a ride into the village in the truck we saw parked outside. I didn't like the idea of returning to the rundown farm and the foreboding structure perched on the hillside, but there was no other choice. We retrieved what equipment we could carry and started downhill, through the dark and silent woodland, our footsteps loud in the stillness.

There was light in the farmhouse windows, and I offered silent thanks for our luck. Bentham went up the porch steps and hammered on the door. Nothing happened, but Bentham would not be dissuaded. The second round of knocking brought a response, not from the old house but from the dark building on the hill—a low, deep rumble that shook the ground beneath our feet. We glanced at each other wide-eyed.

"What the hell was that?" asked Yeung.

"Sounds like a herd of elephants in there," Nielsen said. Bentham took a cautious step back. The roaring noise came again, louder this time, accompanied by a heavy thump against the side of the structure, something trying to break out. I felt a lead ball drop into my stomach; my legs felt rooted to the spot. If there was something moving in the barn, it had to be bigger than an elephant. Much bigger.

"Maybe we better—"

There was a creaking noise and the door opened as far as the thick safety chain would allow. A man peered at us from inside—thin and sunken-cheeked, lank black hair curling around his ears; he looked to be anywhere between thirty and fifty. His dark eyes scanned us with a flat, cold gaze.

"Mister, eh- Whateley?" Bentham extended a hand in greeting. Seeing it ignored, he made an awkward attempt to turn it into a vague gesture at the darkening slope. "We ran into some trouble with our van up there. Sure could use some help."

"If you have a phone we can—" Yeung began, but the noise from the barn drowned out the rest of the sentence. It was like no sound I'd heard before, like the tread of colossal feet across an unseen horizon. It was followed by a series of sharp cracks, the wooden walls of the structure creaking and breaking. In the dull glow from the windows, I saw the blank look in Whateley's eyes change to terror.

"Shouldn't have gone out there." He jerked his head toward the hillside, staring somewhere past us. "You need to leave. The time ain't right. Not yet."

The door slammed shut, leaving Bentham with his mouth open. I couldn't say why, but suddenly I knew we had to get out of there, and right away. Nielsen had gone into some sort of daze, and Yeung was as white as a ghost, his eyes riveted to the bulk of the barn.

"Hey!" Bentham's confusion had worn off; anger rose in its place. He kicked at the door, but it remained closed. A stirring rustle reached us from the immense structure, hundreds of sharp-taloned feet scraping across a stone floor; Nielsen clapped his hands to his ears and whimpered.

"Come on," I said to Bentham. "If we have to spend the night out here, we do. We'll walk back to town in the morning."

"That bastard." Bentham's fists were clenched. I'd known him for years and never saw him lose his temper before. But there was something about the place that set your teeth on edge, worked on your nerves. "He's got animals in the barn, and I'll bet he's dumping manure straight into that stream. Let's see how he likes it when we slap him with a fine."

Before I could stop him, he took off up the hillside, his tall, lanky figure disappearing into the gloom. We followed him to the side of the structure. Up close, the resemblance to a temple was even stronger—the foundation was hewn from massive stone blocks, the walls made from heavy timber sections. It towered above us like some battlemented castle of the gods. Bentham waded through the water and clambered up one of the huge joists to a grid-covered hole. When he turned toward us, his face bore a grin I didn't much care for.

"Just taking a look inside," he said, and peered through the grate.

A shifting, slithering sound came from the other side of the wall as whatever was in the structure moved with a hideous eagerness to meet him. Bentham gave a strangled half-cry and lost his footing; the grate, bearing his full weight, tore off its frame and he splashed into the shallow stream. Yeung went to help him up, grabbed one arm, and let go with a shriek. Bentham was dead, his lips pulled back from his teeth, his face twisted in a grimace of absolute horror.

Out of the corner of my eye, I caught a glimpse of the dim interior, lit by a wan, pale light; there was a vague notion of something immense rearing on many legs—as tall as a cliff, but without constant shape, an amalgamation of all the nightmares dreamt up by humanity. Beneath the sound of its roar I could hear the flapping of leathery wings and saw the raw, flesh-colored things leaping and fluttering between its colossal legs. I felt the sight claw at the back of my skull, offering insanity. I tore my gaze from it and staggered away from the barn, only to see Whateley—or whoever the man in the house was—walking up the slope with a shotgun pointed in our direction.

The shot rang out, loud as thunder between the cliffs. Yeung's hands went up in front of him, a half-hearted attempt to ward off a blow; a pink cloud blossomed at the back of his head and he pitched into the stream, next to Bentham's corpse. Whateley raised his weapon again, slowly. His lips moved as if forming words, but all I could hear was a low, inane mutter. Nielsen was kneeling, face turned up to the dark, windowless monolith; his mind was gone. I yelled at him to run and tried to tug him to his feet, but he outweighed me by a good thirty pounds.

"Time ain't right," the madman said, and pulled the trigger. The bullet dug into the ground, inches from my right ankle. I let go of Nielsen and ran for a tangle of bushes, thorns and brambles scraping my face and hands. There was another shot, but the darkness had already hidden me. I lay flat on the ground, cheek pressed into the dirt, paralyzed with fear, as all hell broke loose around me.

The walls of the great structure groaned and burst apart, showering splinters into the stream and the bushes. The thing inside had crushed it like a box of matchsticks. For a moment, its vast, inconstant bulk was outlined against the starry sky—it was invisible, flickering in and out of existence like the image from a broken projector, but its presence seemed to bend light and space. I only glimpsed it for a moment before I averted my eyes. It was insanity become flesh— towering, walking insanity that had frightened Bentham to death and stricken poor Nielsen from his wits.

I felt a rush of air rustle through the bushes, as if from the stirring of something immense, and heard the shrubs and trees on the hillside crack and flatten as if trampled by a tremendous weight. The night filled with a leathery flapping as the winged creatures scampered away from the ruin of the barn. One crashed through the bushes beside me and I screamed at the touch of its slimy, rubbery flesh; it scrambled through the undergrowth, emitting an odd, high-pitched piping.

Up the hillside the unseen horror shambled, leaving a wide swath of destruction in its wake, the ground trembling and trees snapping like toothpicks. Nielsen cried out; rising to his feet, he ran straight toward those Cyclopean tracks, arms open in rapture, and flung himself in the path of the lumbering horror. There was a sickening crack as the unseen feet trod him to a bloody mass. But this I didn't see— both the man and the tracks had passed beyond my field of vision, toward the top of the hill, where a pale light leaked into the night sky.

This was where the shambling obscenity was heading, following some unheard call from the circle of stones. For a moment I saw a great shadow squatting in the middle of the circle, and the stars above me seemed to gather in weird constellations. Reality teetered on the brink of a black gulf.

The sequence becomes garbled at this point. I remember seeing

Whateley fling the shotgun away and run after the monstrosity, chanting strange words in a shrill, inhuman tongue. I remember the unearthly roar that rent the night, part agony, part unfulfilled rage; for a moment the thing's grotesque shape was limned against the pale light—seething, writhing, gibbering, unraveling with every shrieked syllable. Then a flash of blinding light seared awful images into the backs of my eyelids; I buried my face in my hands, my fingers twisting with a will of their own. It took every shred of self-control not to claw my eyes out to stop the visions from coming. A great tumult swept down the hillside, tearing trees from their roots, slamming me against the ground.

When I crawled out of the bushes, shivering and bleeding, Whateley was gone and not a trace of the horror from the barn remained, save for a trail of absolute devastation that led up the hill. The decrepit farmhouse and the barn had been reduced to a heap of splintered planks. Whatever unclean secret Whateley had called upon to summon and bind the shambling monstrosity was buried under the ruins.

They found me wandering the barren fields around Dunwich two days later. I was almost catatonic, near death with exposure. Of what I'd seen up at the farm I refused to speak. Which was just fine, for the villagers were in no hurry to ask questions; they had seen the weird lights and heard the distant rumble from the forbidden place on the hill. They fed me and gave me blankets and kept their distance until the police arrived from Dean's Corners. The policemen—two elderly part-timers who were as eager to leave the village as the silent, sullen crowd was to be rid of them—took my babbling statement in the musty general store, their eyes dancing uneasily between the half-effaced symbols on the walls behind the shelves and the brick partition that walled off the former chancel. From Dunwich I was taken to the sheriff's office in Lowell, and from there to Boston.

A big investigation followed—the FBI got involved, as did the police departments of several counties. I was brought in for questioning several times, but my account of events was dismissed as raving and unreliable. For a while I was the chief suspect, but the discovery of Whateley's shotgun exonerated me from Yeung's murder, and the coroner's office found no evidence of foul play in the bizarre deaths of Bentham and Nielsen. An APB was issued for Harlan Whateley's arrest, but that was six months ago, and nothing has come of it. The same can be said for the Agency's probe into the dumping of waste into the Miskatonic, which has been placed on hold indefinitely. I took a few weeks of mandatory R&R and still see a shrink twice a week, on Tuesdays and Thursdays. It's not helping—at this point, nothing can—but it makes me feel like I'm putting up a fight, and one has to hang onto one's delusions, right? All the way to the bitter end.

There's something in those hills—a doorway, an opening into some dark and unknowable place—and the inhabitants of the valley know about it. The knowledge of the old ways, knowledge that was ancient before man walked the earth, is still alive. Sooner or later, another will come in Whateley's place and bring something through that opening, some unnamable denizen of the other side. Something vast and hungry, born of insane dimensions and weird planes of existence. Something that feeds on those tainted waters, fetid with offal and blood.

It can afford to be patient. Time and space as we know them mean nothing in the universe it inhabits. There are others—trapped in the nighted chasms between worlds, dreaming madness and chaos. But this one is the first, the opener of the way. It that waits on the other side of the breach, on the other side of those silent, brooding hills, watching, waiting.

My mind is a gate that keeps the insanity from spilling through into this world. I know that, and the thing from the other side knows it too. Sooner or later I'll have to close the gate forever.

PAUL C. BOWEN was a senior analyst with the EPA's National Headquarters in Washington, D.C., and the prime suspect in the deaths of three EPA personnel and the disappearance of a local farmer in Dunwich, Mass., in February 2013. A joint investigation by the FBI and Massachusetts State Police found no evidence connecting Bowen to the crime. In the months that followed, Bowen was diagnosed with sudden-onset schizophrenia and paranoid delusions; all attempts to obtain a coherent statement from him about the events in Dunwich proved fruitless. He was found dead in his home in June 2013. His death was ruled a suicide.

DAMIR is an aficionado of weird and macabre tales, presently residing in Arlington, Virginia. His reading interests range from horror and fantasy to pulp and science fiction. His short stories have been published on the *Tales to Terrify* podcast, in the *Schlock! Bimonthly* magazine and in anthologies by *Schlock! Webzine*, Source Point Press, Parasomnia Press, Apokrupha, Villipede Publications, Miskatonic Press, and the Black Library Bolthole. He earns his living as an accountant, a profession that lends itself well to nightmares and harrowing visions.

IN DEFENSE OF PROFESSOR FALCROVET

AN ACCOUNT BY
PROFESSOR HALWARTH STEPHEN FALCROVET
edited and presented by Darin M. Bush

The following are excerpts from the personal journal of my dear friend, Professor Halwarth Stephen Falcrovet. Hal—he refused to let anyone call him Halwarth if he could help it—was a great help to me many times personally, and in my trials as an aspiring writer. He was a boon to his students, and to the faculty of Miskatonic. I cannot find a way to say that he will be missed without slipping into trope. He was a sharp contrast of a man; his reputation for delving into the occult and collecting bizarre artifacts from all around the globe was sharply contradicted as cliché by his constant presence in the life of the campus. He delighted in his students and his lectures more than his clay tablets, horrid tomes, and grotesque statuary. He presided over many social activities, both for faculty and body. He seemed hardly to differ in physiognomy or aura between preparing students for the exam on voodoo cults of the Caribbean, and opening the spring formal by dancing with his facetious nemesis, Professor

Lauren Hubberd of the Comparative Theology department.

Some of you will recognize most of the above paragraph from the exordium of my eulogy for Hal. I repeat it here to set the proper tone for what is to follow. I am not alone in refuting the hypothesis that Hal's death was a suicide. I reject this notion—utterly. His investment in life, not just his but others, was obvious to all. It has been said, with humor, that Hal lived to know death and foresee the end of the world, and his studies sometimes did leave me nauseated or disturbed, but these horrors were "abstractions entire" to him. He took them no more literally than he took my science fiction short stories. While neither the Essex County authorities nor the attorney general of Massachusetts will return my interrogatives, I continue to work to find some physical evidence—the so-called "soft" sciences being of no use in this case to the forensic practitioners—that Hal could not have taken his own life.

Having consulted with an attorney, I find no reason not to publicize the following excerpts from Hal's private journals. He leaves neither widow nor children from whom to gain consent. I have avoided any possible personal embarrassments for his peers or students. His professional journals have been discussed and pored over, both in and out of the halls of justice, but I think they only distract us from the real solution: something terrible happened to my friend, something inexplicable.

If he had died of coronary failure or a stroke, those of us who loved him could put his spirit to rest. I have no sense of accomplishment with these feeble paragraphs, only outrage and frustration. I must believe that Hal was exactly who he showed to the world, and I must provide that world with the evidence, no matter how subjective or bizarre. My only consolation is in the sure knowledge that if Hal himself could comment, he would immediately, affectionately, deride this quasi-hysterical fable as unworthy of my efforts, and beneath even vanity publication.

୮ଠ

Here begin the excerpts from the personal journal of Professor Falcrovet.

୮ଠ

30 NOVEMBER

Thanksgiving is over, thank goodness. I shall not desire turkey for weeks. I cannot even see myself eating it so soon as the time of Yule, but I seem to recover that appetite every year, so I shall bow to history. What was Franklin thinking, asking us to embrace this bizarre monster of a bird as the national metaphor? What are we: weak, stupid, food for the slaughter?

Oh! It must be said before I forget—speaking of slaughter—I have received word just today that the expeditions in the East are fruitful! I am the owner—well, the curator—of the *Necronomicon*! Not the original, thank goodness, as even I cannot think to stomach such a horrid tome. Insanity surrounds its mere conceptualization: bound in skin, written in blood. (Note to self: Add sanguinography and anthro-sanguinography to future vocabulary tests.) To make a book in such an inefficient and fragile manner, to risk its obliteration merely by travelling through destructive years, is madness. However, it appears that some long-dead maniac or genius—or both, why not?—copied the cryptic inscriptions so as to disseminate its apocalyptic directives to all corners of this real estate investment of the Elder Gods, that we call Earth. (Note to self: Get the geography kids to give me a word to replace "corner"—that euphemism should have been crushed under the pressure of spherical evidence by now.)

Kids. Why would I have my own children, when I am flooded with the delights of near-parenthood, without the burden of wiping their noses? For example, I have all the freedom of pedagogical discourse with my good friend, Darin, and I usurp mentorship over him and his artistry. (Note to self: I must remember to tell him his work currently reads as if he slept with an H. G. Wells book on his face, and it poisoned his mind.) And then, at the end of the day, I am able to expunge him from my home, with all the good will in the world, and return to my solitude, knowing he and others will return in time. I cannot possibly be any luckier, and perhaps I celebrate Thanksgiving heartily not so much for its version of history, as for my personal interpretation. I am getting a bit emotional in my age, apparently.

13 DECEMBER

One of my students, possibly intoxicated by exams and the following winter furlough, asked in class if she could qualify for extra credit by completing an audio-only version of the *Necronomicon* text, possibly for use by blind students. I do not know if this was her idea, or if she was put up to it, but she was so earnest that I did not recognize the prank for what it was until a few young ladies in her row began to titter or bite down on their lips. I have a reputation to maintain, and so therefore I rewarded the charlatan with praise, but the explanation of the witticism to the majority of the class created quite a distraction. Some of my less serious students seemed to see this as justification for their opinion of my field: hokum.

I would not have it generally known, but my greatest concern was in the fact that the students somehow knew I was going to have one of these texts in my possession. Only two or three people on staff knew I had acquired it, and only recently. Why would they discuss it with students, or discuss it at all? And why does it send a shudder through me to think of this horrendous tome as a topic of general conversation or humorous inspiration? The idea of reading the *Necronomicon* aloud to blind students: I laugh to injury, but cannot avoid dread, too. I must separate these thoughts, and understand the latter better, and soon. The book itself arrives any day now.

ƒo

22 DECEMBER

Delays! Delays! Where is my package? Promised a week ago, and no sign of it. I am told by letter that the book arrives on time, but then where is it? My frustration knows no bounds, is cyclopean in scope!

ƒo

25 DECEMBER

What a strange occurrence. The *Necronomicon* arrived on my doorstep on the 24th—Christmas Eve to some—and I did not hear the knock on the door nor see the package on my step. So, there I was, on Christmas morning, confronted with the strangest Christmas gift ever. What would Jesus of Nazareth or Saint Nicholas say about my opening the box with all the thrill and expectation of a small child opening an air-rifle-shaped package, or the sarcophagus-like box of a new doll? How would they react if they could see what my Christmas blessing contained?

The book is not at all what I expected. It is huge, a true tome in all senses, and it is made of some material foreign to my experience. The pages are thick and inconsistent in texture. The ink is dark, not black, but very dark. I made myself dig around in the workshop for gloves. Some subconscious part of me yelled in concern for myself, and the book. It certainly looks like it is bound in skin, written in blood. But I know for a FACT that it can't be the original. It is too small, and too young. It looks old, make no doubt, but not centuries upon centuries old, unless I am deceived. My only hypothesis is a very clever—or mad—imitation of the original. Perhaps the copiers assumed the book's authenticity, and allowed the requirement of skin and blood as spell components.

And that brings me to the largest fright of my professional career. Despite all the care of the graduate students who packaged the book—not knowing what they held, only that I valued it greatly—the box on my doorstep was open to the elements, even if only a sliver. I'm no expert on shipping containers or vermin, but it almost looked like it was set upon by a dog, torn at the corner. If a carrion eater smelled the book and thought it a hearty meal, it stopped short of actually touching the book itself. Perhaps I have just averted disaster. It could certainly have been worse. It was not snowing, today or yesterday. In fact, the winter weather is incredibly dry, perfectly dry, although bitterly cold.

26 DECEMBER

Obviously I was exhausted. I awoke late this morning. My eyes opened to the N lying in my lap, my hands upon a page of visceral turmoil and alien diagrams. I am not squeamish, nor easily startled, but I could not help myself. I cried aloud on waking, shocked by the sight of human suffering so eloquently illuminated. I cannot remember turning to this page last night.

Cold, shivering, I tried to set my mind to the delights of a Boxing Day consumed by my new research. Several puzzles distracted me, and I cannot make sense of them. I had forgotten that I had dragged mud in the house with me the previous day, during the excitement of the unpacking. Not terrible in itself, but so much wasted time cleaning the rugs. On impulse, I threw the muddy wash water into my garden. The horrors of N are so vivid to me now, no wonder that I overreacted to the sight of a dead raccoon in the wood just beyond my fence. Some large predator, maybe one of the dogs that go unleashed in my community, had killed it and made a mess of it. The pictures of the N came instantly to mind, or I would not have even made note of it.

ठ

27 DECEMBER

I hope this is not going to become a habit. I awoke again, N in lap, in my favorite chair. At least this time I have the comfort of not being caught in a moment of pique. I did not cry out. I merely chastised myself aloud. My voice sounded dry and hoarse, weak, squeaky almost. I pride myself on a professor's voice. Hot tea and honey will answer, and that will be that.

But first, I must comment on the page: I see a winged daemon of hideous proportions and distorted limbs, apparently peeling the skin off living human victims. My goodness, how melodramatic can you get? I am sure that if I took the time to read the corresponding script, it would delight in the screams of the innocent souls rent asunder, yada, yada, yada. I laugh, and feel myself a wit today, but sometimes I see the page out of the corner of my eye, and wonder if that daemon is not putting the skins on something, instead of taking them off?

Why would I allow such grotesquery to haunt my vision? The simplest of answers: the pages are dry, the cover brittle. I will not touch the N, nor turn the pages, disturbing or no, until I have purpose to do so. I risk damaging what cannot be repaired: my reputation and career. Again, I cannot contain my own wit. I laugh in the face of evil.

ठ

[DMB: The following line of script is written in a shaky, erratic hand, in large, blocky characters, indistinguishable from Hal's own handwriting.]

ᚱ

Fhtagn! Fhtagn!!

ᚱ

28 DECEMBER

I am singularly lucky. During another night of obvious mental wandering, as evidenced by my habit of sleeping with the N in my lap, open like a gaping yet ponderous mouth, almost beckoning me to fall into it, I seem to have scribbled words in my journal that were part of my studies. How devastating if I had written in the N during my half-doze! The damage I would have done, to the priceless book, to my reputation, to the school's!

In my weakened state, exhausted with study, isolation, and cold, is it any wonder I would write such words? My subconscious calls out to me to sleep, and maybe I should. These words could easily be a cry of, "Sleep! Sleep!" but maybe the script suggests an instruction or even command, "To sleep! To sleep!" What is the Cthuvian for, "Perchance to dream"? And what of dreaming? I expect my nights to flow with horrid nightmares, residue of these studies, but no! I have not dreamt for days. If I sleep so deep, why so tired?

And I am not just tired; I am exhausted, devastated. I can barely catch my breath this morning, despite taking my ease, doing what I want when I want—which is to crack this ancient cypher. It is no situation to tax the strength of a man such as me: not yet old, not young, but not yet too old. However, the "not old" man that looks out at me from the mirror is pale, paler than I ever thought possible. I yearn for the sun to stop his frolic in the Indian Ocean, and return to New England.

ƛ

29 DECEMBER

Again, awaking to find I slept where I worked. My armchair is very comfortable, of course. I did not buy it for mere decoration.

The N lay in my lap, open again to a page I don't understand, and have exerted no effort upon. Some creature, winged, horned, three-toed and three-clawed, swipes at a human-like figure, spills the poor victim's blood upon a symbol or ideograph that appears to be a scroll or perhaps a shroud. The diagram is disgusting but not surprising, as many primitive cultures believed, including some in Europe not so long ago, that the blood was the conduit or source of power of the human spirit, or perhaps even the spirit itself. This ritual seems only to feed an artifact for another purpose, or perhaps to prepare the blood for use in an unholy recipe.

Speaking of bodily fluids, I seem to be having trouble with, well; I am embarrassed to write, even to myself, about having trouble with excretion. Urination. The exhaustion I have been experiencing for weeks has finally settled on my digestive systems. I drink water as normal, but my body seems to refuse to process it or expunge it. I sense no bloating, no water retention, no kidney pressure or pain. The lack of a second symptom concerns me more than anything. I am resolved to go to the Miskatonic medical school their first day back after the holiday, to let them practice upon me, and see if their teachers are as good as they claim to be.

ƛ

30 DECEMBER

That figure: it's not a scroll as I thought. It is the symbolic language of the N, referencing itself! The blood is pouring INTO the N!

I found the answer to the riddle, finally searching for that same symbol. It was as I feared, as I knew in my subconscious. Every ritual in the book shows a figure, man or beast, holding that symbol in its hand or claw.

The book names itself by that image! *Necronomicon* is not just the lexicon or cookbook of evil; it is the focus, the lens, perhaps even the "demon egg"!

ƨ

[DMB: What follows are several pages of indecipherable script—I dare not call these words—and diagrams that are unreadable even to Hal's contemporaries in the field. It is unfortunate that they are smeared with small marks of Hal's blood—macabre support of the state's suicide theory.]

ƨ

31 DECEMBER

I see the crazed writing of this early, early morning of the eve of the New Year, and I begin to despair. A week ago I would have laughed at any suggestion of the validity of these topics, these studies, these magics. Now, seeing the forms my subconscious mind drew on paper, I know not what to believe any more. I fear my soul and my body are already lost. I feel a presence sitting on my shoulder, and it is not an angel. It is only known to the west as a devil, but what it may really be, who can tell? Will I discover it? See it in a sideways glance at a mirror? Or do I merely delude myself due to illness unexplained, untreated.

ƨ

1 JANUARY

Today my vague fears coalesce into concrete, undeniable madness. I now doubt my every sense, my every waking thought and memory. I record here, in the haze of confusion, hoping pen and ink will bring sanity back to me in some future moment, or at least show to posterity my horror, my humanity, and my reluctance to be dragged down into this hell of self.

So, perhaps I should explain, knowing the agony it causes me to write this, even the same amount as when I look around my besieged abode. Enough stalling!

I awoke not in my armchair, not even with the N on my lap, as has somehow become my unfortunate habit of late. I awoke naked and prone on the floor, on my carpeted living room floor. Somehow, in my sleep, I have contrived (and my aching body attests to the evidence which my rational mind rails against, perhaps in futility, perhaps in pure stubbornness) to move all my furniture to the walls, clearing the center of the room, without order or sense, even blocking all the doorways out of the room.

In that central space, madness. Deliberate, competent, practiced madness. A circle of power, a diagram of evil magic, a gateway or portal, lay on my carpet, seven feet in diameter, with my body as centerpiece, sprawled like Da Vinci's *Vitruvian*, with my hand amongst the pages of the cursed N.

Circles, figures, lines, around and centered on my body, flowed out in all directions. They must have come from within the instructions of the N. I am sure of it, but cannot yet bring myself to search that tome to discover which ritual has been invoked in my home. I say ritual because it is not a study or a theoretical analysis. The candles are in place. I don't remember owning tapers of that size.

And why would a diagram drawn on my floor disrupt my sanity, make me doubt myself, question aloud my long-held skepticism against the supernatural? The diagram is sanguinography! I fear it may even be anthrosanguinography! No, no, no—

ᚱᛟ

[DMB: This page is smeared with blood and what I assume are tears. Hal leaves most of this leaf blank, and skips to the next.]

ᚱᛟ

I must not obfuscate. I must not hide myself, from myself, behind a wall of words. The marks on the floor are blood. I have no idea from where the blood came. I cannot find a dead animal anywhere. Most of my brain (and soul) is locked off from the certain knowledge that the lesser spells allow for the blood of any warm-blooded creature, even one dead, even one killed for food days before, while the great spells, the true evil, require blood from a living PERSON—blood collected while the sacrifice is still breathing!

I looked the house and yard up and down for another dead raccoon or something similar. I doubt a squirrel holds so much blood. And while my conscious mind would not allow me to search for a dead person, I found none. I am the only animal in or near the house, in any state of life or death, of any size worth considering. As I write this, I confirm I am not dead. Sick, yes! Weak, yes! Insane? Perhaps… I would rather be insane than a murderer of such skill and cunning and cruelty. (Are the two mutually exclusive, as I suggest?)

What have I done? Or, what have I allowed to be done? What have I, against all my science and learning and experience, unleashed into the world?

Again, I beg the air and the page; what have I done?

ᚱᛟ

IBID.

I have taken some long minutes to clean myself and dress. I cannot find my clothes of yesterday. Neither can I find any wounds on my person. I wrote the earlier entry awash with what I feared was my own blood, but it cannot be. I have no cut, no hole, not even a missing toe nail or molar to point the bloody stylus at me. Small consolation, as now I must wonder who or what served as the hapless ink bottle to this mad inscription.

I made myself eat a little, but my bodily functions seem to fail me today, and I am already exhausted, having done no more than snuff the candles and clear the doorways. I shall not wait for the holiday to end. I shall go now, weak as I am, and take the N to the University. I shall lock it up safely in the book vault—am I not its curator?—and think on what to do, whom to consult. I must end this evil now, and I need to get this monstrosity away from me, now, immediately, and perhaps forever.

ᛯᚖ

Here ends the personal journal of Professor Falcrovet.

ᛯᚖ

As is well publicized, he was found dead on the morning of 2 January by staff of the library. They found him locked in the book vault, dead on the floor directly below the display for the *Necronomicon*. He lay in a pool of his own blood. His body was almost completely drained, despite not having any obvious wounds or cuts. The police continue to maintain the belief that this blood must have come from self-inflicted wounds.

The authorities choose to ignore the implications of the trail of blood that led out of the vault for almost one hundred feet, into the stacks, and ended abruptly in a pile of broken glass, amidst which Hal's key to the book vault was found. A high window, directly over the key and final drops of blood, had been smashed out, probably on the same night as Hal's death, but that cannot be confirmed.

The solution to the blood trail is obvious to me, when you see Hal's personal notes to himself about his waning health. He was not a weak or unhealthy man. His symptoms, seen in hindsight, point easily to hypovolemic shock from severe loss of blood. I know that Hal himself would eventually have seen what the coroner takes as a flight of fancy; Hal was losing that blood for days before his death. His lack of wounds does confuse the matter, but not for me. The medical experts ignore all else but the blood on his carpet, and the blood in the library.

This line of reasoning now brings me to the details of the blood trail itself. The trail was marked by footprints of a most unusual nature. The footprints were not Hal's, as he was wearing his normal dress shoes. The human-sized prints—both left- and right-footed—had three large toes each, perhaps ending in very long nails, but actually appearing to have animal claws. The prints appeared inside and outside the book vault, all the way along the blood trail to the vault key and the pile of broken glass. Again, the police regard this as either a hoax or a coincidence, somehow trying to convince themselves we only wish to see animal prints, instead of random blood marks.

Hal's account is further discredited by the book itself. The Head Librarian reported days later, during the investigation and interviews of her staff, that Hal's notes in his professional journal could not possibly describe the *Necronomicon* in her vault. That book was not dry, brittle, or fragile, she stated. The book appeared to her to be in excellent condition, and she doubted Hal's estimations of its antiquity. Her primary concerns were to get the "disgusting thing" out of her library, to hand it over to the authorities to investigate the trafficking of such frauds, and to prevent further loss of University funds to charlatans.

However difficult the evidence is to read, however bizarre Hal's final state of body and written mind, I am not dissuaded from my hypothesis that Hal was murdered. Murdered not by human hands, but murdered all the same. The "daemon" of three toes slew him and took his blood to feed the *Necronomicon*, in order to revitalize it, or perhaps to prepare it for some immediate task of apocalyptic proportions. The book slumbers now, but it is visited on rare occasion by scientists of the University and the courts, as they attempt to identify the materials of the book binding and ink, with a frustrating but telling lack of success.

It is obvious to me now that it is constructed of human skin and blood, as the book itself told Hal, but not from some recent murder or delusion of sacrifice to an Elder God. They will not find the victim or victims, because the book is indeed centuries old. It is protected by its own infernal powers, and by denizens of a world we fragile humans barely touch, who appear rarely, and then only to do the important work of their masters.

If it were not for the love I hold for my late mentor, Halwarth Stephen Falcrovet, I would not dare to work to turn over these ancient and slimy rocks, to see what unearthly worms lie beneath. My loss at his death is overshadowed by the fear and dread I feel every waking moment, as if something were watching me, biding its time. I expect any night to be awakened, all too briefly, by the scraping and scratching of three long, bloody claws at my window.

PROFESSOR HALWARTH STEPHEN FALCROVET has served as the professor of Occult Studies at Miskatonic University for over thirteen years. He has advanced degrees from Miskatonic, Harvard, and MIT. He has published over one hundred scholarly papers. His book, *Analysis and Timeline of the Transition of Extrasolar Entity Worship*

Cults from the Levant to the Caribbean is taught in universities worldwide. He is President of the International Body of Xenobiologists and Xenopsychologists. He is an Arthur Murray dance instructor and enjoys cryptograms, logic puzzles, riddles, and cooking exotic foods from all over the world. He resides in Arkham, Massachusetts.

DARIN M. BUSH became a life-long fan of science fiction and fantasy after seeing the original *Star Wars: A New Hope* in the theatre as a child. He is the author of the short stories "Hot Steel, Cold Irony" and "Abducted by the Librarian," available on the Kindle. He has adapted Shakespeare for community theatre. His poetry has been translated into Norwegian and Japanese. He is a certified Toastmaster, having served as a mentor and officer many times. He has worked in special education and information technology. He can be found on Facebook at www.facebook.com/darinmbush. He lives in Atlanta, Georgia.

ARKQUARIUM

AN ACCOUNT BY WES HICKMAN
as provided by Folly Blaine

During my junior year of high school I volunteered nights and week-ends at the Arkquarium—technically the Arkham Aquarium, but nobody ever called it that. I told my parents I was volunteering to boost my college application, but really it was because of Ellen. Smart, funny, awesome Ellen Jasper. Ellen was in my biology class and worked at the aquarium's coffee cart. I'd been in love with her forever, since second grade at least, and by setting myself up as the only other male high school junior in her vicinity, my plan to make her notice me was foolproof—until I discovered you don't get much quality flirt-time when you're busy wiping fingerprints off glass all day, scrubbing algae out of tanks with a ratty sponge, and scraping wads of dried chewing gum from the faux-rock walls.

Ellen's coffee cart was in the lobby between the tide pool replica and the ticket office. Just past that you'd enter the dim, winding halls where I spent most of my shifts wiping down endless panes of smudged tank glass. But I lived for the opportunity to clean out the tide pool—people were always dropping their sunglasses and jewelry in there, just out of reach—because it meant talking to Ellen. Gentle, wonderful, thoughtful Ellen who, back in the second grade, walked me to the nurse's office after a fourth grader busted my lip and my shirt got drenched in blood. Ellen never even flinched.

I was up front one day, trolling the tide pool with my net on its long metal pole, trying to think of something to say. "Have you checked out the new exhibit?" I asked.

Ellen shook her head. "I've been stuck up here all day." She scrolled through her phone, laughing occasionally. I could tell she wasn't really listening. "What's the exhibit about?"

"Octopi, squid. It's just a bunch of posters so far. There's a cool one about how all octopuses are venomous from some *National Geographic* study. The aquarium's supposed to get a couple live ones next week. Should be pretty awesome. I hear Doctor G's got a knack for finding rare ones."

"Doctor G?" Ellen looked up from her phone. "Don't you think there's something strange about that guy?"

I shrugged and scooped a piece of floating popcorn into my net. Doctor G was the aquarium's marine biologist, one of those pale academics Miskatonic U was so fond of matriculating.

Ellen continued, "Gail in janitorial says all kinds of noises come out of his labs late at night. Like heavy furniture moving and squealing sounds. You know," she lowered her voice, "from those back rooms."

Ellen, who I happened to know was a vegetarian, went on to tell me her theories about Doctor G and what went on in his lab, mostly involving fish torture. She leaned against the coffee cart, screwed up her mouth, and rambled about how intersecting ocean currents off Martin's Beach meant Arkham had a lot of displaced sea life washing ashore or making their way up the Miskatonic River, getting stuck— blah blah something about global warming, vents along tectonic plates, or whatever. I tried to pay attention, but I was too distracted by the little downy hairs on her tanned arms. I wanted so much to touch them.

Ellen's eyes narrowed. Doctor G, she said, received all kinds of weird deliveries in the dead of night. Nobody knew what those deliveries were exactly, but they made the staff nervous, and Ellen—she tossed her long brown hair over her perfect shoulders—said she knew all this for certain because everybody chatted around her like she was invisible when they came to refill their coffee.

"I bet I can find out what's back there," I said, because I'm an idiot. "I know where they keep the keys."

"You do?" she said.

I stood up tall, puffed out my chest. "In the ticket office. In that gray cabinet against the far wall." I'd found the keys by accident, all carefully labeled, while looking for paper towels.

"I'd feel so much better if I knew all the animals were being treated with respect, you know?"

I didn't really know what she was talking about, but I said "Absolutely," and returned to the tide pool before she saw the blush creep into my cheeks. I plucked a waterlogged penny from the sand—heads up!—and slid it into my pocket.

I could use all the good luck I could get.

ᚱᛂ

Here's what I told the cops, later, about that night, before I realized it was easier to lie. This is straight out of the police report:

After I borrowed the spare key from the ticket office, I waited for Doctor G to take a bathroom break. It was a lot easier than I expected, actually. If anybody asked what I was doing, I figured I'd just say I was looking for a mop or something. But nobody did.

I was really nervous and not paying much attention, but the main thing I noticed when I finally got in there was a tub at the center of the room. The same kind of heavy plastic tub they use for transferring bigger stuff between tanks and you know it looked kind of like a squid through the clear lid—like the ones on the posters in the new exhibit—not that I was an expert or anything. There were a few dead fish floating on the surface of the water, all decomposing and peeling scales, like they'd been in there a while.

And the tank smelled bad, even fishier than usual, if that makes any sense.

The squid-thing though, I remember it had long wavy tentacles and a balloon head that was kind of a long, narrow triangle and a massive black eye in the center of its skull. Skull isn't really the right word... Anyway, the creature hardly moved. I thought it was sick? Legs just drifted around its half-deflated balloon head, a spongy whitish color. I hadn't seen many cephalopods up close, but this one though, I knew enough to tell it wasn't a traditional squid or an octopus because... well... at the end of each suckery tentacle was a small, white hand. Eight hands, *with thumbs*, slowly opening and closing independently. I leaned over the tank as a viscous, veiny lid slid shut over its single black eye and opened again, watching me watching it. Then one of the tentacles darted to the surface and the hand on its end *grabbed* one of the dead fish. The hand hauled the fish down to a black beak at the base of its head-foot, and then the beak gobbled up the fish. Freaked me out.

Then a toilet flushed down the hall—pipes always do this shuddering, clanking thing every time you flush a toilet in there. You'd think an *aquarium* would have better plumbing. And I got the hell out of that room before Doctor G or anybody else saw me. That was the first time. The second...

ᚱᛟ

The next morning I wanted to forget it ever happened. Well, I sort of wanted. On my way to grab a vacuum, I passed Ellen setting up a fresh batch of coffee and I stopped to say hello.

"Hey," I said.

"Hey, Wes." Ellen measured out a tablespoon of ground coffee, dumped it in the filter. "Did you—"

Ellen trailed off as Doctor G pushed through the front doors and strode across the lobby. The doctor's hands were stuffed deep in his pockets and he was muttering, like usual, but he was followed by two squat, thick-necked dudes, which wasn't usual. Affecting nonchalance, I picked up a pen sitting on the counter, and spun it a couple of times between my fingers before it clattered to the counter. Doctor G and his goons never slowed.

After they disappeared down the hallway, Ellen whispered. "What did you find out? Is he torturing animals?"

"I saw—" I started to say "nothing," but the way she looked at me with those huge brown eyes—every detail spilled out before I could stop myself. It was stupid, really. If I could've just said from the beginning, "Hey, Ellen, want to hang out?" I never would've had to break into Doctor G's lab to impress her in the first place. But now I couldn't stop talking, even if part of me felt like I should've kept the creature a secret.

I'd be such a shitty spy.

When I finished, there was only the gurgle of drip coffee brewing. Ellen brushed a strand of hair behind her ear. "I want you to show me," she said.

I blinked. Seriously? She'd believed every crackpot theory she'd overheard for months and *now* she wanted proof. Just the thought of seeing that thing again made my stomach roil. All night I'd had nightmares about pale hands dragging a bloated pale fish-corpse up and out of the tub, getting closer and closer, tentacles filling my nostrils with salt water and seaweed, until I woke up choking on my own spit. No way was I going in that room again.

Ellen put her hand on mine and batted her insanely long lashes at me. "Please?" She drew out the word, especially the "eeeeze" part. I swallowed the sour bile rising in my throat.

"How about tonight?" I heard myself say.

"I'll bring flashlights," said Ellen.

ᚱo

After our shifts ended, Ellen and I hung out on the floor of the ticket office, half-assedly studying for biology. The borrowed key was pinned hard and cold inside the pocket of my jeans, and it was a relief when Doctor G finally left through the lobby to the parking lot and Ellen confirmed his car was gone.

Reentering the lab, first thing I noticed: the creature was no longer in the middle of the floor. That brought a huge rush of relief, and I would've been fine calling it a night then, but Ellen wanted to investigate, so I followed her into the adjoining room reluctantly.

The overheads were off, but we could see by lights inside the tanks that lined the walls—enough to make out the edges of a long, narrow room, and a whole lot of occupied tanks. Water gurgled all around us. Ellen inspected the tanks, cooing at the different fish. I switched on my flashlight and swung it around the space. Waist-high elevated pools, shallow like the tidal pools out front, took up most of the room. I leaned over to see what was inside.

Behind me, Ellen shrieked.

I spun to find Ellen trying to back away from the wall of tanks. Her long brown hair had caught on something, something—I stepped in close for a better view.

Small pale fingers gripped Ellen's hair. Fingers attached to hands attached to tentacles, attached to a pale, long, bulbous, and eerily familiar head. My heart jolted into full-on freak out mode and my muscles screamed to run, but the sight of Ellen struggling stopped me. I lurched forward instead.

Ellen was yanking her head around too much for me to pry the fingers open, and they were tangled too tight in her hair anyway. What I needed was a weapon. Nothing in reach—except the light in my hand. Light. Dark. That could work. I aimed the flashlight into the creature's single black eye. Its viscous lid snapped shut like the thing was in pain and I hoped it was. Ellen swatted the loosening hands free, stumbled, and then sprawled on the ground.

"Are they off? Are they all off?" Her hands jerked through her hair, fingers raking through to the ends.

"They're off," I said. "You're just lucky none of the suckers got you. They looked pretty nasty."

Ellen groaned and tucked her chin against her chest. She was shaking.

"*Did* they touch you?" I crouched in front of her.

Her mouth opened, closed. "I don't know. Maybe?"

"Let me see."

I shone the flashlight at her face. Dime-sized welts trailed down the side of her chin to her neck.

"Holy crap," I said.

"Is it bad?"

I cleared my throat, determined to speak calmly. "Does it hurt?"

"A little," she whispered. "But it's my fault. I shouldn't have scared her."

"I'm sure it'll be fine." I glanced at the tank. A whoosh of sand went up like a grainy cloud. "We should probably get a doctor to look at it though, just in case."

"I just wanted—Oh!" she hugged her knees. "I dropped it."

"What?"

She was rocking back and forth now, rubbing her chin against her shoulder, scratching the welts.

"What did you drop, Ellen? Tell me."

"I dropped my phone in the tank," she muttered. "I just wanted a picture." She rose unsteadily to her feet. "I have to—"

"I'll get it," I said. "Scooping stuff out of tide pools and tanks is pretty much what I do."

I took a deep breath and shone the flashlight along the walls. Half-way down the room, on a hook between tanks, I found what I needed: my old friend, a pole with a net on its end. I grabbed the pole and returned to the tank. The water was still cloudy where the creature had swirled up sand.

"Hey," I said, soothingly. "I don't want to hurt you, little guy. I just need my friend's phone."

I raised the flashlight at the octo-squid. The creature cringed and lifted Ellen's pink phone above the water, its pale hand glistening in the shaky beam. That was curious. I didn't want to frighten it, so I set the metal pole on the ground. Slow movements.

"Careful," Ellen said. "Don't be scared." I wasn't sure if she was talking to me or the creature.

I reached out and gently took the phone. The case was wet and the screen black. I handed the phone to Ellen, looked back at the squid. Sediment was settling around its head-foot, its tentacles undulating around its base.

The creature lowered its now empty hand below the surface and then, slowly, slowly, waved at me.

Waved? *What the hell.* I waved back.

Then I made a thumbs-up gesture. The creature mimicked the gesture.

"Shit," I whispered. "Ellen—"

"Something's wrong." Ellen scratched her neck. "My face feels funny." The welts had thickened, expanding into overlapping lumps. I kept the alarm out of my face.

Over the water gurgling, I barely heard the outer door open and close. I held my finger to my lips, cocked my head to listen. Footsteps.

"We have to hide," I whispered.

Ellen shook her head. I grabbed her by the shoulders, and pulled her towards the waist-high pools. They were wide enough for cover, and I hoped we could stay concealed in the shadows when the lights turned on. I crouched under the table with Ellen pressed against me. Her hair smelled like strawberries.

At the last second, I realized I'd left the metal pole in the aisle. I stretched out my arm and grabbed it just as alternating rows of fluorescents flickered to life, leaving long pockets of shadow between them. I huddled deep in the shadows with Ellen. Doctor G entered, followed by the same thick-necked men we'd seen earlier in the lobby. The men pushed a wheeled cart. All three stopped before the tank with the octo-squid and, with effort, managed to slide the tank onto the cart. As they wheeled past us, I prayed Ellen would stay calm. The lumps on her face had grown to the size of softballs.

But she was brave. They didn't see us.

I eased Ellen back on the floor, wadded up my jacket, and stuffed it like a pillow under her head. "Stay here," I said. I was worried. The lumps had turned a vicious purple-red and she was blinking double-time. What if she'd absorbed some kind of venom through the tentacle suckers? She obviously needed medical help, but if I waited a bit longer I might be able to get us out without being seen.

I peeked out from under the table, careful to stay in the shadows as much as possible. The doctor and the men had stopped at the far end of the room, and appeared to be discussing something. They were turned away for now, but they'd definitely notice if I dragged a half-conscious girl towards the exit. I looked around for an alternate exit, crawling forward with the only weapon I had: the metal pole with the net attached.

I scanned the room from my hiding spot. The ceiling caught my eye. A red pentagram had been painted directly above where the three men stood.

Well, damn, I thought.

Growing up in Arkham, you hear things. Ghost stories wrapped in magickal moon lore with a heaping helping of elder gods and forbidden books, all swapped between boys and girls over dwindling campfires. We collected alternate histories like kids on TV traded baseball cards. As a child of Arkham, you just took for granted you lived in a special town, but seeing that difference up close and personal, in the place where you gave up evenings and weekends so college admissions might think you were well-rounded and responsible, well, seeing that kind of truth was an awful big shock.

The three men began chanting in a guttural language. This, I knew from the stories, was really, really bad. The men stepped aside to reveal the octo-squid splashing wildly in its tank.

I shivered and glanced up at the pentagram. I wasn't sure if it was my imagination, but the air below it seemed to shimmer and rotate, grow thicker, and take on a grainy texture.

Something shuffled across the floor behind me. I turned. Ellen was dragging herself across the concrete in my direction. I tried to wave her away, but the chanting was growing louder, and I became distracted.

Between the men, the octo-squid slammed its fists against the glass again and again. Waves sloshed over the edges of the tank.

Doctor G produced a knife from his waistband and raised it with the clear intent of plunging it into the creature. I reached for Ellen, to stop her from reacting, but it was too late. She was already screaming, "No!"

The men froze, turned, and then Ellen was careening towards them, unsteady. The men had no trouble restraining her, she was already so weak. One of them just pinned her hands behind her back.

"Keep chanting," Doctor G screamed, over the rising wind. "Don't stop."

I couldn't just sit and watch. Not while they had Ellen. I crawled out from my hiding space and stood, gripping the metal pole firmly in my right hand. "Hey," I said.

"How many of these kids are out there?" said one of the men. "Thought this place was locked."

"Say the words!" Doctor G yelled.

"You can see she's sick," I said. "Let me just take her and go. We won't tell anybody what we saw."

The men ignored me and continued chanting at the ceiling. Swirling air whipped my hair against my cheeks, filling my nose with the acrid scent of salt and low tide.

"The portal is opening," Doctor G said, standing alongside the tank. He raised the knife again. Ellen released a blood-curdling scream and clutched her face—just the distraction I needed.

I ran up and hurled the metal pole at the tank. Glass shattered, water rushed over the sides of the cart, and there was a terrible angry shriek from the sky.

Massive white tentacles spilled through the swirling clouds on the ceiling. Huge fists attached to those tentacles slammed into Doctor G and his men, sending them skidding across the floor. A different hand clutched each man and swung them upwards one at a time into a waiting black beak poking just beneath the cloud cover. Each man was ripped apart above our heads.

Meanwhile, Ellen fell to her knees, spasms wracking her body. What once were welts had become huge blister-sacs. Something inside each sac writhed against her neck, her face, strained, and then exploded outwards in a gush of yellow fluid. Tiny octo-squids swarmed from the sacs and skittered down her body, across the floor, and towards the small creature now flopping on the floor.

Ellen passed out before the end. She missed the massive tentacle-hand from the sky retrieving the octo-squid and all its offspring. She missed the shimmering clouds dispersing and the winds fading, and she missed the chunks of partially digested man meat hitting the floor of the lab with a series of red, wet thuds.

But I'd never forget what I saw that night. My dreams made sure of that.

Later, Ellen would claim not to remember a thing, and the marks on her face would be dismissed as an allergic reaction to shellfish—so much for being a vegetarian. Her parents would take her on an extended vacation, we'd exchange a few letters, but there wouldn't be any substance, and we'd drift apart.

Local authorities would announce we were all victims of a slow gas leak caused by shoddy pipes. Nobody would question it.

We were all high and none of it was real. Or we weren't high and all of it was real.

As a child of Arkham, facts didn't really matter. What mattered was this: I, for one, would never volunteer again.

WES HICKMAN currently lives in a landlocked state. Aquariums make him nervous.

FOLLY BLAINE lives in the Pacific Northwest. Her fiction has appeared at *InfectiveInk.com*, *Mad Scientist Journal*, and in the anthologies, *Dark Tales of Lost Civilizations* and *Fresh Blood, Old Bones*. As the Podcast Manager for *EveryDayFiction.com*, Folly has narrated over 80 stories for weekly podcasts. See more at www.follyblaine.com.

DR. CIRCE AND THE SHADOW OVER SWEDISH INNSMOUTH

AN ACCOUNT BY CALLIE-ANNE CERES
as provided by Erik Scott de Bie

I was walking down a hallway, which in itself was pretty damn peculiar, considering. The sound of rushing water surrounded me, echoing off the walls of the sewer tunnel.

Things crept in the dark—slithering things I couldn't see or understand but could only hear and feel, like a persistent cold I couldn't quite shake. Mold hung thick from the ceiling, dripping brackish condensation like blood. It fell on my bare skin, leaving oily wormtrails where it dripped. The mildewed stone felt slippery under my bare feet.

That's right. I had actual *feet*, which was past-the-bend strange.

Nonsense words echoed along the walls. "La yk ullm la," they said, and "la la fhtgan!"

I was moving toward something that had no name, something that made no sense. Biologically, physically, psychologically, it could not be. Every step was a step deeper into madness. And yet there I was, gladly walking into it like it rung the supper bell.

A deep croon resonated through the tunnel, caressing my ears and weakening my bowels. Nothing human could make that sound.

A part of me—and not a small part, mind—wanted to see. Wanted to understand. Science is my whole life, and I live with the certainty that all knowledge is valuable. Truth can hurt sometimes, but the pain's worth it. I pressed forward, even against every instinct cursing me for a fool and screaming at me to turn back.

I came at last to a curtain of murky water, through which I saw a dim green light. Shadows moved through the water, cast by something unseen. For some reason, I thought if I could just *see* the terrible thing, I'd understand… *everything*. I felt it, deep in my gut.

I reached into the water, which parted hesitantly around my hand like cream.

Something lunged at me in the dark and I sucked in a breath to scream.

ᚱᛟ

My eyes popped open and I found myself staring out the window of my second story boarding house. From here, the storied town of Innsmouth reminded me a bit of a pie my momma once took out of the oven too early: drooping at the edges and soggy in the middle. The snow looked like sugar half-melted into a congealed mass and dripping. Dirty water trailed from the icicles on over-hangings like par-boiled filling made from cherries about two months past season. Wisps of oily smoke trickled up into the sky, escaping from crumbling chimneys that looked like slits in the houses, completing the pie metaphor and making my stomach go all queasy. Not a great feeling, first thing in the morning.

Cheerful neon lights in some of the less dilapidated storefronts promised hot cocoa and cookies to passersby, of which there were of course none. No one was out on the streets in the early morning, and aside from a few lights and rusted out cars that hadn't moved in years, the place was a snowy graveyard. Down-right homey, for a vampire. Or a serial killer.

"Oh, *gurl*," I said to myself, in my lazy Louisiana accent that has prompted so many to underestimate me. "Coulda picked a better spot fer sweet dreams."

I climbed out of bed, flexing my strong arms against the splintery bedframe. The sweat-damp sheets pooled around my hips in an indecent manner and the air hung thick with the greasy tang of a coal heater. The dream was unsettling, for sure, but I'm a biochemist. I've seen a lot of strange stuff in my time—and created a lot more—but rarely did it intrude on my personal time. And that language, both familiar and alien-like. It drew me and repulsed me, and I just could not put it out of my mind.

"Where are those cotton-pickin'—ah." I fumbled around the head of the bed and my fingers landed on a smooth shaft of plastic about four inches in diameter and two feet long. Adorning the top was a padded leather brace I designed myself for maximum comfort. I pushed the covers off my missing legs and strapped on the prosthetics one at a time, then rolled up the stockings that had slipped down to the ankles. Momma always told me to dress proper.

A discreet knock came at the door. Marian, my landlady at the Innsmouth Jellyfish B&B, always seemed to know when I wanted breakfast. "Hang on, Sugah!"

I shrugged on my B&B-provided threadbare robe, which was a little improvement over the chill. Like all things in Innsmouth, it seemed about a hundred years old. I positioned my sweet self in the middle of the room, smoothed my curly strawberry blonde hair as best I could without a shower, and beamed.

"Ah'm decent. C'mon in."

The ancient curled handle turned, and the door creaked open. Marian—I never did catch her last name—was a stocky bear of a woman, her rectangular body the same width from shoulder to knee. Dark eyes under gray eyebrows hinted at a life spent weighing and judging people. She reminded me of Doctor Marta Rosenbaum, my favorite Advanced Particle Physics professor, but without the degrees and Swedish rather than German. Same crazy eyes, though.

"Breakfast." Marian's accent was a collision between a Massachusetts drawl and Scandinavian flow. She held a tray of steaming oatmeal, bacon, eggs, and blood pudding. The dream had gone and left me as ravenous as if I'd run ten miles on my blades. Which, in point of fact, I did once. Can't recommend it.

Marian set down the tray on the little table and looked around me at my desk, which was haphazardly strewn with papers and glass jars with murky contents. It'd be impolite to mention it, so I just shifted my weight to the side to block her, and smiled when Marian looked up at my face.

"You out, today?" Marian asked. She weren't never one to use four words when three would do.

"Just a walk out on the beach," I said. "Take in the sights."

"You walk on the beach every day." My landlady looked suspicious. "Good beach?"

"The best." I smiled even broader. "Sit an' stay a spell?"

That made Marian back up a step. It was a dance we went through every morning: Marian got all nosy for a hint about what had brought the highly degreed bio-engineer to Innsmouth, I tried to engage her in polite conversation, and she retreated like I insulted her. She nodded, mumbled something, and headed out the door.

I set down to breakfast at the work table, brushing aside papers covered in mathematical scrawl and a short-hand only I could work out. I left the blood pudding untouched, being not terrible strong of stomach, but devoured the bacon and eggs, and set to work on the oatmeal, which could use a little more protein, in my opinion. As I munched, I glanced over my latest notes thoughtfully.

It was probably for the best that Marian hadn't seen any of the papers. Not that my research would mean much to anyone but the reviewers at an academic journal, but to the untrained eye, my work could look... unflattering. The sketches were bad enough, but certain words caught the imagination in all the wrong ways. "Hybrid," "amphibious humanoid," "membranous anomaly," and—most of all—"deep ones."

That last came from pre-mission research, back in Boston where the web still existed. I knew as much about Innsmouth's past as could be gleaned from the Wikipedia page, which had last been updated over twenty years ago, apparently by a thirteen year old Lovecraft fan. Lots of legends of creatures in the sewer, who held court beneath the dark waves and exchanged gold and fish for blood sacrifices. I knew about the governmental bombing of 1928, which apparently the Bureau could not verify, and about the town's economic hardships since then. Apparently it had seen a boom in the early twenty-first century, returning to the ship-building that had made it successful two hundred years before, but all but collapsed after the economic collapse of '08. Now, fifteen years later, it was a ghost town, though recent reports of "Deep Ones" had spurred a tourism revival the last few seasons.

I set the spoon down, the filling oatmeal warm inside my belly. "Ancient magic, antediluvian earth goddesses, bio-engineered man-cheetahs, yes, but primeval alien gods from beneath the waves? Now that's just plumb crazy."

Still, the Bureau demanded results, and I wasn't finished yet. In a world where magic is a verifiable reality, who knew if these sightings were just hearsay to bring in gawkers, or the genuine article? And if they were real, then they might be a threat.

What I needed was a sample, something other than the moldering pieces of fish carcasses I'd collected from the shores of the bay or the streets and stored in mason jars. I'd analyzed the samples in detail, but found nothing out of the ordinary about them.

I bundled up against the New England chill and headed out.

ᚱᛟ

In my fashionable red coat, spotless white scarf, and multicolored wool cap, I reckon I cut an odd figure walking down the streets of the moldering port town. I trudged through drifts of brownish snow, my red-stocking legs shockingly bare against the cold. Breath steamed from my mouth as I went, and I could feel it turning greasy against my cheeks after less than a second in the polluted air. Over the last decade, Innsmouth had resumed its use of coal to heat its homes and rolled out gas-guzzling, oil-dripping cars that dated from the industrialization era. Not since the second Civil War that smashed the Union had I been in a place quite so filthy. It was as though Innsmouth had returned to a previous incarnation: the dark soul of the place, timeless and inescapable.

As the sun rose a little higher—it never seemed to get particularly bright in Innsmouth—I started to see a few others on the street. Mostly tourists, who ranged from boisterous, mostly drunk college students to foreign tourists here to see one of the most haunted cities in America to the occasional pale, dark-clothed teenagers or twenty-somethings, who lurked in the alleys and soaked in the ambiance. Many of them lurked near one of the storefronts advertising "Ghost Tours" or "Lair of the Deep Ones" or some other gimmick. Actual natives of Innsmouth were a rare sight: stooped, shuffling forms in dark coats and hats, crossing to the other side of the street when an outsider came near.

During my whole stay, I can't say that anyone native to Innsmouth—a town that seemed to take xenophobia to the speaking-in-tongues and cuddling-with-snakes level—seemed to like me very much. With my red hair and freckles, my propensity for sundresses, and of course my missing lower half, I stood out among the drab, wilted inhabitants of the coastal dive like a painted rabbit in a pack of 'coons. None of them made much of it, though, except to stare at me a trifle uncomfortable-like when I smiled, spoke, or otherwise did anything that required breathing.

That suited me—and my work—just fine.

I headed along the mostly frozen over Manuxet River down to the docks, which had gone through more than one reconstruction and collapse. The rusted out corpses of motorboats shared moorage with the moldering hulks of century-old cogs. A few seaworthy vessels were tied up at the docks, but even after a few days they would start fading to match their rotted neighbors. I saw one such yacht, which had been in town only a couple days, which bore the unlikely name of the *Hydra*. It was a luxury vessel with impressive lines and a deep draft. I'd never been much on the sea—my daddy always said if God wanted man to swim, He'd have given us flippers—but I had a sudden sensation of wind in my hair, a salty breeze on my skin, and an awesome sort of freedom. I shook my head, however, and returned to the dreary task at hand.

I made two circuits of the nearby coastline and found plenty of broken shells, garbage, and one dead jellyfish. The sea stretched out before me, gray and languid but for sharp white caps that appeared every so often. I stooped in the gray sand to investigate a pile of sludge, prodding it apart with a metal probe, but it was only a fish skeleton and some tattered cloth. Nothing I needed.

"Well, don't that beat all," I said. "A week freezing mah arse off, and what've ah got to show fer it? Squat."

I started to stand, but I caught sight of someone else on the beach and froze. He was standing at least a hundred yards away: a tall dark figure, black coat flapping in the cold breeze. It was the stark contrast of his visage against the sand and sky that caught my attention, as well as a blood red scarf that flowed from around his neck. I don't think he saw me; he was just gazing out over the waves, like a romantic vision from a long ago past.

Much as I would have loved to be all sociable-like, I had a job to do, and the Bureau's per diem wouldn't last forever. I made my way back into Innsmouth and along the Manuxet River, paying especial attention to connections to the sewers. The town had been built long before environmental protections, so most of the city's sludge got dumped straight into the river, where it then flowed to the sea. In the winter months, when the river mostly froze over, the ice radiated stink, as though the putrid water beneath was diffusing up through its patina of normalcy. The river was a stinking cesspool that no sane person with a fully developed sense of smell would go near.

I didn't expect to find anything, and for a long time I didn't. I headed along the river in my loping gait, peering over the grimy crenellations down at the gray ice. It stank to high heaven, but it wasn't so bad with a scarf wrapped around my nose and mouth. Amongst the piles of rubbish and feces, I saw a surprisingly large rat that scurried across the gray ice, looking for something. It was an ugly thing, all bushy fur and asymmetric features, with one big milky eye. I tracked the rat's progress until it settled on an object in the middle of the river, something that made my neck prickle and my bowels go all watery. Whatever it was, I needed to get a closer look.

"Hey!" I shouted at the rat. "Scat, y'mangy thing! Shoo!"

The rat looked up at me, sniffed the air, and went right back to gnawing.

I grumbled and headed over to the nearest entrance to the river: a rickety ladder that looked as if it hadn't been used in half a century. The rungs were slippery with collected lichen, sludge, and ice, and half of them looked of dubious load-bearing ability at best.

Didn't wear my climbing legs today. I sat on the ground and detached my legs one at a time. These I tossed down onto the icy stone below, then levered my diminished body onto the ladder. Least I was lighter this way.

Hand over hand, I made my slipping way down into the river. I grasped each rung tightly, and I could feel the grime soaking through my mittens. "Sorry, Aunt Paula," I murmured. "You'll have to make me another pair—"

The sixth rung groaned and buckled under my weight. I slipped right off.

My stomach curdled. I hit the frozen stone six feet below, and the impact jarred the air right out of me. I stayed on the ground a while, blinking up at the gray sky, gasping for breath. When I could move, I curled my fingers, and was relieved to see them do it.

Then I heard a squeak, and I remembered where I was. "Darn rat."

I flipped myself over to see that the creature had left off what it was doing and come a few feet in my direction. At least no one else was around to witness my entirely undignified distress. The rat stared at me, its matted fur bristling. It hissed, and I'm not ashamed to say I hissed right back. The rat scampered away, its claws clicking on the ice.

After a moment to compose myself, I put my legs back on and took a shaky step out onto the gray ice. Years of operating on two prosthetics had given me an excellent sense of balance, and at least I'd remembered the crampons this time. The ice groaned under my weight, but held.

"Here we go, then," I said to steady myself, and headed toward the object.

Ten feet out onto the river, it poked up through the ice, half entombed in a frozen grave. It looked much like the other hunks of trash in the river, wrapped in something gray-black that looked like old fabric. And yet somehow, I knew it was what I was looking for. Slowly, I knelt down beside it, just within arm's reach, and touched it with my metal probe. With a waft of stink, the wrapping peeled away like a gelatinous membrane, leaving...

A hand.

It was mostly skeletal, reduced to bones and sinew by the elements, and frozen in place as it reached toward the sky. It had three fingers and one digit that looked more like a dewclaw than a thumb. Patches of scaly flesh clung to the thing, molded and mostly rotted, webbing the fingers together like the fins of a fish. But it came from no sea creature I had ever heard of.

I retracted the probe and slid it into my pocket, then replaced my mittens with latex gloves. The hand had stood out here on the river for quite some time, but one couldn't be too careful. I repositioned myself nearer the hand and took out a Mason jar as well as a small chisel. Archaeology had never been my favorite field—too slow moving—but I recognized the value of some of the techniques. I tapped experimentally on the ice, which flaked off around the hand without sending any significant cracks outward. Good. Diligently, I freed up the hand until it could just move, then gently closed my fingers around it and pulled. No luck. More tapping, breaking the ice little by little like a piece of crust left in the oven too long, and the hand started bobbing. I took hold of it again and worked at the base.

"C'mon, Sugah," I said. "Just a little bit..."

The hand closed around mine in a sudden grip tight as a bear trap.

I must have shrieked in surprise. I tried to jerk away, but the hand held me in a death grip. I flailed on the ice for a second and heard a cracking sound. Then I was in the water.

The sluggish dark waters of the Manuxet closed around me like a cold blanket, and I was sinking in a world where all I knew was cold. My body fought to breathe, to move, to keep functioning. But even if I could swim, I saw only an endless expanse of gray ceiling, like clouds without air beneath them. The chill burrowed into me like a thousand voracious insects, digging under my skin to the warm flesh beneath.

My legs and sodden clothes became dead weight, worse than useless, pulling me down, down into the dark reaches.

There was something down there. The thing I'd almost seen in my dream. If only I could grasp it. It was pulling me down by the skeletal fish hand I still grasped tight, and I couldn't have let go even if I wanted to. Words echoed in my brain—nonsense syllables I could almost parse, if only my mind would open to them. If only...

Something caught my other hand, close to the surface, and pulled. My muscles stretched in both directions, toward light and toward darkness, and for a second, my body screamed in protest. I fought against rescue, longing to get down to that... that *thing*. To know it and understand it. My shoulders and arms strained to the breaking point. Darkness uncoiled beneath me.

Then I felt something give: the scaled corpse hand broke off, and abruptly the force pulling me down vanished. I shot toward the surface, slamming my numbed midsection into the ice even as my face broke into the air. A dark figure hauled me up and out of the frozen river, grabbing me by the shoulders for a better grip. The world felt icy and everything was white and I couldn't breathe.

"Thank—" I said to my rescuer. I focused on a floating pair of bright emeralds, which happens to be my birthstone, and which at the moment provided the core of a frost-choked world. "Thank you—"

Then a massive force seized my left leg and ripped me back under the water. It dragged me down with an irresistible strength that brought my rescuer crunching down to the ice to maintain his hold. This time, not a single part of me wanted to go down to join the thing beneath the water. The world vanished in a sea of bubbles and shadows. The frigid water stung my eyes and exposed skin, and a great pressure closed on my chest. My lungs were running out of air and my prosthetic tore painfully into my hip.

Slowly, I pulled one hand away from rescue and reached down to the straps of my left leg. I unclasped them, and the leg tore violently free. A dark shadow darted through the water under me, and then I was up and out of the putrid river, my one remaining leg dangling limply from my shivering body. I looked up into a dark face with vivid green eyes and tried to breathe.

ʕ̓ο

The next few minutes were a blur. There was a long period of muddy light and moving shadows, and then I was somewhere comparatively warm, where the wind no longer howled. Warm hands stripped me down to my unmentionables, then lowered me into a chipped tub where water flowed over me. It was cold at first, but it gradually warmed up, and that was good—a shock to my system would have knocked me flat.

Instead, I shivered gradually back into awareness and found myself in a Jacuzzi bath in a small but comfortable bathroom, with warm water flowing over me from a copper shower head above. I wore only my sodden underthings, and I heard a small clothes dryer rumbling away in the corner. The world rocked gently from side to side like I'd gotten into granddaddy's rye again.

A fuzzy white robe that looked very warm hung on a peg by the tub, and one of my walking legs was leaning against it. Reckon the other was at the bottom of the river. There was a pair of crutches too, which looked a little big for me. I put my one leg on, then shrugged into the robe, took up the crutches, and hobbled to the door. Outside the little room was an airy room, and I could see out the big windows that I was on the water. The gray clouds hid the sun, but it was still day.

"Explains the sea legs," I murmured.

"Oh, you're up," said the man in the little kitchenette. He ran one gloved hand through his dark hair. Steam rose from an old iron kettle on the rusty stove. "I just put the kettle on."

His dark, threadbare suit blended so well with the furnishings of the room that I hadn't seen him before. He was lanky with dark hair, handsome in a tortured artist sort of way. Now that he had turned to me, I saw his green eyes like polished stones worn smooth in a river bed. Somehow, they'd seemed brighter when I was drowning. He was the man I'd glimpsed on the beach, staring out across the waves as though looking for something no one else could understand.

"Reckon you're my hero, then," I said. "Callie-Anne Ceres. Circe, if you like. Pleased to make your acquaintance."

"Edwin Olms. Most people call me Ed." He gestured around. "This is my boat. Your clothes are in the dryer." The kettle whistled angrily, as though it didn't like being ignored, and he pulled it off. "Tea? It's English breakfast."

"Much obliged." I was still shivering a little and that sounded excellent. If he'd had warm cherry pie, I might have lost my marbles entirely.

"Sugar? Honey? Vodka?" He opened a very extensive liquor cabinet. "Absinthe?"

"Just two sugahs, Sugah."

Ed poured us two cups of steaming tea, and his own got a little shot from a flask he kept in his breast pocket. We sat down by an observation window, where we could see Innsmouth squatting like a cold sore on the coastline. We sat in companionable silence, sipping our tea.

"Weird, ain't it?" I asked at length. "The two of us complete strangers, bein' so familiar, like ah didn't almost die an' you rescued me. Thank ya kindly, by the way."

"Don't mention it. I'm just glad you're all right." He inhaled the warm vapors of his tea. "I heard you fall down the ladder and came to investigate. Thank God."

"You heard that, huh?" I cleared my throat. "Not mah most graceful hour."

"Could have happened to anyone." He gazed out the window

toward the decrepit town. "Not a lot interesting happens around here. Thanks for livening up an afternoon."

"Ain't what ah heard," I said. "All manner a'strange creatures luring tourists. Monsters from the black lagoon an' the like. Or have ah heard wrong?"

Ed was still staring out the window, and he betrayed no reaction. He didn't seem to notice that I'd spoken. "You aren't from around here, I take it?" he asked. "You couldn't pay locals to go near the river, much less walk out on the ice."

"It was an exploration of a scientific nature," I said. "I'm lookin' for..."

Again, Ed looked away, as though the topic not only held no interest for him, but simply didn't compute in his brain. I thought I saw the slightest twitch in his neck muscles when I pressed: a single nerve impulse screaming at me. A warning? Wish I'd paid more attention in behavioral psych.

I changed the subject. "You're a native, then?"

He nodded. "I'm in town visiting relatives for the holidays. It's miserable. I couldn't wait to get out of this town when I was a kid. Haven't been back practically since I started at Miskatonic."

"Oh? What do you teach?" I asked.

He looked at me oddly, and I bit my tongue. Of course he was too young to be a professor. Just because I got my first PhD at fifteen doesn't mean everyone's on the same schedule.

"I'm a grad student," he said. "Archaeology."

"Ah see." For a second, I thought of my dream—of the dark thing I couldn't quite see. Mentioning either the dream or the creature beneath the water seemed like a bad notion just then. Again, I changed the subject. "This has got to be the longest conversation ah had all week, not to mention the strangest."

"Why so?" Ed looked intrigued.

"We get this far in the conversation and you haven't mentioned

mah condition." I gestured down at my bottom half, with one prosthetic leg and the other missing entirely. "Most gentleman callers at
least say something about it within about twenty words."

Ed seemed unfazed. "I grew up in Innsmouth, where you're
strange if you *don't* have a disability." Ed held up his stiffened left
hand, and drew the glove off one finger at a time. He only had a thumb
and three fingers, two of which were webbed together. I flashed on the
desiccated hand in the river. Damn traumatic stress.

"Fascinating. Is that hereditary?" Instantly my cheeks felt warm
and I practically kicked myself for my rudeness. "Sorry. Scientist."

He shrugged. "Yes, all the men in my family have it." He put his
glove back on and gave an awkward little smile. "Do you always blush
this easy, or just in the presence of deformity?"

I had to bite my lip to keep from laughing. "Ah'll have you know,
ah'm a lady. Ain't nuthin' about me that's easy."

"How about drinks and a night on the town?" he asked. "Promise
I'll work hard."

"You always go for the girls this hard, or just tourists? Redheads?"
I gave him the one quizzical eyebrow raise. "Ah could come up with a
dozen more characteristic vectors, but not knowing your post-phero-
mone receptor configuration, ah can't rightly say."

Ed leaned in close. "Why don't you say that again, and I'll pretend
I know what it means?"

Cute. "You know me goin' on five minutes and already you're
asking me out."

"Well, fifteen, but you were unconscious for most of it."

"Ah'm mighty obliged for savin' mah life and all," I said. "But that
don't make me owe you."

"No," he said. "Of course not." He looked faintly flustered, as
though he hadn't considered that at all, and the very concept made
him very uncomfortable. Point in his favor.

I couldn't help but smile. "Well, ain't you just the tom-cat's kitten?"

"I'm rusty on my southern," he said. "Does that mean yes?"

I was about to flirt some more when a sharp knock sounded on the door to the ship's deck. Bundled up against the bluster was none other than Marian, my blockish landlady. Her dark eyes glared at us through the window, and I realized they were the same as Ed's eyes. Shared genetics. Obvious.

"Excuse me a moment." He touched my forearm gently, and his fingers felt very warm. Then he excused himself to go speak to Marian in a series of short, choppy sentences.

I drank my tea, feeling the warmth swell inside me, and looked around the richly appointed cabin. At first it had seemed like a homey sort of place, but upon further inspection, I saw it was full of oddities. I got up and hobbled around as best I could on one leg and crutches, checking out his boat.

What I'd taken for framed landscapes were in fact exquisite if strange abstract pieces depicting doorways of many different shapes and sizes. All of them were done in the same hand, with the initials "E.O." at the bottom. One in particular caught my eye: a round, black gateway with what looked like green slime that ran from its top down the middle. I reached out my fingers to touch it, then saw something else: a sculpture of some kind, about the size of a gallon jug, sitting on the counter. It had to be an abstract piece, but I thought I could see limbs and fins in its strange curves and folds. The dryer beat out a recurring rhythm. My mind stretched...

A hand grasped my arm, shocking me back to myself. Ed stood beside me, his expression halfway between anxious and worried. There was a paper bag on the table next to him that hadn't been there before. "Ms. Ceres? Are you all right?"

"Never better, Sugah." I looked away from the statue to where Marian was walking away up the dock, casting the occasional glare in my direction. "Mah apologies. I didn't mean to cause a fuss."

"Maybe I should take you back to my aunt's place," Ed said.

"Maybe you'd best do."

At just that moment, the dryer dinged, signaling my clothes were done.

ᛉ

As we walked through the streets of Innsmouth, with the snow-choked buildings drooping around us, I was keenly aware of everyone we passed. Most tourists regarded us with speculative glances—a one-legged woman limping down the street on a gentleman's arm—then looked away. It was the Innsmouth natives I particularly noticed, because they were all looking right at me. Whatever they were doing, from sweeping stoops to chipping ice to emptying garbage cans, they turned silently to stare at me. Unsettling to say the least.

Ed patted my arm in his. "People here don't like me much either," he said, voice soft. He was limping slightly, which explained why he had crutches sitting around in his boat: they were his.

"Guess that's a thing we have in common," I said.

We got to Marian's B&B in just a few minutes, as Innsmouth wasn't particularly large. We paused on the steps, like a couple returning from a day out.

"Strangest first date ah ever had," I said. "And shoot, you already seen mah unmentionables."

"True. Most of my dates don't lose a leg on the first date. You going to be ok?"

I nodded. "Ah'll put on a spare. You need these back?" I offered the crutches, but he waved them away. "Thank ya kindly."

"I'll pick them up later." He flashed me a winning smile. "Dinner? Pick you up at eight?"

"Good Lady willin' an' the crick don't rise." I grinned at his frown. "Means yes, Yankee Boy. See you then."

He nodded and made it down two of the icy steps before he

stopped and turned back. "I almost forgot." He held out the slightly crumpled paper bag he'd carried from the boat. "You were holding onto this pretty hard. Probably for science reasons. Figured you'd want it back."

"Thanks." I took the parcel, and instantly felt colder. When I looked up, Ed was heading away faster than I could manage on one leg and crutches. There was a definite limp there, but he was being a gentleman, and I let him.

I got inside the B&B before I looked inside the bag. Sure enough, the desiccated fish hand was in there, torn raggedly away about three inches above the wrist. My breath caught. How had I forgotten about this? I hadn't even asked Ed.

I sensed someone staring at me, and saw Marian looking at me rather suspicious-like. Then again, she always looked at me that way. I gave her one of my best smiles, then headed up the stairs.

Back in the safety of my room, I set the fish hand carefully in a metal tray on the work desk and stood staring at it for a moment. "Well, might as well fish or cut bait," I said, which was very apt.

I dove right in. As I worked, I recorded the dissection on a series of note sheets, then a series of notebooks. In all my studies to complete four doctorates and a smattering of master's degrees, I'd *never* come across something quite like this. Both a mammal and a fish, in a kind of melding I'd been unable to manage in my own lab. The work was too perfect, as though nature had crafted it, rather than man. The sample seemed simple, but the cellular structure was surprisingly complex, reacting in ways to different chemicals that defied understanding.

At the end of four hours, I still couldn't say what it was, but that made me no less curious. My mind lay open to all possibilities, and I felt like the answer was right on the next page, just waiting, if only I could find a way to *turn* the page.

I knew I should report in, but what would I say? That I had a sample I couldn't identify? I needed an answer. My mind craved it, even as part of me grew increasingly uneasy.

The truth was buried in this thing, somehow.

ᚱᛟ

The sun had set, and the world was black as death outside the window when a knock on the door woke me back to the world. Was it eight already? And here I'd barely showered or done anything with my hair. Momma'd be ashamed.

"Coming!" I called, which was a damn lie. I leaped around the little apartment on my muscular arms, putting on my best—that is to say, least dirty—dress. I put on my spare legs—the blades, which were technically for running, based on a South African design—and hoped my jeans would conceal them well enough to deflect any odd questions. I even gave myself a once over in the mirror for good measure, though I'd never been much for makeup.

The knock sounded again on my door, more insistently, and I hurried to answer. "Now Sugah, just hold on—"

Something big and dark stood on the other side of the door, and it lunged at me out of the shadows. I had the sensation of something striking my forehead—hard—and then my head hit the floor. My vision swam, and I saw the thing looming over me, smiling wide. My mind stretched…

ᚱᛟ

Somewhere water was dripping, an unsteady *plink-drip-plink*, and I couldn't sleep anymore. I've been given a lot of sedatives in my life, and so I know the feelings of one wearing off: a kind of gradual numbness slowing resolving into a persistent itch, my thoughts swirling around a central concept like water circling a drain. The haze lifted, and I was able to think and see.

I was in a dank, disused sewer chamber, hung heavy with mold and strewn with cords of something foul that dripped from the ceiling. A little bit of light bounced off the walls from a deeper chamber. In the near darkness, I couldn't tell what it was, and probably I didn't want to know. A rusted over metal cabinet on the wall glinted, a few feet out of reach. I pushed myself up, and in the process discovered a heavy iron manacle attached to my left ankle, bunched around my jeans. A short chain attached to a ring set in the wall.

"Well that's just inconvenient," I said.

Whoever had chained me up must not have known my legs were fake, because I just detached the one and left it locked to the wall. I hauled myself over to the metal cabinet, which boasted a mostly mold-obscured "high voltage" warning. Balancing on one leg, I pulled it open and hit the power, and lights buzzed on throughout the complex. Now that I could see the room better, it looked less intimidating, and the strands hanging from the ceiling became not entrails but frizzy ropes stained with grime. Hung beside the box was a cabinet with a sign that said "In case of emergency, break glass." I reckon this counted.

I took off my dress, already dirty from lying in a sewer, and balled it up around my hand, then punched through the glass. The fire axe balanced pretty well in my hands, and worked well enough to hack apart the chain to my blade. Half-clothed, armed, and mobile, I headed out the passage and into the sewer.

I walked through the corridors, axe ready, looking for an exit. Despite the season above, the sewers were remarkably humid, and sweat slaked my skin. Rustling sounds echoed off the walls, flesh against stone, and the hum of ancient light-bulbs. My breathing kept spiraling out of control, and my heart gradually increased its pace until I could barely hear anything else. My thoughts made no sense, bouncing around in my brain like a thousand confused fire bugs.

A light-bulb whined overhead and flickered out, plunging me

into darkness. The sounds suddenly became louder and closer. I whispered an unladylike curse and took one hand off the axe to reach up and tap the hot bulb. My fingers tingled with a shock of pain, but I tapped and twisted until the element flared back into life.

A figure loomed out of the shadows.

I fell back a step, overbalancing on the blades, and yanked back the axe. The light-bulb swung crazily, alternately illumining the both of us, one after the other. I managed to focus on the looming figure by the second swing, but it moved away, out of the light, and was gone. I saw movement at the entrance to the next chamber.

Heart thundering, I pressed on that way. Suppose I'm a fool, but I wanted to know.

I came into a large central room, lit by a single flickering light-bulb that hung from the center of the ceiling. It buzzed and faltered in an arrhythmic strobe. Four flowing streams of sewage met here, and it stank fit to make my nose shrivel up in protest. The walls glistened with something green and sweating beads of moisture. My mind flashed suddenly to back when I was a girl in Louisiana, frog-fishing with my grand-daddy, when we watched a school of pollywogs bust out of a clump of eggs.

"You can't be here."

The voice was soft and not at all threatening, but it was so sudden I whirled, eyes wide. Marian stood not five feet from me, wearing what looked like a velvet black robe. It looked hot and uncomfortable, but the landlady hardly seemed to mind. She was staring at me intently.

"What is this place?" I asked. "Who brought me here?"

"This is their home," Marian said, her Swedish accent cold. "The Deep Ones. Put down the axe."

The wall moved. My heart raced, but I'd never been able to turn away from knowledge. I looked closer at the membranous wall, which swelled toward me, stretching like plastic wrap—like the belly of a very pregnant woman. I reached out a hand toward it.

"Circe," Marian said. "Don't—"

As if her warning was a cue, the wall of grime split and an arm, green-black and muscular, snapped out at me. Claws the length and shape of a man's straight razor snapped at my face, and I fell backward out of the way. I overbalanced on my prosthetics, which went out from under me and dumped me unceremoniously into the putrid flow in the middle of the room. Stone struck the back of my head, and everything went blurry.

Hands were grasping at my face, and I clawed them away as best I could until I realized it was Marian. The big woman was kneeling beside me, a worried look on her face. "You all right?"

I nodded, tried to stand, but only succeed in flailing my prosthetics to no effect. The world was still swirling around a drain. "Terrible sorry," I said. "It's just the floor's gone all catawampus."

"I told ya," Marian said. "Deep Ones, dontcha know."

"Ain't no such thing," I said.

"Tell that to them."

Half a dozen things moved in the semi-darkness, the flickering light only partly illumining their horrid features. They looked like four-foot tall frogs with legs and arms, hulking things of muscle and madness. The one that had attacked me slipped out of a fissure in the slick sewer wall like pus from a swollen pimple. It looked at me with maddening eyes.

"Well, if that don't beat the band." I put up my hands in a peaceful gesture, but I really didn't know if the creatures would understand the concept. "We got some sorta plan, Miss Marian?" I looked around and froze. "Marian!"

The woman stood unmoving before one of the frog-men, which looked at her with a swiveling eye that blinked with two sets of lids. She put out a hand, and it touched its chin to her palm.

"These are the Deep Ones, the children of our Lord Dagon and his consort, Hydra," she said. "They have ruled Innsmouth for centuries, and they will rise again. The time is coming when they will pour forth into your world and seize it once more for their own. But first, they need mates."

The frog-man put out its tongue and licked her lips, and Marian shivered with pleasure.

"Thanks, but ah'll pass, if y'all don't mind." I breathed a sigh of relief.

Marian looked back to me. "You don't seem scared," she said. "Or even all that impressed."

"Listen, Sugah." I couldn't help but smile. "Ah turned a platoon a'the South's finest into half-man, half-cheetahs—amphibians ain't all that different. Though ah'm curious how y'all solved the aeration process. And why do they have ears *and* gills? What kind of amphibian DNA did you use? Ah tried West African frogs once but the rascals had this tendency to—" The nearest fish-man nudged me with its fanged mouth, and I caught myself. "Sorry, ah'm babbling, don't mind little old me. You were saying?"

"And this makes sense to you?" A scowl turned Marian's face into something like a rotted squash. "You don't think I'm insane? Monstrous?"

"Now that's just down right closed minded," I said. "It all makes perfect sense, now don't it? Tourism's in a bit of a slump these last years, what with the Dissolution an' all. So y'all thought you'd combine a little viral marketing with a little mutagenic experimentation. Create yer own Nessie, or Bigfoot, or Ronnie Reagan to stir up some talk. Knowin' local legends, a'course you'd do scary fish things."

Marian bristled. "What I have done, I have done out of devotion to He Who Should Not Be," she said. "The Esoteric Order of Dagon has served our Nameless Lord throughout the ages, and now we return him to a world where the Interloper God has been slain and the heathen Earth Goddess grows weak." Her eyes were fever-bright. "The time of his rise is at hand."

"Huh." I tried not to laugh. "Just 'tween us girls and the fish-people, are you *sure* y'all ain't doin' all this for purely capitalistic reasons? Can't imagine this Church a' the Dragon thing puts much in the communion plates. 'Cept for sick-up and bones, a'course, an' those don't sell too well, ah reckon."

"Esoteric Order of... you know what? It doesn't matter." Marian reached out and stroked one of the fish creatures, which rippled and burped a grateful noise. "You're here now—you and all that fancy book learning of yours, dontcha know. Your skills will be invaluable to our profane task."

"Doubt it." I pointed to the tunnel where the light was coming from. "Ah think y'all are gonna let me pass, unless you prefer I don't report into the Bureau and they send a force to conquer Innsmouth, like they did a hundred years ago. Y'all don't remember that, ah reckon, but it's on Wikipedia. The river's even froze over again." I looked around at the Deep Ones. "Your frog-men make great tourist attractions, but how are they against Navy SEALs?"

Marian's confidence faltered. "You'll just report us anyway. Why should we let you go?"

"Wouldn't do nothin' of the sort," I said. "If only out of professional courtesy. An' ah give y'all mah word, as a Southern gentlewoman. Good enough?"

We faced off for a while, all of them trying to stare me to death. Marian considered, then bowed her head. The frog-men around her did the same, their black eyes tracking my movement. I strode through their midst, trying not to think about their black eyes. I was never coming back here. Not ever.

I saw a ladder at the end of a long hallway and headed that way.

About midway along, though, I stopped. The feeling of scrutiny had intensified. All the frog-men had stayed behind in the central chamber. The feeling was coming from a different corridor, where a circular waterfall glowed with greenish light. The humidity drained away, replaced by a chill that drove into my shaking bones.

I took a single step into the corridor, and heard a familiar crooning, which made my bones shiver and my skin crawl. This was no scientific aberration or anything created by nature. This was something else. Something that would make my mind expand beyond my dreams.

"Nuh uh," I said, and turned away from the hallway. It took all of my willpower, but I did it.

ʕ

Out on the street, grainy, soot-blackened snow was falling. Innsmouth squatted around me, desolate and rotting, a sore on the New England coastline. I never wanted to return to this place.

Ed was there, wrapping a blanket around my shivering body. As he led me away, I looked back at the manhole I'd climbed out. Remembering. Dreading.

"What is it?" Ed asked.

"All knowledge is worth having," I said, "but some things y'all just can't handle."

The controversial bio-engineer **CALLIE-ANNE CERES** is a product of her time and tragedy. A child-prodigy born in the waning years of the American Republic, she lost her parents in the great flood that claimed New Orleans in the mid-2000s. She acquired her third degree from M.I.T. at age 15 and made a name for herself creating genetic soldiers for the Confederate forces during the second American Civil War. After a building collapse left her crippled, she went into self-imposed exile for a time but has since begun work with the Northern Intelligence Service (NIS) as a paranormal researcher.

ERIK SCOTT DE BIE hails from the West Coast and a variety of alternate dimensions, all of them much darker than this one. He has written for the famous Forgotten Realms, *Pathfinder*'s Golarion, the Iron Kingdoms of *Warmachine*, among dozens. Owing to his ability to fold space and especially time, he is publishing three novels this year: a space opera set in the *Traveller* universe called *Priority: Hyperion*, the twisted happily-never-after fantasy *Scourge of the Realm*, and his epic full metal fantasy *Shadow of the Winter King*. He currently abides in Seattle where he is married with pets.

A DOG NAMED SHALLOW

THE TESTIMONY OF LILYA REDMOND
As provided by Erick Mertz

Back then I had a dog. Her name was Shallow. We lived together in a fifth-wheel, parked on a two-acre plot way up on Passmore Road. All around us there was this wide-open meadow, hemmed in by a deep, dark pine barren.

Those there were good days.

Shallow and I walked each day. We would strike across the meadow then down along the tree line. She loved walking, always mindful of my voice. As a reward one spring morning, we took a different path. We left the trailer before dawn, under a canopy of fog stretching out as far as the eye could fathom.

Instead of crossing the meadow, we walked through the barren. We were turning back just after daybreak when we come suddenly upon this man out walking alone. I had never seen him before, burly type with a stare as distant as the horizon. Had an exotic accent, a quality I've always felt attracted to. Shallow loved him. Couldn't pull her away. I remember a sense of lost time; although our talk lasted only a minute or two, it felt like eons.

What did we talk about? As I recall, we discussed the fog.

What I remember best was his manner of speaking. Maybe something got lost in translation, but to hear him describe that fog, it was like a living, breathing thing. I listened until we reached a particular moment in our conversation, then he simply vanished back into the woods. How odd, I thought.

That morning changed Shallow. Couldn't keep her close on our walks. She'd paw at the door all day while I was at work. I'd come home and find our space torn apart, like she was desperate to escape something. After nightfall, she'd pace up and down, keeping me awake, growling and barking.

One morning, I recall driving in to work. It was early October, time of year when the light starts changing. About halfway into town, I was overcome with a sudden, dreadful sensation that I couldn't shake. I felt like I had left the stove on, so I turned around and went back.

I approached the trailer and found the door ajar. As my hand went to the knob, a fear worse than a hot burner was confirmed: Shallow had escaped. I ran like mad through the trees, yelling her name at the top of my voice. All afternoon I looked, dragging through every blackberry tangle and creek bed in that barren. Around 4:30, as the fog settled, I gave up. My only hope, I thought, would be that she returned to the trailer out of either fright or hunger.

On my way back, I passed through a birch grove. The leaves were golden, still clinging to the branches. One gust would have stripped them all clean. In the center there was a clearing and a rock, unlike any I'd seen in that barren. It was hip high, big around like a dinner table and certainly did not form there. Seemed to me that rock had been dropped into that clearing from somewhere beyond.

There were footsteps in the mud, going every which way. I crept around to the opposite side of the rock where I found Shallow. She wasn't sleeping. She was just curled up, lingering on the brink, completely unaware of me. I whispered her name, "Shallow," voice trembling. She didn't budge though. Not even a slight twitch of her nose. A chill consumed me and it wasn't the cold.

After a moment, I picked her up. She was heavy, legs dangling as I carried her body away. We went up that hill through the gloaming, back toward our trailer. When I laid her down to open the door, I had a vision.

That man. As clear as day, his face washed over me. He's been down by that stone recently, I thought. He's behind this.

Shallow passed that spring. Don't like to talk about that time too much, except to say in those last months, I was by her side, night and day. I stayed away from work so I could care for her. I chose a spot on our customary walk to bury her body, in her favorite trail wayside where she would run up ahead and root around. Chose not to mark her spot. I dragged branches over the mound.

I'll remember where she rests, I thought.

This part I will tell though. On my way back from burying Shallow, I passed through the clearing where I had found her months before. As I arrived amidst those trees, I about fell over with fright. That stone had vanished with neither hole nor crater to mark its place. A patch of grass-covered earth lay undisturbed before me. I looked around, thinking there had to be a sign of how, tire tracks or perhaps bark burned by a rope pulley; there was nothing. As that thought trailed away, I was overtaken by another vision. I recognized more than that man's face. He knows that I'm here, I thought, as I ran from the clearing.

There was no doubt in my mind, detective.

I think of Shallow every day. She had spirit. Once she encountered that man though, everything sapped away. After Shallow passed, there was no use keeping the land. I allowed my lease to lapse and sold our trailer. I married some guy in town so I could be closer to work. The way I'm telling it now, suppose I was starting over, trying to forget.

I seemed to move on too, until the other day, when I seen that man again. He was on the news, the one you arrested for digging. You know whom I'm describing? The man who dug a grave down in that pine barren, only to discover there wasn't a body.

Right. Him. That was the man who spoke about the fog like a living, breathing organism. That was the man who stole my life away from me.

LILYA REDMOND ran away at the age of eleven. She was gone a week before returning and never spoke about her experience. Lilya has never been honest regarding her age. Some peers have placed her as a junior in 1982 although this she has denied.

She attended three terms at MU before dropping out. She has worked at a group home since 1987, never rising above the position of direct care worker. In 2001, she married Edwin Black, a long haul trucker from Toronto. In 2003, she made an allegation of verbal abuse against Black, but has since recanted her initial claim.

ERICK MERTZ writes fiction, screenplays, and poetry while living with his wife, dog, and cats in Portland, Oregon. He graduated from the University of Oregon with a degree in English and Comparative Literature in 1998. He writes full-time while also working with persons with disabilities and mental health challenges.

Recent short stories have appeared in The Los Angeles Review of Los Angeles and Mad Scientist Journal. His short story "The Measurable Blood" has been adapted into an audio book. His new novella The Pelican is due in the summer of 2014. Follow along @emertzwriting and his site: www.erickmertzwriting.com.

SO PRAISE HIM

AN ACCOUNT BY WESLEY STRANG
as provided by Samuel Marzioli

I, Gloria Stromm, a surviving member of the First Church of Arkham, bear witness that "The Revival," written by Mr. Wesley Strang, is an honest and true record of the events that did transpire on April 6th through April 12th, 1950.

Signed,
Gloria Stromm
Arkham, Massachusetts, 1955

ᚱ

Excerpted from "The Revival," by Wesley Strang

Mr. Todd stood, again, poised over the paraffin candles on the altar, thumb upon the flint wheel of his Zippo lighter. To his right, Pastor Stromm held his arms out, shaking as if he were supporting some enormous weight. Around me, the congregation lifted one or both hands, eyes shut as they focused on that single word of invitation, "Come!"

That evening, on Pastor Stromm's insistence, we used a new approach to praise and worship—loud and ostentatious, like carnival barkers enticing passersby. He said he'd been researching the practice for years before bringing it to our attention and that it was the key to our success. But so far it'd been four nights of raucous praise and prayer, met by an apathetic silence from above, and our own discontent. Despite it all, we pressed on.

"So praise Him," Pastor Stromm shouted, attempting to stir us up into deeper supplication. "I can sense some of you are holding back. He wants to hear you, so praise Him!"

Voices lifted in a wall of sound. I tried again to join them. I closed my eyes, put my attention on that spot behind my eyelids where red and black swirled in an endless corridor of concentration. My praising spot. After another earnest attempt, I sighed and settled into my seat.

Guilt tugged at the muscles of my gut. No matter how much I wanted to participate, something held me back. Perhaps nerves. Perhaps confusion about what this was supposed to accomplish. But most of all, the fear that our desperate cries for attention were no better than a pack of noisy dogs, barking and scuffling up the trunk of the wrong tree.

At the beginning of the fifth day's service, disappointment ran high. Though I chose to remain quietly indignant, the grumbling from others in the parish came in a widespread baritone murmur. Pastor Stromm reacted quickly. He raised a hand and everyone fell quiet.

"I can sense the doubt among you, but you *must* hold steadfast if you wish to reap the benefits."

He put his hands behind his back, began pacing the stage with eyes downcast. Equal parts Charlie Chaplin shuffle, and a death row march to the electric chair.

"You've heard me mention this story already, shared with me by the great granddaughter of the man, Francis Seymour, himself. In 1850, the Ten Faithful of Vinewood Street met in Pastor Seymour's house to collect in prayer. It was a humble house, not much more than dust and hardwood flooring. Hardly a temple fit for God. I dare say, for five weeks, nothing happened beyond good old fashioned fellowship and a whole lot of *sore knees.*"

On cue, a chuckle from the crowd.

"But on the sixth week, the last day of a planned three-day fast"—he slammed a palm against the pulpit, with a wood shivering crash—"the Divine Presence shook up that house and everyone inside it. *Changed* them somehow, once and forever."

His theatrics did their job. The congregation responded with an enthusiastic, "Amen!" that had them shifting in their seats.

"Now, Seymour's wife left the group soon after and took their daughter with her. She lacked the faith, lacked the conviction, to carry on. As a result, both wife and daughter lost out on the blessings poured out from that day forward, something I gather they both regretted until their dying days. But *this* close to the finish line, we can't be guilty of the same, can we?"

He fell still, turned toward the audience and dropped his arms into a loose shrug.

"Of course not… So praise Him!"

The response was instantaneous. Our voices lifted in accord and hands shot up so fast one might have thought Pastor Stromm had threatened to jump into the crowd. Soon, the sanctuary filled to bursting with hopeful cries and singing.

Everywhere, people began to shake in turns, as if a low electric current progressed from person to person and pew to pew. Pastor

Stromm fell to his knees. Mr. Todd rested his chin on his palms and his elbows on the altar. He lit his face with a closed-eyed smile, having quite forgotten the ritual lighting of the candles.

Even I wasn't immune. I could feel heat gathering in my chest and in my palms. A buzzing started in my brain and the world teetered like an ocean. For a moment, I was a raft thrown about by violent, cresting waves, which threatened to swallow me up in its vast waters. I choked, if only on the idea. But then I realized the sensation wasn't breathlessness after all, rather strange words attempting to rise unbidden from my throat.

"Kamsssa isss-cryp sssak-reepee—"

The spell soon broke for me when Anthony, the Leftkes' boy, turned around and stared. Amid the maelstrom of similar gibberish shouted by the other parishioners, I could feel his gaze—those twin beams of absent-minded distraction—burrowing into my skin. When our eyes met, he shoved a finger into his nostril and dug around. It didn't come out alone. And I couldn't bear the thought or sight of it drifting to his open, waiting mouth. I hurried from the sanctuary to stem the rising tide of sick.

As I stepped into the night, I took in a deep breath. The light of the only working lamppost wavered from half a block away and then fizzled out. After that, the street teemed with a dark and eerie silence, transforming trees into giants caught in a ceremonial sway, cars into crouching beasts waiting for unsuspecting passersby.

Once my stomach settled, I focused on the waning moon. Letting my eyes absorb its soft trim of glowing blue.

We were a church of the Calvinist tradition, and for the most part held ourselves proper and restrained. Though we were open to outward shows of worship, they were never anything on this level. And never before had there been such a demonstrative response to our efforts.

Whatever it was, it'd brought more than just mesmerizing

warmth, disorientation, and the compulsion to make strange utterances. There was hunger in it—a need stronger than the pulse of our collective desire, maybe even stronger than our will.

I didn't bother going back inside.

ƿ

On the sixth day, I almost didn't attend the service. The experience from the previous night left a hollow ache inside me, as if I were a battery drained of all its juice. It wasn't so much physical weariness, but like some indistinct quality deep within me had gone missing.

Nevertheless, my sense of obligation was the stronger pull. I'd been attending the church for nine years, had grown fond of many of its members. We may not have been blood, but we were family even so. And it was a small congregation by most accounts, only fifty strong, including children. No matter what I believed had happened, it seemed wrong to leave them now.

I arrived a few minutes late. The left of the heavy double-doors groaned shut as I crept inside the sanctuary and found an empty spot in one of the rear-most pews. Pastor Stromm was already in the middle of delivering another micro-sermon to start up the proceedings.

"It'll be a *hundred years*, tomorrow, since the Ten Faithful left Arkham behind for good, to preach the Good News throughout the world. From the testimony of the great granddaughter, power and signs preceded them, the likes of which mankind had never seen before. That could be *us*. We're on the brink of something truly extraordinary tonight."

We all clapped, though mine seemed by far the less enthusiastic.

"Tonight, we claim our heritage by walking the same path set out for us by our spiritual ancestors. Storming the gates, as it were, until God can't *help* but answer our call—can I get an amen?"

"Amen!"

"So praise Him!"

It started simple, same as the previous nights. But then the presence returned and it became different, progressed into something... wrong. I opened my eyes, took a look around the sanctuary. The strips of halogen above us winked out and Mr. Todd lit the candles one by one. The stained glass windows behind the pulpit—brightened by the setting sun—sparkled like jewels, bathing us in beams of primary colors. All around me voices rose, low and throaty, high and tinkling, laughing, sobbing, screaming babble.

I could feel it trying to force its way inside me—a sensation like warm water blasting from a nozzle. Only it was everywhere, all at once, and not even clothes or skin could hold it at bay.

"Stop," I said as it poured through hidden channels into the reservoir of my soul. My tongue lolled in my mouth and I bit the tip hard when the word "kamsssa" slithered from my throat. At the same time, I grabbed my arms, forced myself into a seat to keep my body from thrashing.

It wasn't hard to guess the presence did the same to others. I heard a growl to my right. Kathy, the Sunday school teacher, dropped on all fours and proceeded to galumph along the center aisle, barking. Martin and Cynthia, a newlywed couple, began to laugh—harder and harder, until they collapsed in their seats, gasping for air. Some roared like lions, others fell prostrate to the floor, and others still convulsed as if caught in a seizure.

"Stop this," I yelled to Pastor Stromm. "It's gone too far!"

He didn't hear me. He tore at his clothes, screaming, "I'm burning with the glory, burning with the glory!" tears sliding down his cheeks.

"No. This isn't right," I called behind me, struggling for the exit.

On my way out, I spotted Anthony. Much like Pastor Stromm, he and all of the other children in sight cried too. But unlike Stromm, it wasn't rapture on their faces. They stared up at the ecstatic display of their parents in helpless, stark terror.

ↅ

For the seventh day, Pastor Stromm booked Mount Harmony, a conference center located in a backwoods southeast of Dunwich. We'd held our yearly church getaway there for the last five years, so it was familiar ground. Beyond the complex proper, dirt paths twisted through the forested terrain, choked by conifers, oaks, maples, laurels, and a dozen other species besides. Less than a mile north from the sanctuary, the Miskatonic River marked the border of the property. And all around, the sanctity of nature: air fresh as new creation, drenched in birdsong, and the moldering scent of litterfall.

Shame that it would be wasted on a thing like this.

The afternoon and early evening had been set aside for free time, family events, and dinner. I arrived late, during the hour of preparation for the evening service. When I entered the conference sanctuary, I found Pastor Stromm's wife seated on the front row pew, lilting her head while singing a hymn. Mr. Todd fixed up a makeshift altar out of a folding table and a tablecloth on which to set the candlesticks. As for Pastor Stromm, he paced the stage, muttering things I couldn't hear over the distance.

Once he saw me, he waved and smiled, causing his white and gray speckled mustache to lift into a lazy M.

"Ah, an eager beaver! Welcome, Wesley. We saved you a spot up front," he said, with a mischievous wink.

I hurried over, greeted Mr. Todd and Mrs. Stromm with a casual nod along the way, and said to the pastor behind a cupped hand, "Do you have time to talk?"

"Of course," said Pastor Stromm.

"In private?"

"If necessary."

We headed outside. Most of the congregation remained in the

dining hall. However, Mr. and Mrs. Bettridge strolled around the complex, their kids chasing after chattering squirrels. Martin and Cynthia, the laughing couple, sat on a wooden bench as they gazed—thoughtful and composed—into the foliage above. All appeared calm and, I must admit, it shook my convictions over what I'd come to say.

"Pastor Stromm, I'm worried about tonight's service."

"Whatever for?"

"I have my doubts about all this, for lack of a better term, strangeness. It has the feel of menace, not the peace you'd expect from something good. Beyond that…" I glanced around to ensure we weren't being overheard and, seeing we were not, continued in a conspiratorial tone. "The way people lost control and the chaos that ensued the last few nights? If it happens again, someone might get hurt."

He folded his arms. "Yes, I admit things got a bit hectic. Tonight will be different, though. You'll see."

"I don't know, Pastor Stromm." There was so much more I couldn't say, feelings and intuitions that had stirred my concern, but resisted all attempts at elucidation. "Maybe we'd be better off canceling the whole thing."

"I can't do that. After all our hard work, how can I tell them it was for nothing?"

"Do what you believe is right. However, I'm not sure I can take part in it anymore."

His eyes narrowed and his cheeks drew up, tight. "Wesley, you can't leave. Look, you have my word I'll keep the service in order. But let's say you're right and things do get out of hand. I could use a level head in the congregation to help keep things straight."

There was just enough logic in his suggestion to make me hesitate.

"Please. Everything will make sense after tonight," he said.

Against my better judgment, I stayed.

ro

Just as the sun set, we assembled for the final service. The crowd sat, anxious, even if the mood was dampened by having to cram into only a handful of pews. Though the outside air held a moderate chill, the conference sanctuary sweltered from our close proximity and accumulated breaths. Many of the service pamphlets were converted into fans, their *swoosh, swoosh, swoosh* accentuating the drone of Mrs. Stromm's pre-service announcements.

After a few other speakers took their turn on stage—with news about upcoming summer programs, and a few testimonials—Pastor Stromm sidled up to the pulpit.

"Welcome, my friends, to the Day of Paramount!"

We clapped. A few whistles rose above the clamor.

"It's been a hard journey. We started out dedicated to a single goal: to make ourselves heard, to demand the presence of the Almighty Himself. The Church of Vinewood accomplished this task with only ten voices. How much more can we accomplish with *fifty*?"

More applause, more whistles.

"I put aside something special for tonight," he said, holding up an old, cracked and warped leather-bound book. "This is the journal of Pastor Francis Seymour, given to me by his great granddaughter."

He flipped to the end among an excited murmur from the crowd.

"I think you'll find this interesting. In Seymour's own words, 'Again, an angel of the Lord came into our midst in the form of a man. He told us not to fear him, but that he came because we had gained the admiration of the Heavenly Host through our prayers and perseverance. As a result, he brought a gift, words that would invite the presence of the Divine whenever recited. Words spoken in the *angelic tongue*'!"

He looked up. "Are you ready for this? 'Kamsa is'cryp sakr'pe dug'luman," he said, throwing an arm out in violent swipes, like he was launching miracles into the congregation. "You recognize them, don't you? The *same words* revealed to us over the course of Revival Week!"

A wave of applause and a few more scattered whistles. Pastor Stromm snapped the book shut and placed it aside, fixing us with a heavy gaze.

"Tonight, I want us to try something different. Instead of prayer, instead of song, I want us to say *these* words. Speak in His own language. And brace yourselves, folks, because this is going to get *intense*."

The hairs on my body stood on end and my insides tingled from a soft vibration, the source of which was indiscernible. I slid from my chair onto my feet.

"Kamsa is-cryp sak-repe dug-luman," they chanted.

The presence returned, filling the empty spaces all around us so that the air felt thick as water. I took a few steps toward the exit.

"Kamssa iss-cryp ssak-reepe dug-luumaan."

A rumble arose like from a gathering storm. I rushed for the open door.

"Kamsssa isss-cryp sssak-reepee dug-luuuumaaaan."

The sanctuary splintered before my eyes, hairline cracks in the fabric of existence, strengthening the presence's power. It attempted to take me over just like before. Sweat poured from every crevice of my body and I began to speak those words despite the absence of intent. Had I not broken past the threshold in that fraction of a second in which it tried, it would have succeeded.

I ran from there, hurtling through the dark, until I found a dirt path and veered into the heart of the forest. All around me, the trees stood silent, a taunting contradiction to the permeating screams that replaced the congregation's chant. Despite the speed with which I traveled, somehow I managed to stay upon that path—and not tumble down the hillside into the canyon below, or ram into a trunk.

But several miles on, the bitter realization sunk in. Everyone I'd known and cared about for the last nine years now stood in harm's way. Because of fear, I'd left them all behind without a second thought. And only He knew what that thing, that demonic presence, had done to them once they'd set it free. If there was any chance, any chance at all, of saving them, I had to try.

I took a deep breath, rolled my eyes up. My heart pounded like a fist against the back of my ribs. I turned and went back the way I came.

ꓭ

Closer to the complex, before the trees thinned out completely, I ducked into a thicket and searched for movement. The power had been cut, and the only light came from emergency back-up lamps—one or two tucked into the corners of every building. Far from easing my fear, it made it worse. Only enough light persisted to accentuate the black pools of shadow, expanding and contracting like living, breathing things.

I cast a glance into the deep of the forest. In the direction of the river, I could hear manic laughter, similar in kind to the sixth-day service, only coarser and utterly mirthless. Interspersed among it was the sound of coughing, sputtering, terrified shrieks. And then more laughter.

After a few more moments, I braved the open space, creeping forward in long, quiet strides. When I stepped into the passage between the dining hall and the (unused) nursery, the darkness ahead of me clarified into a figure. It was Anthony, the Leftke boy, standing alone in the middle of the walkway.

"Anthony," I whispered. "Are you alone? Where are your parents?"

He didn't respond, didn't move. If anything, he held himself more still.

I crept closer. The second I could see the details of his face—his empty eyes and the thin line of his mouth—he lifted a finger and plunged it in a nostril. It didn't stop. The wet sound of sliding gave way to a hollow crack and the nostril split from the fat of his knuckle. When finally he pulled it out, something big, red, and meaty clung to its tip.

"Oh dear God," I said, and he sneered at my words, lipping the chunk and pulling the finger away clean.

I ran past, giving him a wide berth. Within moments, I tripped over something soft lying across the walkway. It was Martin and Cynthia, and they were dead. Their eyes bulged from their sockets, mouths stretched out in cheek-splitting grins, baring every tooth. Their skin was tinted a shade that could have been gray or blue, as if they'd choked on their own laughter.

There was no time to react. A series of growls alerted me that things prowled close by. Perhaps humans emulating animal noises, but nothing like the embarrassing display of the sixth-day sermon when Kathy scampered down the aisle on hands and knees, barking like a dog. These were unrestrained, violent, and debased articulations—the sounds of madness. And they were converging on my position.

I backtracked toward the forest, but more growls came from that direction. So I turned again, retreating down the walkway that skirted past the sanctuary. There, beside the entrance, Mr. Todd stood behind the makeshift altar. The sight of him flooded me with relief—until I noticed what he was doing. It snatched the breath from my throat and I skidded to a halt, incapable of moving.

In place of the candles lay three severed heads, hair slicked up in even spires. Mr. Todd studied the closest one, flicked his Zippo and put the flame against its tip. Each time, the spire sizzled and smoked, but never stayed lit. That didn't stop him from trying again and again.

"What is this?" I said.

He looked up in surprise, as if he'd only just noticed me.

"Ah, Wesley. There you are," he said, his voice soft, even gentle. "Pastor Stromm is looking for you. He said to say, if I should come upon you, that he'd failed to live up to his promise. But if it was any consolation, you were right and had every reason to be worried."

"Pastor... Stromm?" I muttered, barely able to think.

"Yes. If you want to speak to him, you'll have to step inside," he said, motioning to the sanctuary door.

More murderous growls, this time from every direction.

"Better hurry. The 'hounds' are drawing near," he said, using his fingers to indicate quotations. "And just between you and me, I think a few of them are angry you missed the doling out of holy gifts."

I nodded, though I don't know why, and ducked through the door. The wall-mounted emergency lamps inside were drenched with blood, bathing the sanctuary in the crimson light of a darkroom. A dozen bodies slumped against the pews, a few poised as if sleeping, others ripped apart and scattered along the aisles. Pastor Stromm stood upon the stage, his arms held out and wavering from an invisible weight—just like during the fourth-day sermon. Only now, they were stumps, severed just above the elbow joint.

"What happened? What did this to you?" I asked, my hands clenched and held out to steady myself against slicks of blood.

He turned his head, nothing else, in my direction. "Oh, Wesley. You're still here? I'd hoped you had escaped all this."

"Where is everyone?"

"Most of them are by the river. Drowning the children and then themselves. I'm sure you heard the rest skulking about outside."

"The Ten Faithful. They never served on any worldwide mission, did they? They got the attention of the other side alright, but it wasn't Heaven. It was Hell."

"Hmmm, yes, I may have been a bit hasty in my conclusions. The evidence was circumstantial at best, but I thought I had it right. In any case, nothing good came of the Ten Faithful of Vinewood, of that we can be certain," he said, stretching his stumps to indicate the state of the sanctuary. "But you're wrong about the latter part."

"What do you mean?"

"It wasn't Hell unleashed tonight. In fact, I suspect things are a *lot* more complicated than we had ever imagined."

He nudged his head, indicating something behind me.

I turned and saw a man, a stranger, standing by the doorway. Naked, his skin lay spoiled by deep gouges dripping red across his entire body. His eyes stared, piercing me with an inscrutable, ageless gaze.

"Come," he said, his voice strong, but nondescript. Everyone's voice, but no one's. "You've earned your rest."

He took a silent step toward me, stretching his arms out as if to embrace me, revealing gaping holes that spanned from shoulders to wrists.

I spun around to face Pastor Stromm, shaking my head to deny the evidence of my senses, attempting to rewrite the memory of what I'd just seen. Confusion muted my voice, but I pressed the question with my body, my mind, and everything inside me—screaming it at Pastor Stromm with all my might.

He nodded. "We called and He came."

Fingers curled around my shoulder, bearing the same weight and pressure as that familiar presence. Though the hand remained solid, something entered me. My insides shuddered; that indefinable energy began to drain away. Then my mind unfolded, and the universe revealed itself—the false dichotomy of things I took for granted. Darkness and light, heat and cold, being and nothingness, sanity and madness, good and evil? Mere forms of the same existence. Different modes of the same underlying power, all bearing the same substance.

And all of it derived from him.

I fell to the ground, staring up at the presence now made manifest. Looming over me, face etched with both eternal indifference and endless compassion.

"So praise Him," said Pastor Stromm, before the void of laughter consumed us both.

ᚠ

A day or so passed in a forgetful blur, a sort of drunken madness. When something like reason returned to me again, I found Mrs. Stromm alive. She told me she'd stepped out to the bathroom shortly after she delivered the seventh-day announcements. When she heard the tumult, she locked the doors and hid inside a stall.

Together, we searched for other survivors, but found no one else, not even bodies. All signs of violence had been wiped clean away, as had the personal effects and property of the missing members of our church. As far as it appeared, they never came.

After that, we parted company and headed back to Arkham. For months, we were questioned about the disappearances by authorities, journalists, and the families of the congregation. Without collusion, Mrs. Stromm and I answered them in the same way, the only way we could—with truth.

By the will of God, they left this world behind.

WESLEY STRANG (1905-1971) was born in Monterey, California. His mother died in childbirth, leaving him to the care of his father, a career military man. They moved all across the United States before settling in Arkham, Massachusetts, in 1921. From 1922 to 1924, Wesley attended Miskatonic University, until financial difficulties resulting from his father's unexpected death forced him to quit. He eventually landed a position as groundskeeper for the University where he worked until his own death. He was never married.

SAMUEL MARZIOLI lives in Oregon with his family. His work has appeared or is forthcoming in numerous publications, including *Apex*, *Penumbra*, *Ares Magazine*, and the anthology, *A Darke Phantastique*. For more information about his upcoming projects and publications, visit his website at: marzioli.blogspot.com.

RIDE INTO THE ECHO OF ANOTHER LIFE

AN ACCOUNT BY CASSANDRA (CASSIE) WOODROOFE
as provided by Kelda Crich

Like the sound of thunder born in the motionless night, I heard the familiar bike pulling up alongside my trailer, rattling its dying throttles into the walls. In another life, I would have liked to have been a biker. The life is freedom. But biking's a man's life. I've never known a gang worth joining that would have a woman as a full patch member.

The trailer door opened. There's never been any formality between me and Sam.

"Cassie," he said, with a nod. As if I was still his woman. As if it hadn't been a good five years since I'd seen him last.

"I expect you're hungry."

"I am at that."

I walked to the kitchenette, glad to have the distraction. Five years on the road, five years of partying, had taken a savage toll on Sam. And there was something in his manner that didn't seem like the old Sam. He looked frail, half-starved. His beard was stained a dirty yellow gray. His head was as bald as the eggs I was cooking for him. And worst of all, although he was wearing his old denim vest, he wasn't wearing any colors. That worried me.

I concentrated on the eggs sizzling in the pan, frying brown in a ragged skirt at their edges. It was a pity I'd got no bacon to go with them. But I'd plenty of beer. I eased a can out of its plastic yoke, opened it, and handed it to Sam. I laid the rest of the six-pack on the table for him. Sam swallowed down the beer in one long pull. I laid the eggs and a bit o' bread on the table for him.

I sat 'cross the table watching Sam Drought eat. I could see the threads where he'd ripped off his patches, his colors, from his vest. The patches on a man's vest are his affiliation. It looked strange to see Sam wearing a vest without any colors. Like he was naked. No. Worse than that. Like he'd been skinned. "Trouble?" I asked, pointing to his vest.

"Yeh, trouble," he said. "I'm running again, Cassie. How old do you think a man must get before he stops running?" I noticed he was clenching his teeth. Sam always did that when he was in trouble. We hadn't been man and wife for twenty years, but I could still read him. From time to time, Sam would step in on me, take the couch in the trailer, running sometimes from a woman, or from the law, or just coming to see me.

"I expect you'll be staying here for a time?" I said after he'd eaten the eggs, mopping up the last of their gold with a heel of bread.

"No," he said. "Not this time, Cassie. I'm thinking I might just get on the bike and ride as far as I can."

"What brings you here then?"

He looked down at his empty plate. "It's about Kyle."

Then all the air went out of the room. I sat down on the chair hard, as if the legs had been kicked from under me. Kyle. I haven't heard from Kyle for nigh on ten years. Kyle: our son. "You seen him?"

"Yes," said Sam. He cracked open another can. "I seen him. I thought you'd like to hear about him."

"You thought right."

"He's in trouble, Cassie."

"Yeh? What's new?"

"Trouble," he said again.

"Just for once in your life, speak plain and tell me what's going on, Sam."

"He's part of a gang running out of Mireslow. And you know, Kyle. He's charmed his way up the ladder. Gotten to be the road leader."

"Yeh?" That didn't surprise me. When it suited him, Kyle could charm the birds out the trees.

"Yeh."

"One of the big four?

Sam laughed. "No. Not the big four. This gang calls themselves The Desolates, Cassie. They ride wild. Into some places I'm afraid to go."

That made me pause. There wasn't much on God's green earth that made Sam afraid. "What are they into, speed? Other stuff?"

"No, not just speed. Bad stuff, like the old days. In fact they're the reason I'm thinking about running. It's a big country. Even so, I'm afraid I might not be able to get far enough."

"I don't see what I can do about it, Sam."

"I've talked to him, and nothing I say makes any difference to him. And I thought… " Sam opened another can of beer. "Just thought that you'd want to know."

"Right," I said.

"Then I'll be getting on my way. And whatever you decide to do, you be careful, now. You hear?"

ᚱ

In another life, I wouldn't have got knocked up at seventeen. I married Sam when we were both eighteen. Got married quick. But our little baby, Annie, didn't make it to her first birthday.

Then I guess I got a little wild. We both did. Me and Sam. Hooked up with some bikers, partied hard, trying to forget little Annie. And that coffin. Tiny, forlorn.

We were okay, me and Sam. Free and easy. Not a speck of jealousy between us. Or perhaps it was something else. Something that I can't name.

Up and down the Miskatonic Valley we went. And then we hooked up with the last riders. And they was strange. We partied hard, real hard. I don't remember much about those few weeks. Can't even remember the name of the gang; I was doing a lot of meth.

But I do know that when we ran, I was pregnant again.

In another life, a new baby would have healed me and Sam. Given us something to love. But when Kyle came along, it didn't work like that.

I always knew that something was not right with him. I never did feel the love for him that a mother should feel. Not even when he was a tiny thing. The sickness didn't help. Kyle was jaundiced, and he just wouldn't stop crying. And Sam was half crazed with fear that we was going to lose him. And I was sick with guilt that the drugs had gotten into the baby and damaged him.

Kyle's sicknesses did wear me out. It was just one thing after another. It seemed that we had to give up everything for him. Not that it was his fault. But the tests, the endless testing, scrabbling around to pay the bills, going cap in hand to the medical charities. And the doctors implying that I was making it all up to call attention to myself: Munchausen by proxy syndrome. That I was inventing diseases for him. But they never heard Kyle crying, thin and wheedling all the night.

And Sam couldn't stand it in the end. He moved out. I couldn't help looking at Kyle and blaming him for his daddy leaving. Except Sam wasn't Kyle's daddy. Perhaps he always knew that, although I never breathed a word to him.

So when Sam left, I had nothing except Kyle. In another life, I might have been a decent mother. I didn't harm him, neglect or abuse or anything. I just didn't love that baby. It was as if anything good I'd had in me was all bled out.

Ƹ

I took the Blue Valley Bus. It was a long journey, stopping at all the small villages, along endless fallow fields and worn-out farmhouses, isolated and lonely. I never much cared for the place where I lived.

Just before the Miskatonic River emptied into the sea at Kingsport, just before the end of the line, I changed buses and got myself to Mireslow, a dozen or so miles from Boston and not too far from the famous witch town. Most of Mireslow is built on swamp. I wandered the town's narrow twisting streets. It was like I'd turned back in time. But money had graced Mireslow at some time. Maybe there was still money, because I didn't see no trailer parks. But the money that had fed the town when it was a resort town had faded. You could see that in the peeling woodwork on the old colonial houses, in the top heavy, gabled houses of moldering gray wood, in the small windows of thick glass painted with grime. It seemed like nothing new had been built in Mireslow for a long time.

I found the abandoned rail line running along a street of medicine shops. I followed the line uphill leading out of town. It ended abruptly in the overgrown grass of a boneyard. A lone white-steepled church stood with its door open in invitation. But there was no comfort for me to be had there. I decided to eat my bag lunch in the boneyard before deciding what to do next.

I'd spent the journey thinking about Kyle. And Sam. And maybe blaming Sam. Rightly so, I reckon. If Sam had stuck around, been a daddy to him, maybe Kyle wouldn't have turned out like he did. And even though Sam had said he'd tried to talk to Kyle, I wondered how hard he'd tried. Sam had been odd, like he was hiding something from me.

When Kyle hit thirteen, all his sickness fell away, just as sudden as if a switch had been flicked. And it made me wonder if the doctors had been right all along, and he'd been faking it. Kyle got his first bike. He began hanging out with a gang of older bikers. He was a good looking boy, and he had a string of girlfriends. He got into trouble, I knew that. I know the kind of bikers he was hanging out with. But all my advice didn't mean a damn to him.

It was no surprise when he cleared off at fifteen. I went to the police, but they didn't find him. I don't suppose they looked too hard. I asked his friends, and all they did was laugh at me.

And then I was on my own, and it was too late to start again. Not like I wanted to. I just went to work, came home bone tired, flaked out with some beer in front of the TV. I've never been a looker. Men left me alone, and that was how I liked it.

And I thought I'd left Kyle behind me, written him off as dead, but like the tooth with a rotten cavity, I kept thinking about him. And although it was fair to say that I never loved him much, I felt the pull of it. Who was going to look after my no-good boy if I weren't?

ᛉ

I was trying to read the names on the crumbling tombstones when I heard the bikes. The roar from an incomprehensible throat. I wondered what they could be riding.

The sound grew closer. The sky grew darker. The sound of them nearer, and still, and still they hadn't reached me. I felt the urge to run, like me and Sam had ran all those twenty years ago, from the surging apprehension of their approach, like the harsh wind bringing the night.

They came. Stopping a dozen yards from the edge of the bone-yard, sitting with their heads pointed in my direction. I couldn't see their faces (I didn't want to see their faces). Their heads were covered in leather masks of rawhide, with slits for their eyes and mouths. Lean men, looking like skeletons, covered in their leather. I must have stood a full five minutes staring at the bikes. I couldn't make out what they was. The feeble sun behind them dazzled my view. All I could make out was impressions. The bikers sat low, on bikes, like choppers, on black metal, languid and lazy as oil. Their rawhide gloves on the exhausts, revving the engines like the warning growl of a great beast. The air was full of fumes. When I glanced around at the church, I saw the doors had shut, and even that sanctuary was denied to me.

I stood, transfixed like a small critter about to be smashed into the tarmac, until the church bells rang out, discordant. The bikers turned and left, leaving me intimidated and small against the diminished sky.

And as they turned their backs on me, I saw the bikers' patches: the sign of the severed hand and the sign of desolation. I knew I would have to face them down if I wanted to talk to my son. And I remembered that I knew them.

ర

I got myself a room in the cheapest boarding house I could find, all the time thinking it was a waste of money. Even if they let me speak to Kyle, I reckoned there wasn't much I could to do help him.

I wanted to think about the bikers, but my thoughts kept slipping off them. I unpacked. I found myself thinking about what outfits I was going to wear, as if I was on a vacation. I remembered that feeling of couldn't concentrate, after me and Sam had run from The Desolates twenty years ago. At the time, I'd put it down to the after effects of all the meth I'd taken. But now I wasn't so sure. Crank can mess up your head, make you psychotic, make you see things that weren't there. But crank's not the only thing that can do that.

I wrote it down. I was afraid that if I stayed in my room too long,

I'd forget all about them. So I tried to write it down, all the details I was thinking of.

Bikers. Oil. Crows. Skeletal Hand. Raw Leather.

And underneath I writ a reminder.

Where are the bikers are holed up?

Clutching that bit of paper, I made my way to the front desk, where a lean woman sat, biting the top of her pen, and reading a Harlequin.

"Help you with something?" asked the woman. Her lipstick just about all rubbed away, leaving her mouth colorless.

"I…" My mind was blank. What was I supposed to be asking?

I looked at the paper. *Bikers. Oil. Crows. Skeletal Hand. Raw Leather.* I remembered what they fed me twenty years ago. I remembered when they planted Kyle inside me. And I never wanted them to take off the mask, never wanted to see underneath.

I looked at the paper again. "Where are the bikers holed up?"

The woman looked down hard at her book. She added a note in the margin in thin spidery script.

"Where they at?" I asked again.

"Oh they come and they go, with the wind," she said. "Honey, you best to stay away from them."

I saw a picture locket round her neck with a photo of a young boy. "That your son?" I asked.

"Yes, ma'am."

"Nice looking boy," I said.

She smiled. "He's doing real well at school. He's a good boy."

"My boy, he's with the bikers. My son, he ain't such a good boy, but still I want to talk to him. You can understand that, can't you?"

She went pale. "They holed up at the old Bass Shore Hotel on the north side of the lake," she said. "But…" She picked up the locket between her finger and thumb, rubbed it like a talisman.

"It's okay. I just want to talk to my boy." That was natural. That a mother would want to talk to her son once in ten years. And for all their costumes and paraphernalia, their codes, and their lifestyle, their silences and intimidations, they was men, and they had all had mothers. Sentimental sometimes. They'd let me in, I'd have a word with him, do what I could, and then I'd be on my way. I kept telling myself that.

゜

In a different life, I'd have stayed with The Desolates, twenty years ago. Instead, me and Sam had jumped on his bike and hightailed it out of there. And me carrying Kyle in my stomach. But all of my life they were there, in the shadows of my life. They colored me, scared me. They spoiled me. Like rotten meat. They spoiled me. Perhaps I wasn't here for Kyle. Perhaps I was here for a taste of what I'd had. Like an old addict whose longing never goes away.

゜

The burnt out shell of the hotel rested right at the lake's edge. The Bass Shore Hotel had been grand once. A seven story block of rooms topped with towers. At the east and west sides there was a hall with a gabled roof. But the roofs were nothing more than slats, the rooms inside open to the elements. I had the feeling that the hotel was contaminated, tainted with something more than age. And the quiet lake was deep, black waters still as a dark mirror. In the distance, the gray peninsula was scattered with massive rocks, out of place like a lake henge of unknown purpose.

I walked along the broken promenade looking for a way inside. When I saw the two dozen bikes parked outside the east wing, I backed off. The bikes repelled me, the strange oil and haft of them. I quickly retraced my steps to make my way round the back of the hotel, where I met an old man, sitting down on the ragged patio, his back against the hotel wall. When he saw me, he laughed, a ragged wheezing through his broken meth mouth.

"Come," he said. "All are welcome here. Especially a woman." His eyes were dilated, the eyeballs yellow. He laughed again. His eyes rolled back in the sockets. When he started shaking, I walked away quickly.

I found my way into the hotel easily enough. All the doors were gone or dangling off their hinges. A quick step through a moldy guest room led me into the long hotel corridor. I heard the noise of a throbbing beat, and I followed it to the east wing.

Once it was the ballroom. Now it was a throne room where the gimp-masked bikers stood in attendance to an ancient, thin man, sitting on a throne made from the carcasses of bikes. And I had the feeling that their owners were no longer around. On the wall was a patchwork of colors, bikers' vests stitched together, a flag of a kind, a trophy. A low throbbing music thudded into the room, an ominous sound that seemed to shudder through my bones. In one corner was a vast pile of weapons, guns, Uzis, even antitank weapons. In the other corner a couple of men hunched over lab equipment, cooking something that smelt both chemical and meaty. I walked with trembling legs to the man on the throne of bikes.

"Say what you want to say," said the man on the throne.

"I want to talk to my son, Kyle," I said. "I've heard he's your road sergeant. I just want to talk to him."

A rippling laughter broke through the men.

"That's all. I'm not interested in anything else you're doing here. I just want to talk to my son."

The king man raised his hand. "Clyte!" he shouted. One of the men cooking, walked over and held a saucer towards me.

"Can I offer you a little something?" asked the king man.

There was crystal in the saucer, but it wasn't white like meth, it was amber, oozing, sweating. The aroma of meat mixed with a chemical tang made me want to gag. I took the saucer. "What is it?" I asked.

"A sacrament," said the king man. "And you took it a long time ago."

"I'd never take this," I said, though I guess I couldn't remember.

"They unwind the thread and let you go so far, like flies on the line, but then they twitch and you come back."

"I just want to talk to Kyle."

"Such a shame when a mother doesn't recognize her own son."

"Kyle?" I took a step forward to the man on the throne, trying to see to recognize him. How could this old man be Kyle?

"It's me, Mother. Would you like me to take off my mask?"

"No, don't do that," I said quickly. It *was* Kyle. But he was so old. So changed. "Kyle," I said. "Let me talk to you alone."

"As you wish, Mother." It was clear he had a position of power in this place. As he climbed slowly off the throne and walked towards the door, the heads of the masked men followed him. I had a feeling that they weren't real at all, simply puppets, skeletons covered in denim and leather.

At the door, Kyle turned and said sharply, "Mother, join me."

Perhaps I could talk some sense into him without the audience. We left the throne room and walked along the hotel's long corridor.

"What are you doing here, Kyle?" I asked.

"We ride, Mother," said Kyle. "We take their sacrament and most of all we ride." He took a piece of the crystal from the saucer and rubbed it over his lips. "You've always wanted to ride, Mother."

"I always wanted to ride," I said. "I've always wanted that freedom."

"But we ride not in freedom," said Kyle, "but in bondage."

"Where are we going?" I asked.

"We're going to fetch our rides, Mother." Kyle smiled. "I'm so glad that Sam sent you to me."

"Sam would never do that."

"Why do you think that we let him go? On the arrangement that he go to you, to bring you here. Oh, he didn't like it here, Mother. But

I think you will. Poor Sam, running, running all his life. But no one goes for long. They twitch the thread and all return."

I thought about how shifty Sam had seemed when he'd come to see me. In another life, Sam wouldn't have betrayed me. I walked along the corridor with my young/old son. This was a bad scene. The worst scene. But I couldn't run. It was something that had to be played out to the end. "Why did you want me here, Kyle?"

"You're my sacrifice, Mother."

"You're going to kill me?" Perhaps this is what I'd always sensed, when he'd been a little baby. Perhaps I'd sensed the seed of my murderer in the baby.

He laughed. "Not matricide. There's a season for violence, but the demands of family demands something more intimate."

"I don't understand."

"Understand that we are The Desolate. Understand that we are the riders. We praise them," he said, "in every kill we make, in everything we do, in every time we ride, dark or light, and eat up the road. The universe is a big road, and we can only see the smallest part of it. Others have travelled here long ago. And every moment of our lives we call to them, riding on metal or on flesh."

"And what do *they* give you, Kyle?"

"Give us? They give us nothing. Don't you understand that they are so far beyond us that they are not to be bargained with?"

"I don't understand." But I did understand, somewhere deep and dirty in my soul. "What you're doing isn't clean, Kyle. And it's killing you. This is madness."

"I am one of them, born of them. And when I was in your belly, Mother, I fed that to you."

"What are you going to do to me?"

"I'm going to make you my sacrifice."

"It isn't a sacrifice if it doesn't mean much to you," I said.

He laughed. "Oh Mother, Mother. All my life I wanted your love, and you never could give it to me. And all the time I hid myself."

My withered heart had never bloomed in love for Kyle. It was a stunted seed. But now, in this dark, derelict, mad temple, I felt something for this child of mine, this flesh of mine. The tides slowly moving in the emptiness of my heart.

My son intended me harm. Yet I walked with him, listened to his delusions. All was too confusing to understand. All was bad/good/ sideways and meaningless. I was not smart enough to understand. All I felt was the unwinding road of emotion. And Kyle was happy. And did not a mother only want her child to be happy? A true mother, one who felt love.

"I came here to save you," I said. "I did wrong by you." In another life, I would have saved him. But there is no other life. Nothingness. I wish I could have been better.

We'd reached the end of the long corridor, and walked into the empty west wing. The room was littered with a trail of bones. The roof was gone, open to the sky. And the host of The Desolates waited for us, wearing their skin masks. They were a fellowship, and that was something. The bikers opened their throats in an obscene chant, building and building. And I thought that they have fellowship. In their obscenity, they know that others are like them.

Kyle turned to me, his eyes shining, the pupils dilated. He smiled. "We call our rides, Mother, the Byakhee. Out of the blackness they come, out of unfathomable places where they ride from cold flame to cold flame. And their body is the sacrament. Only those who have eaten their flesh can ride their roads, their roads, strange, looping in and out of the places deathless and eternal. And as we ride they eat us, until we become part of them." He raised his face to the open sky and let out the most terrible scream.

Like oiled leather they came, with skeletal flesh, wearing harnesses strung with bone. Hybrid creatures, bat and bone, buzzards, crows, ants and skin, and creatures dreamed only by nightmare. And the men jumped on their backs and one by one the creatures flapped their membranous wings and rose into the air.

Until only two beasts were left.

"The sacrament, Mother, take it willingly. Remember the feel of the weird in your veins."

My son, my old/young son, jumped onto the Byakhee's back and stared at me, willing me to follow him.

And I swallowed down that morsel of tainted flesh. I mounted the back of that unwholesome creature that screeched as it rose into the air.

And I rode into the coldness, the never echo of my other life stretching forward into the long road of the night.

CASSANDRA (CASSIE) WOODROOFE née Ruggles lived in the Miskatonic Valley all her life. She was gainfully employed as a waitress at The Happy Burger, Arrowshaft, for the last five years. Colleagues of Mrs. Woodroofe describe her as a quiet woman who "minded her own business." Mrs. Woodroofe's mobile unit in Nirvana Park, Arrowshaft, was left abandoned in April 2014. Her estranged husband Sam "Solid" Woodroofe is wanted for questioning by the Miskatonic Valley Sheriff's Department concerning her whereabouts.

KELDA CRICH is a new born entity. She's been lurking in her creator's mind for a few years. Now she's out in the open. Find her in London looking at strange things in medical museums or on her blog. Kelda's work has appeared in the *Lovecraft E-zine*, *Journal of Unlikely Acceptance*, *Mad Scientist Journal*, and in the Bram Stoker-Award winning *After Death* anthology.

THE GHOST CIRCUS

FROM THE JOURNALS OF JORIS SEVEREN
as provided by Philip C. Gonzales

It only takes a bit of pressure," the Ringmaster explained, "and the head should come right... there."

The child's head rolled off the filthy table and landed among the sawdust and viscera.

The Ringmaster let a contented sigh escape his lips, lifted the bespattered goggles from his eyes, and mopped his brow.

"Well," I said, snapping a picture with my battered Leica, "that was certainly an enlightening experience. And the child's spirit is where now?"

"Why, floating through the ether!" the Ringmaster explained, shedding his stained apron and exchanging it for another. "Playing with angel clowns and angel trapeze artists and angel trained poodles even as we speak! She is a part of the Ghost Circus now!"

I chanced a look down at the small head resting near my feet. The pathetic creature had put up a bit of a fight there near the end. Years of exposure to some of the harsher elements of the strange had inured me to the oft-times brutal and bloody practices I might encounter in my journeys. I had, after all, sat through more than one public flaying, several trans-piercings, and more than my share of poetry readings. And yet my gorge still rose. I tamped it back down by focusing my thoughts on the importance of investigation, the ideals of journalism, and the rent on my modest flat. The quiet repose on the dead girl's face betrayed none of the terror it had displayed earlier and stood as proof of the Ringmaster's hypothesis. At least, it would for my readers. I snapped another picture.

"And how many children have you sent to... the Ghost Circus?" I asked.

"Oh, several," the Ringmaster responded. "Tens of several. Dozens? Many dozens? I have a catalog in my tent. All of them transient and orphaned, so my work can be seen as a necessary service on both sides of the equation. The children get a happy future and society at large is unburdened of one more member of its increasing criminal class."

"And the body?"

"My dear sir, we have lions!" the Ringmaster declared and let out a hearty laugh. I laughed along. It was a somewhat amusing answer.

The William Price Circus had first come to the attention of *Unbelievable World Magazine* through the whisperings of our network of mediums—the few living human beings capable of interpreting the shudderings and wailings of the deceased and deranged—who formed a sort of psychic relay across the United States and who passed along rumors and speculations of disturbances in the "connective tissue" of the netherworld. In recent years, these "few living humans" had bloomed from several dozen into several hundred. A fact that I suppose should have touched off a few alarms. But hindsight and all that.

In 1931, several mediums began reporting "traveling fluctuations" that eventually revealed themselves to be following the railway schedule of a relatively unknown circus owned by one Mr. William T. Price. The traveling show would set up outside small towns, promising the usual flea bitten animals, lackluster side show deformities and tired feats of mediocre derring-do. But rumors had been circulating that well-paying audience members were being offered the opportunity to witness in private what was coming to be referred to as "The Ghost Circus"—a vision of spectral wonders that left witnesses in a state of rapture for days on end.

A state of rapture or drooling half-consciousness—depending on the source of the rumor.

This being exactly the sort of story *Unbelievable World* trades in—and frequently has to invent whole cloth—my editor Pattison Blake dipped into our dwindling budget and had me on the first train to parts undesirable.

The Miskatonic River Valley was not unfamiliar to my editor or to me. This blighted northeastern area of Massachusetts had been the location of several of our more popular features. The towns of Arkham, Innsmouth, Kingsport, and Dunwich (and please don't ask me if the 'w' is silent; no one knows) had all seen their share of strange goings-on in the past decades. Miskatonic University housed many ancient and terrifying tomes—as well as ancient and terrifying faculty—that had worked their way into the pages of *Unbelievable World*. Those who managed to flee their upbringing in the Miskatonic Valley rarely returned. It was, in short, a miserable little part of the country.

I'd located the William T. Price Circus with relative ease—they had set up operations on an ashy expanse just west of the town of Arkham—and arrived shortly before the evening's show was to begin. The faded tents and jerry-built animal cars dotting the area did little to elevate the oppressive and claustrophobic air of the damned spot. A few listless clowns slumped near a battered water barrel and a small congregation of families filed slowly into the Big Top. I purchased my ticket from a sullen pig of a woman and followed the swelling crowd.

The performance itself was as underwhelming as I'd expected. Introduced by an under-rehearsed and possibly mentally-deficient master of ceremonies, a few mildly trained animals cowered under the whips of a cabal of less-trained humans to the tuneless pooting of a pipe-organ. Bareback riders—who probably spent more time bare and on their backs than practicing the equine arts—flounced about the ring on horses that would have been better put to use hauling logs after the show. And clowns "entertained" the children in the crowd with japes and jokes that would have been considered failures if the clowns hadn't seemed so willing to accept the nervous whimperings of small boys and girls as proof of success.

In all, an average traveling circus.

Until the end.

As the final clown shuffled out of the ring—and presumably into a bottle—a spotlight illuminated a lone figure standing with arms outstretched in the center of the ring. This was not the man who had introduced the show and announced each act. This man was a true Ringmaster. He wore the garb of a salesman from a medicine show broadside: top hat, long coat, twisted mustache. In one hand, he held a megaphone and in the other a metal rod.

"Ladies and gentlemen," he'd boomed. "Children, too. Especially children. Thank you for attending our little entertainment. The evening is ending, but before you head back to your homes. Before you tuck yourselves in for the night. Before you drift away into that landscape we call 'Dream' I have one final treat for you."

The Ringmaster hoisted the metal rod into the air and held it so the crowd could see.

"Science!" he bellowed. "Science is a beautiful thing!"

And with that, a pair of burly troubadours wheeled a wagon into the ring. The wagon was covered in a tarp, which concealed something the size of a small elephant or a large cow. The way it rigidly jiggled as the cart bounced over the rough floor suggested something stiff and mechanical, but certain aspects of the way the tarp hugged various contours suggested a biological component as well. Whatever it was, the audience grew noticeably quiet as it reached the center of the ring.

The Ringmaster handed his megaphone to one brute and took the corner of the tarp in his free hand.

"Tonight, ladies and gentlemen, you will all bear witness to the fruits of seventeen years of research, experimentation, blood, sweat, and… many, many tears."

The Ringmaster lifted the frayed corner just enough to reveal a round gray plug-hole. He raised his metal rod once again, giving the crowd a "do you see?" look before plunging it into the waiting socket, creating a shining toggle-switch.

"And now," he said—and although he whispered, we all of us heard—"gaze upon… The Ghost Circus!"

The Ringmaster, in one practiced flourish, flipped the switch.

Ten years ago, in a remote corner of the African continent, I found myself imbibing a revolting mixture of pig's blood and tree sap that froze my senses and sent me into convulsions that threatened to snap my limbs. Two years later, in a dilapidated Parisian apartment, I devoured whole a fecalith bezoar the size of a modest orange, gagging on its putrescence, but choking it down that I might glean the knowledge it protected. Just last winter, in darkest Sweden, I participated in the birthing ritual of an Evangeline Witch—the creature emerging fully grown from the nether regions of a crucified orang-utan—which involved the consumption of an acidic compound known to produce terrifying hallucinations, quite possibly including the emergence of a fully grown human from the birth canal of an orang-utan.

I present these charming anecdotes simply to convey to any reader that I am no stranger to the strange. I witness the bizarre on a semi-regular basis as a part of my research and, as a result, have grown difficult to impress regarding strange sights.

So allow me the courtesy of accepting that the sights I saw at the William Price Circus were particularly strange.

Having thrown the switch, the Ringmaster stepped back a considerable distance as whatever the tarp concealed commenced to undulate, throb, pulsate, and grind. The tarp itself—a heavy beige sheet of canvas—rose and fell with each pulsation and, in places, began to dampen. With what, it was not clear.

An odor permeated the interior of the tent—coppery, like blood, but with a whiff of ozone and something else. The smell of a men's gymnasium after a wrestling match. A primal smell. The hairs on the back of my hand began to tingle. I cast my gaze about the crowd and noticed people shifting uncomfortably in their seats. Several small children had begun to silently cry. No one spoke. Silenced gripped the audience.

The space above our heads… dissolved.

It was as if a hand had reached through the very fabric of the air itself, grabbed a fistful of reality, and pulled. Light bent inward and, where it bent, certainty itself seemed to resolve into a—I hesitate to use the word "truer"—but "truer" version of what we usually see.

I lived for a time undercover in China, acting as a visiting poet in order to infiltrate a cabal of American expatriates who sought to bring about the end of the world through an inscription hidden in a Song Dynasty portrait of Yue Fei. When I had arrived, my knowledge of the language had been nonexistent—I found myself at a loss to communicate with anyone outside the boorish group of expat cultists—but each day I spent several hours meditating along the banks of a river and eavesdropping on the small-talk of several tradesmen who frequented the area. Their discussions were a garbled jumble of nonsense to me, but one day, about six months after I had arrived (and three months before the tragic events covered in my feature story "Blood of the Jade Moon") I realized that the men were discussing a local politician and some of the trouble he had gotten into regarding a young woman and ten casks of rice wine. Their words sounded no different, but I was suddenly able to perceive the meaning behind them, and it revealed a heretofore-unseen layer of the world around me.

I can find no better way to describe what we, as an audience, collectively witnessed in that Big Top. Through a bending of light and reality, we perceived, for no more than ten or fifteen seconds, a glimpse of our world as it actually is. The truth as we know it was translated into a higher truth. And behind that truth?

Something moved.

It flitted past with the energy of a hummingbird. It existed in my range of vision for no more than a second, but it was there. I saw it. And, for a brief moment, I was terrified.

Then the window closed. And we were left in silence.

If you were expecting me to describe a pandemonium or panic following the spectacle, I'm sorry to disappoint. The crowd applauded wildly, the Ringmaster bowed, and the families proceeded to file out of the tent as if they had witnessed nothing more than a particularly impressive high wire act. The Ringmaster held his position on stage, scanning the crowd, a look of intense concentration on his face as if searching for something. Or someone.

Seeing my opening, I hurried down the rows of bleachers and approached the man.

Twenty minutes later, I was watching him strap an orphan child to a table and remove her head.

ℽ

Later that night, over dinner in the Ringmaster's private tent, he showed me photos of each of the young victims. Boys and girls, ranging in age from three to about thirteen, each appearing filthy, half-witted, and desperate.

"I see it as a charitable cause," he reiterated, his mouth full of ham.

"Indeed," I said. "Still, it seems an awful risk. Certainly, there are people in authority who might find your actions reprehensible at best, criminal at worst. How can the gain possibly justify the peril?"

The Ringmaster paused in his chewing and stared at me. After a long minute, he swallowed and sat upright. With his shift in demeanor came a shift in the atmosphere of the room.

"The Ghost Circus, of course. The Ghost Circus is worth any risk. The Ghost Circus will…"

Here, the Ringmaster cut himself off.

"I believe," he intoned, "It would be in all of our interests to have you witness the Ghost Circus firsthand."

"Is that not what we observed under the Big Top?" I said.

"That?" the Ringmaster responded. "Good heavens, no. That was simply the bait. Typically, I can attract the attention of one or two people who really *see* what my device is showing them. I admit to being disappointed in tonight's crowd. I'd expected more from this region."

"Any particular reason why?"

The Ringmaster gazed at me with a look somewhere between pity and envy.

"I have borne witness to events far beyond anything you could ever imagine," he said, "and I am compelled to share them with the world. Ten years ago, I was hired on by Mr. Price as a barker for his sideshow. It was not a dream of mine; a scandal in my home town caused me to take flight and seek employment on the open road."

"Scandal? What sort of—"

"I was a doctor of some reputation," the Ringmaster said. "My methods were unorthodox, but they produced results. Certain 'squeamish' members of the local council disapproved of my practices, however, and the later discovery of… unmarked burial plots led to the wrong sorts of attention. Pausing only to gather up certain belongings and books that I had pilfered from the local university library,

I slipped away in the night, following the railway and, happily, the William T. Price Circus."

"When did you start killing children?" I asked.

"Understand, my findings are only made possible by these small sacrifices."

Striding to the back of the tent, the Ringmaster threw back a flap, revealing the cart from earlier in the evening, its contents still obscured by the large, beige tarp.

"Accessing the unknown," he said, "seeing the truth behind the truth, answering the oldest questions known to man… this responsibility can no longer fall to spiritual leaders, men of faith, or students of the human mind. No. You do not travel from Arkham to New York by wishing; you travel by machine. And what I have discovered is not a new way of *seeing*; it is a new way of *travel*. The children are a mode of transport. I discovered this when I was practicing medicine and a child died under anesthetic. As his spirit sighed away, a hole opened in my mind. But this was no fluke. I experimented on more children and discovered ways to harness their energy using the techniques of modern science. Chemical. Mechanical. My inventions were small and simple, but very effective. After I fled, they lost much of their power and I had to build larger and more complex machinery to generate the forces capable of rending the fabric of reality. I supplemented this with certain esoteric codes and chants derived from the scribblings I'd discovered in my stolen books. These weren't the magical incantations scholars had always assumed them to be. No, they were formulas, keys to hold open the hidden gateways. But it wasn't enough.

"You see, what my researches hadn't taken into account was geographical location. My discoveries had initially occurred in my hometown and, unbeknownst to me, that was the secret. I had been traveling with the circus and, while it offered me a seemingly endless source of energy for my creations, it was actually pulling me further and further from the location of the originating energy. I was building larger and more powerful machines just to stay in one place. But now..." he paused.

"Now you're home again," I finished.

"Indeed," the Ringmaster said, and he pulled the tarp.

The machine was an abomination to the human eye. It resembled a stationary steam engine, such as one might find in a mill or factory with a piston, crank, and flywheel. But these superficial similarities were the only bridge between a piece of workaday machinery and the monstrosity that squatted upon the cart.

For squat it did. On legs cobbled together from the limbs of who knows how many young people. In fact, the entirety of the machine was composed of the limbs, skin, organs, and musculature of humans. Presumably young humans. And still, it was identifiable as an engine.

"I found my smaller devices had stopped working and so I built a larger engine. Each time it weakened, I added to it. I built and built and built. To compensate, I had not realized, for its increasing distance from the Miskatonic Valley. Something here—something in the very air of this region—feeds the engine. Now that we have returned, you can imagine how powerful my machine is. Normally, what you witnessed under the Big Top would have required the plugging in of several fresh 'fuel cells,' but here in the Valley, my machine runs practically fuel free. Here in the Valley, I will finally be able to achieve what I could not out in the wilderness. Here in the Valley, I will finally not only be able to see through the veil, but *travel beyond reality itself!*"

Sensing movement behind me, I spun and saw the Ringmaster's two goons entering the tent. One carried a wrapped bundle, the body of the young girl from earlier. The other carried the head.

The Ringmaster gestured to his monstrous assistants and they laid the remains gently on a sideboard that had sprung from the side of the cart. With a practiced deftness, the Ringmaster pulled two fleshy cords from the tissue of the machine and drove their bony ends into the neck stump of the body. He extracted a thicker intestine-like cord from another part of the device and worked it up through the neck of the head.

"Please," he said, "stay and witness history in the making."

The assistants turned and faced me. I realized they were there to ensure my compliance. The Ringmaster would have me bear witness to this event whether I desired to or not.

I shrugged. My editor has a saying that he employs whenever a writer betrays any trepidation about entering a dilapidated house, reading a book of forbidden text, or invoking the name of a homicidal entity: "Just get the goddamn story or you're fired." This philosophy has served me well over the years and I decided it was in my best interests—both financial and physical—to follow it.

"Understand," he said, "that what you are about to witness is a privilege. The culmination of my life's work. The Ghost Circus may function as an entertainment for most who gaze upon its wonder, but it is, in fact, sacred to me. The strength afforded me by the land of the Miskatonic Valley should allow me to not only see the truth, but to cross over into it."

He removed from the cart the metal rod from the evening's performance and inserted it into the aperture on the cart. He pulled down on it and the device began to... churn. Honestly, what that machine did cannot be described by any word or turn of phrase that would make sense to a sane reader. Imagine the most horrible thing a body can do to itself and multiply that by infinity and you are no closer to understanding what I saw. And with the churning came a sickly hum that grew in volume and insistence.

"What you are about to see may alarm you. But do not cry out. Do not speak. Do not draw attention to yourself. In the realm of the Ghost Circus, you are more than a spectator; you are a potential participant. Now relax. And let the show... begin."

The Ringmaster's final words were lost in the hum, which now filled my head and built in dimension and pitch until it seemed the very fabric of my brain was about to come unraveled. I squeezed my eyes shut to prevent them from erupting from my skull. And as soon as it seemed the noise and pressure would send me screaming from the tent, it stopped.

A cold silence filled the room.

I opened my eyes.

The Ringmaster, the machine, the goons... as still as stone. Behind the Ringmaster, a hole in the truth. A physical, tactile hole.

Things moved beyond it. Things a part of this world and apart from this world.

And I thought of the movement I'd seen behind the truth in the Big Top. The flitting thing.

And I saw them. I saw the flitting things.

And they saw the Ringmaster.

And I fear they saw me.

And they entered.

They were not angels, the beings that floated through the tent walls, unfolding around impossible angles, vibrating at impossible frequencies, singing impossible songs with impossible lyrics that bled impossible rhymes.

They were not angels. They carried no streak of the divine. They brought no comfort. They offered no understanding or comprehension.

They brought the children with them.

The children did not frolic; in their hands they held their severed heads, the eyes empty yet shining with a greasy light.

The shimmering beings led the children in a pattern around the room, their feet lightly brushing the ground.

White, pulsating, floating, mysterious, gelatinous objects flitted about and through my head.

The machine on the cart ceased its pulsating motion, rose on its two misshapen legs and stepped down onto the dusty ground. Flesh, muscle, and viscera pulled and stretched as it tentatively maneuvered toward the frozen Ringmaster.

It opened. I don't know how, but it opened. I saw at its core a face looking back at the old world, the world rarely seen by the beings that dwelt in the truth. The machine took the Ringmaster up and into itself and added him to its outlook, its input, its timetable.

A year passed, then two, then a hundred, and the objects filled the tent, always in full view and yet always just out of my range of vision. I saw a field of eyes. I witnessed alien numbers and letters spilling out of the too-open mouths of the children.

A child's face, held low in its untiring arms, brushed my hand and I emitted a small gasp.

The room grew still.

I do not recall what followed. I do not believe a properly functioning brain would allow a man to recall what I endured.

I came to, alone on the blasted heath.

"Well, I cannot say that was entirely unexpected," I said to the ashy landscape.

My name is Joris Severen. Most of my life has been given over to the investigation and exploitation of the unexplained and the unexplainable. I have risked life and limb in order to bring tales of the deranged and whimsical to an increasingly jaded and disinterested readership. I have never turned my back on a story.

Until today.

I write these pages that I may close the book on this chapter of my life. I will no longer witness and report. Things have broken loose into our world that should not be here. And I, as one of the only surviving witnesses to these events, am duty bound to find them. To stop them. And, if need be, to put them down.

I may lose my life in this quest. However, I find the fear of death no longer applicable. I do not dread succumbing to the inevitable embrace of oblivion. Rather, I dread the embrace of things far more sinister. Should I fail, Joris Severen may find Death's claim on him to be outmatched by the machinations of the Ghost Circus. And he may find that eternity holds for him a place among that damnable kermesse.

But, I hope not.

I've grown to somewhat dislike circuses.

A Belgian by birth, **JORIS SEVEREN** has proven a valuable asset to the word of American extra-natural journalism. His experiences leading Congolese savages against the Krauts in Togoland toughened him to the hard life of a reporter as his numerous and shocking articles for *Whimsical Wonders, Tantalizing Tales,* and *Unbelievable World* can attest. "The Ghost Circus" is Mr. Severen's final piece of journalism for *Unbelievable World Magazine,* a publication that folded in 1941. Severen disappeared soon after the events in the enclosed piece. His journals were discovered in a trunk purchased at auction in 2012. The enclosed account has never seen publication.

PHIL GONZALES's story "Cool Cats" was a winner of the HPLFF 1st Annual Lovecraftian Micro Fiction Contest. In between performing, directing, and scribbling horrors at zengroans.wordpress.com, he earns his living as a Public Awareness Associate for the Minnesota Brain Injury Alliance and struggles to find time to spend with his beautiful partner and two lovely daughters.

AUGUST AND AUTUMN

AN ACCOUNT
BY DOCTOR SCOTT RANDALL THORNTON
as provided by Jenna M. Pitman

I pushed at the heavy oak door though it was already abundantly apparent my efforts were in vain. The wood was dry and the veneer had worn away over the years. I suspected that was the direct inverse of what the rust on its hinges had done. I was going to have to accept it. These doors were as immobile as the white stones that lined their lintel.

I cursed, frustrated, but gave myself permission to let go of this particular avenue of entry. I took a step back, eyes traveling along the face of the old manor home, searching for a side door.

August wasn't here yet. The gravel of the drive was thick and smooth, overrun with sprouting foliage. No one had been here in at least a month, if not longer. August would have keys, and he knew every door and window, but I didn't want to wait for him. Well, specifically I didn't want to deal with the head games he carted along everywhere, just as surely as he carried his cell-phone. I wanted to get at information, at least some of it, on my own before August had a chance to sour it.

Not that a discarded old mansion was likely to have much to find. At least nothing juicy. Even acknowledging that fact, however, I was betting that there was something out here to make the trip worth it. Just one trophy to justify the travel time, that was all I asked.

That was the mantra I kept repeating in my head. If I didn't, the guilt would eat me whole.

My feet crunched into pebbles so deep I was practically wading through them. Thankfully there was no need for secrecy.

I followed stone molding that cut a path through the still-rich red bricks of the house's exterior. There was a carriage house peeking out from around the corner, where it seemed likely that I would find a staff entrance.

I came around the corner, so singularly focused on my intention, and nearly collided with a broad, sculpted chest. Chiseled from something as immobile as steel and as fine as sandstone. Perfection. August had always been attractive, there was never any denying that no matter how much personal pain was tied up in the man. But in the years since college, August had bulked up, his shoulders and chest widening, enhancing the slender "v" of his torso, cutting suggestive lines hinting at even more muscles through the thin cotton of his too-small t-shirt.

I swallowed. Had August always been that tall? Or had he put on extra inches upward as well as outward in the years since we broke up? It wasn't just physical, there was something more, something almost primal and magnetic... I swallowed harder.

"Oh." I didn't mean to sigh but the sound punched from my mouth unbidden. I brought Henry to the front of my mind. Thin and fragile, abruptly so, so old in his hospital bed back at the university. Henry, who was too weak to make this trip, laying in a well-lit room with nurses and tubes flowing from his body and the strange bouquet of holly and wormwood and unidentified greenery August had sent along with the invitation to meet him out here. Henry *was* the reason

I was here, in so many extremely literal ways. In other figurative ones as well. These were the thoughts I held on to, I *had to* hold on to, to get through the day.

"Hey there, Scott," August drawled in a voice that had haunted the edges of my repressed dreams for more than a decade. "Where are you off to in such a hurry, partner?"

"Off to?" I repeated blankly. How was it possible, or fair, for him to still affect me like this? I told myself that I had simply forgotten just how overwhelming he was. "Not off. Just... looking..."

August arched an eyebrow and quirked his lips. It was an expression I remembered well. Not fondly. Just well. It was amorphous, managing to appear either indulgent, affectionate, amused, or condescending all at once. I could never tell if it was the expression of just one of the feelings or an arrogant amalgam of all four. When we were freshmen, I always made myself believe it was affectionate amusement, but age and experience left me almost certain it was neither.

"Looking?" August prompted.

Suddenly, I was very conscious of how close we were standing. Body heat radiated from August, seeping through to me. I took one step back. Then another. Before he could take offense, I thrust out my right hand, determined not to let it tremble.

"Looking," I said with more confidence this time. "For you. The estate is rather large and I wasn't entirely sure where you had expected to meet me."

Ignoring the outstretched hand, August stepped forward, pulling me into a tight, somewhat uncomfortably intimate, hug. I froze, blood chilling and my body icy stiff. For a moment, just a brief, breathy hush, I thought I smelled the suffocating dust of holly and a taint of sulfur. But August flexed his arms, constricting the hug, pulling me closer, and it was gone, replaced with my body's embarrassing response to the proximity of such a charismatic slice of my history.

"It's so good to see you," August said. His entire body pressed along the planes of mine. I could feel the carved plates of abs and the subtle bite from his hipbones where they rocked into me.

For a third time I swallowed, ordering my hormones to stand down. They fought me, drawn to something deep within August I wasn't sure I could even explain. But I won out over them, peeling myself out of August's embrace. My teeth worried at my lower lip. It was already chapped and I pulled off a strip of brittle skin, the metallic taste of blood rising to where it had been.

"It's been a while," I said. The most diplomatic thing that came to mind given the circumstances.

"It has," August agreed, looking me up and down slowly. Boldly. There was an eerie light to that look, predatory, but beyond that nothing. "What's it been? Five, six, eight years?"

I looked away, consciously keeping my breath steady. I focused instead on the carriage-house-turned-garage, staring through the grease smeared window at the dirt-smudged bumper of August's Aston Martin. I noted, not really seeing, the lichen that coated the building both inside and out, the paint that had faded to an unidentifiable hue on its doors. A thin but unbroken blanket of dust had been distributed across the gracious curves of August's luxury car. Somewhere deep in a dark, hollow room of my mind, an alarm bell started to ring but I couldn't say why. An insect began whirring in my ear, distracting, far more obnoxious than the ephemeral sense of dread that hovered over me in much the same way.

It had been eleven years. Or near enough. Eleven years and three failed marriages (to women), a string of jilted (female) mistresses, no children, five DUIs, four public scandals, two arrests, one community service sentence—half-filled—and an uncountable number of tabloid stories that flirted with dragging out the truth, kicking and screaming. Even if they never actually did. For me, those eleven years had included one heartbreak, one subtle wooing, three therapists, a switch in majors from comparative religions to local history, four degrees, tenure, five papers published in peer-reviewed journals, one novel co-authored with Henry, and one quiet wedding along the Massachusetts coast. And half a million in hospital bills to keep Henry breathing.

"Something like that," I said. I manhandled an easy, friendly smile onto my face, where it vibrated with brittle sincerity.

"Either way, it's been too long. Let's never do that again."

"Let's." I hoped the tone was agreeable. I didn't feel agreeable. "So you said you found some old ledgers? From the eighteenth century?"

"Did I?" August asked in perfect August-like boredom.

It's always nice when the universe confirms that there are some things that can always be counted on as a constant. The sun rises in the east, rain falls from the clouds to the earth, the moon waxes and wanes, and August never speaks straight if there is a power game to play.

"Yeah, you mentioned something like that."

"Oh. Yes. I think I *do* know what you mean. It may take me a bit to dig those out."

"Alright." I almost cut August off. Almost. "Well, while you are doing that, would it be too uncouth of me to explore a little?"

Most families as old as August's were private to the point of paranoia. The Winsingtons were no different. If anything, they were more rabid about keeping their name clean. It was frankly awe-inspiring that they hadn't disowned August. Personally, I believed all that prevented such a thing was the fact that August could publicly step out of the closet at any moment. Probably would out of spite. Or boredom.

But it wasn't modern scandals that interested either Henry or me. There was a rich mystery the family harbored, something that had happened between 1620 and 1790. Even the oldest and WASP-iest of families generally weakened their death grip on that sort of history. Not the Winsingtons.

I flashed an incredibly shallow smile, one my time with August had taught me to wield, and continued. "It's not every day one gets the opportunity to visit a gem of history like this. Especially not with such an attractive and knowledgeable host. I would hate if I were to miss a single brick."

August's expression darkened, but I did not allow myself to cringe. I didn't think I had overdone it, but maybe I had guessed wrong. Not that it should matter, August no longer had control of my life. I was a grown, married man. I wasn't a naive, self-conscious freshman in such dire need of approval anymore. I just needed to act like I still was.

"Is it all business then?" August asked. His voice took on the whiny quality that used to make me leap to his side, full of apologies and favors. Now it just seemed petulant and spoiled. And kind of immature. It kind of... kind of made me angry.

I stepped around August, feigning nonchalance, as though I could ignore him entirely. Moving down the path, I walked toward the kitchen door as casually as possible. I set my sights on the unruly, overgrown mess that had once been a perfectly manicured garden, marching in that direction as though it had been my destination all along.

"I thought business was what you had in mind. I mean it's been eleven years and—"

A hand fell heavy on my upper arm. A shiver shuddered down through me, raising goose pimples down my arms. There was something to them beyond the excitement of forbidden sex.

"You should know me better than that."

"Should I?" I should shut up. Right now. Just stop talking and walk back to the car and drive away. Right now.

But I didn't. Instead I found myself turning, heels digging into the gravel, gouging perfect circles as I spun. I shook off August's hand like a horse disengaging flies. Whatever I had been feeling a second ago had been replaced with shockingly searing anger. "*How?* How should I? We had what? One year? Maybe eighteen months? And the whole time, you kept me at arm's length or you debased me in public.

And for what? Your family's reputation? Because a coke-snorting party-boy with a string of disgruntled, underage girls in his wake is way less embarrassing than admitting there's a homo in the family?

"But that's ok! You loved me! Loved me so much I had to learn from the headlines in a supermarket checkout line that you were engaged! To a woman!"

I was shaking. Shaking so hard that I couldn't speak through the clattering of my teeth. So I finally stopped talking, clenched jaw, clenched fists, muscles pulled so taut I worried they would pop right off my bones.

August sighed and ran a hand through his Clark-Kent hair, staring soulfully at some space over my head, flamboyantly dramatic. The edges of his eyes shimmered thickly with tears and he drew a ragged breath. It was amazing that this man had managed to keep anyone in the dark about his sexuality. He radiated such stereotypical melodrama.

"I know," he said. "I'm such a fuck up. I am. But things were different then. I couldn't—*we* couldn't... People like us? We can get married now!"

I snorted, fingering my wedding band.

August continued as though he hadn't even noticed the interruption. Maybe he hadn't. "I loved you, Scott! More than anyone. More than any*thing*! But I fucked up and now—"

"Just stop talking," I said, deflating as quickly as I had snapped to rage. "Just... It's done. It's the past."

"But I—"

I held up a hand, cutting off August for real this time. "It's done. I'm married and I love my husband."

August made a rude noise and finally moved away. He stepped up to the servants' entrance and pulled an impossibly old and elaborate set of keys from his pocket. He started flipping through them, making more noise than necessary.

"Oh yes," he snapped as he searched. "*Him*. Professor Henry Thornton. A 'historian.' Whose only role in life is apparently to harass my family. But it's ok, he's not the paparazzi because he has a god-damned degree and tenure at Arkham's most vaunted college."

It probably wasn't worth it to point out that August and I had met when we were both attending that same infamous college. The one August had graduated from. Though it wouldn't surprise me if August's degree had been granted less on merit and more because of checkbooks and promises. Maybe school seemed less impressive when you didn't actually attend to learn anything.

"That would be him, yes."

The air around us grew cold, though the autumn sun still hung high in the afternoon sky. There was no dimming to indicate a cloud had passed overhead; indeed, there were no clouds in the sky at all. The chill seemed to emanate from August himself.

Metal groaned as rusty, long-ignored tumblers fought pressure from the key. Then it clicked and August pushed the door open with a surprising amount of ease. He stepped in and walked a few paces before turning back. He cocked his head, but the gesture wasn't inquisitive.

"Well?"

The entry gaped like the maw of an ancient, soulless effigy. The dirty, darkened windows to either side loomed like deep eye sockets. Not alive, not anymore, it was as though we had opened a corpse. Blinking, I looked to August, suddenly less sure of myself and this self-imposed mission.

"Did you want those ledgers?"

I nodded. Once.

"Then come on." August jerked his head to the side, toward the pitch black back of the room. Maybe it was a trick of the shadows and how they fit together in a puzzle with the light, but when he moved it seemed that his eyes changed color—the whites going dark, irises swirling red and purple, pupils flickering white and green and gold like a cat's. Then he righted his face and his eyes were normal again, that bright, cornflower blue.

"Right." I nodded again, determined this time. Forcing myself forward, jumpy as a fox.

The kitchen was as gray as soot and lit only by what streaks of light could leak through the grimy window panes. It was full of dust and ash and leaves and what I knew were animal droppings, though I pretended they weren't. The debris lay in a heavy cloak over the counters, the stove, the preparation tables, and the floor. It was like they had just closed the house in 1983 and never bothered to even check in at any point in the last 25 years. Which couldn't be wholly correct, right?

"This way." August was suddenly standing at the entrance of a servants' corridor.

"Really?"

"Faster."

Something about that statement seemed off, but I followed anyway. August knew better, he had actually been here before. I should trust him. In this at least.

The servants' halls were mildly intriguing, though they weren't really anything new. Most manor homes and mansions had them, and there was little variation from house to house. Most were in better condition though. For a brief moment, I hoped that their disjointed state would lend itself to the discovery of some forsaken personal effects, but no such luck. Just more natural deterioration.

It *did* seem a little strange that this far into the bowels of the house there were so many leaves and so much mud, etched in rusty arcs and splatters along all the walls. And the cloying stench that hung suspended in the air seemed all too incongruous with the long-ignored nature of the environment. But between animals and storms and time it made a certain sort of sense, so I began scanning for any clues of the family that had once lived here, trying not to let the mess get to me.

When we emerged, it was into a library so large the entire first floor of my townhouse could fit inside without straining. It was too dark—it seemed like too much time had passed while we were in the halls and the sun was starting its westward descent. A glance at the windows only seemed to confirm that thought. The light hung at much lower angles than it had when we were outside. It hadn't taken *that* long had it? My hand reached toward my pocket, going for my phone, to prove to myself that I hadn't somehow lost time like a fairy kidnapping. But August chose that moment to speak.

"I think they're over here."

August was standing behind a large desk, the most intact object to be seen in the near vicinity. He was facing some recessed bookshelves along the wall. It was as though he had once again simply materialized there—he couldn't move that fast. Could he? I shook my head, blinking, as though that would somehow fix whatever was wrong. What *was* wrong?

"Oh. Alright." I approached slowly, giving myself time to survey the room. It was amazing how much had been left behind. But then, if I recalled correctly, it had never been the intention to abandon this estate permanently. It was just that no one had ever bothered returning. I don't know why the family had initiated the extended retreat in the first place. This might be my only chance to answer that question, and others like it. It was just that with August right there, I wasn't sure how I was going to accomplish that.

Other than extreme neglect and imposing size there was nothing remarkable about the room. At least not when taking into account that this house was owned by one of the oldest and most powerful families in the country. The sheets used to cover furniture and books and wall art were yellowed and filthy, and more than a couple had fallen away from their charges. At some point in the last quarter century, someone had found their way in here and sprayed some occult symbols on a few of the swathes of fabric. There were more, barely discernible, on the faded wallpaper. It was practically inconceivable, given the grief I had experienced at the front entrance, that anyone could have broken in. But perhaps I am just not as persistent, tenacious, or resourceful as rebellious teenagers. Especially not teenagers who had gotten it in their heads that they should be practicing fringe, anti-culture religions in the spookiest house in this portion of the valley.

I searched the room for more signs of vandalism. Like the nubs of wax that had once been candles arrayed in front of the fireplace. Or the sheet that had been torn in the haste to pull it away from an ancient carving above the mantle, revealing an ornate twist of limbs and waves, of viney boughs and faces, and of... bones? It was chilling. Something stirred in the back of my mind, a vague recollection of something I had seen years before. Just not where or any pertinent details.

"Scott?"

When I looked, the trick of shadows and light was playing on his face once more, turning August's features gaunt, changing his eyes again, teeth sharp and menacing. It lasted longer this time, just long enough to force me to consider that maybe it wasn't an illusion. But then it was gone and I *couldn't* wrap my mind around what I had just seen. I dismissed it, literally unable to give my vision any more weight than an eerie flight of fancy.

"Yeah. Sorry. You found them?"

August held out a large, leather tipped book with warped and weathered pages. "There's a lot more where this came from, I think there are some journals as well. Why don't you come over here and take a look?"

The promise of a treasure of information tugged me forward, motivating me with greed. It was ridiculous, but I couldn't help the surge of childish desire bubbling inside of me. *These* would make Henry's day. Or year really. Maybe we could actually finish a final book before Henry died. Tears sprang to my eyes and I sniffed as a goofy smile spread across my lips. He would really like that.

"Journals?" I asked, striving to keep the over-eagerness I was feeling tucked away. I took the ledger and flipped it open. The ink was faint in places but some was still legible. Most expenses appeared fairly mundane, but immediately an inordinate number of purchases from a holly farm jumped out at me. And a good number of goats and sheep. This hadn't been a proper farm had it?

August placed a smaller book on top of the pages. The tail end of an extremely menacing grin was disappearing when I looked up. My stomach deteriorated into a churning mass of queasy sludge.

"Journals," I repeated. The hair along the back of my neck and down my arms stood on end inexplicably. Torn between panic and awe, I wasn't sure which emotion to give free reign.

"This should make you and that snoopy husband of yours pleased."

That got my full attention, though it knocked into me too hard to respond. August was studying me with a clenched jaw and narrowed eyes. Panic began to win out, echoing through me in crescendoing reverberations that held me in paralyzing spasms.

"You know you didn't have to invite me here if you didn't want us to have this," I choked out through a parched throat, barely able to hear my own voice over the thudding of my own heart.

"Would that have stopped you?"

"What? If you hadn't invited me? If *you* hadn't offered the information and a tour I wouldn't even be out here. I don't really have the time for a frivolous day trip right now."

"What is it about my family that makes you so inquisitive?"

I shook my head and placed the books on the desk. They slid a little, belying a subtle imbalance, but they came to a stop before I had to grab them to keep them from crashing to the floor. The diary bounced a little, flipping itself open to a random page.

"It's not just the Winsingtons, you know," I protested. A little guiltily. "It's all notable colonial families."

It was true. Mostly. But I had met Henry *because* of the Winsingtons and my connection to August. It was shortly after August's first engagement announcement, the impetus for my leaving the fraternity and frat house where I had lived with August. More to the point, leaving the room we'd shared. I had been considering leaving college entirely when Henry, a professor of New England colonial genealogy at Miskatonic University, had tracked me down. He was hoping for an inside scoop on the heir to a bulk of the Winsington fortune and this dump of an estate. I may have never been allowed to be open about my relationship with August, but I *had* been to their houses and to all their private places.

When I met with Henry, we found inconsistencies, things about the Winsingtons that the other families didn't do, things they hid that others didn't. It was intriguing to look at the big picture and opened the door to so many more questions. Questions we both wanted answered.

August snarled. It had to be my imagination that gave it the monstrously threatening, throaty rumble. Had to be.

I stumbled backward, eyes wide, heart thudding a loud staccato, pounding in my jaw, at my temples. My feet collided with something both firm and lumpy on the floor behind me. I wobbled, arms windmilling as I toppled over, my back cracking against the wooden arm of an old settee. I exhaled a giant *woosh*, and my eyes clasped tight as pain bloomed along my spine. I fought to catch my breath. The room was reeling, even with my eyes closed.

I forced myself to look, pinning my eyes wide, trying to focus.

I needn't have worried. August was gone. For some reason, the fact that he was just *gone*, without a sound or a hint of his passing, just disappearing into thin air, was less unsettling than the *why* behind his absence. That was sobering and, despite the prickling of fear, I sat up, ignoring how my back clenched. I slowly covered the room, eyes eventually returning to the fireplace. The hanging wooden carving seemed to leer from its many hidden faces. I blanched and looked down. The fireplace was full of charred ropes of what had once been plant life. I squinted closer, making out scalloped points on once-waxy-but-now-crispy leaves.

Holly.

I looked toward my feet, time drawing out like taffy. The object I had tripped over was dark and still. It was tucked between the side table, an easy chair, and the matching settee I had just slammed against. I couldn't have seen it from where we entered. It was tough to make out the details in the dim light, but it seemed as though the lump was wearing jeans.

Holding down bile and a sudden urge to run I leaned forward, rocking the lump by its... shoulder. I knew what it was—even before I touched it I had known, and now I was certain.

I rolled the corpse onto its back and choked back a piercing sob. It escaped in a strangled squeal like helium from a deflating balloon. August's rigid stare was fixed to the ceiling. Once bright blue eyes now dull and glossy. Lips and cheeks brushed with a pale, purple pallor.

"Oh no," I breathed, voice coming apart at the seams. I gaped stupidly at the lifeless body of my first lover. August had been a cruel, self-centered, spoiled playboy, but he was also the first boy who had drawn me into admitting who I really was. In middle and high schools, I had been far, far too shy. Even if I had been straight, I doubted I would have gotten laid before university. I had always been more comfortable with a computer between me and any social interaction, but somehow August had known what I had not and coaxed me into coming out. Or at least coming into his bed.

I might hate August for the way he treated me like an inanimate accessory, dragging me around like a purse dog for a year and a half, but if it hadn't been for him, I would have been alone for so much longer.

And no matter how much anger and how many hurt feelings I had stored up, August was dead. Lying on the ground. Right in front of me. The enormity of the situation struck me like a fist. I brushed a hand over August's face and his half-lidded eyes shut easily. So it had been at least a full day, obviously quite longer, since August's death.

Something whistled down the chimney and up the corridors, stirring leaves and dust and reminding me that even one unexplained dead body was a sign of danger. I scrambled to my feet and crouched low. There was nothing to be seen, but I felt eyes on my back. I glanced over my shoulder, that strange carved wreath once again commanding my attention. I shuddered. It was, beyond a doubt, well past time to leave.

Four hours had passed, maybe more, and Henry would be worrying. I didn't want his fears to become realized. With only a moment's hesitation, I darted back and scooped up some of the ledgers "August" had shown me, snatching a few of what I assumed were personal journals from a shelf as I did. I noticed the journal I had been holding earlier, still lying open on the desk. A sentence from the page seemed to reach out and grab me.

The ritual last night proved effective.

I paused, ticking off what we knew about the Winsingtons. Their reclusiveness, even from their peers, the way luck always seemed to follow them, and the scandals that never seemed to break. How rivals always seemed to fail and enemies disappear. How slaves and servants and contractors refused to talk to outside sources, even decades after leaving the family's employ. How there were never chapels on their properties and even when they donated money to local churches, none of the Winsingtons were members or were ever buried on consecrated ground. How could I have been so blind?

Once again The Ilexiataent have silenced the rumors and my family is safe from harm or intrusion. It is just too bad that my brother could not contain himself without this intervention. I wish there had been a better solution to dealing with his indiscretions, but after years of his dalliances threatening to sully our reputation, this was our only course of action. His funeral will be held in three days' time, best to get this trouble out of the way now. And the witnesses are already falling away. I expect the last will be gone before the week is out. Our gods are truly powerful. Given the extent of this season's profits, our next sacrament will be an exceptional event. Yet again The Ilexiataent have blessed us with…

I knew I had heard of The Ilexiataent, but in that moment I had nothing. They were gods of some kind, thankfully the passage made that clear, but from where?

There would be time enough later to sort that out. In theory. If I hurried. I slammed the book closed and added it to my pile, preparing to flee. It was a little awkward, as encumbered as I was, but then I didn't know where I was going anyway, so I couldn't have done too much better had I not been weighed down. I moved sideways through the door to the main hallway, scuttling crab-like.

If anything, the halls were darker than the library, maybe even darker than the servant pathways. They were tall and wide and lined with giant, streaked windows, but it was evening now and the gray of twilight was throwing itself across the walls and lengthening shadows with abandon. There was more graffiti here, paint carelessly smeared across expensive wooden paneling and thick European wallpaper. Knowing what I now did, the etchings filled me with dread. How much of this work was the result of faceless vandals and how much came from the deliberate worship of the Winsington gods?

The seconds ticked by, itchy fingers tapping at my skull as my feet smacked compressed carpet in clouds of what I hoped was merely dust. I wished my legs were moving faster or that time was moving slower, but it seemed neither wish would be granted. This house was a mistake—visiting it, stepping inside, exploring, even my interest in it. This whole trip was misguided. But how could I have known?

I hugged the books tighter to my chest, as though their acquisition and the knowledge they possessed was enough to make this horror show worth it. The pools of graying light that cut through the darkened hall speckled the manse's interior in a menacing merle arrangement. I was sure that at any moment, gods of indeterminate forms would be waiting to ambush me.

Which only served to draw out another question. *Why had the damned thing disappeared in the first place?* Wouldn't it have been a perfect time to kill me when I was in the other room, off kilter from the discovery of August's body?

The fetid smell was more pungent in the rest of the house. I had assumed that the stench had been the fault of the corpse—the sickly sweet way it clung to the air seemed to confirm that theory—but if that were the case, it should be growing less apparent the more distance I put between myself and the library. It made me wonder if maybe August's wasn't the only body in the house. Maybe animals? It was a real possibility, wild animals taking refuge in an abandoned house and dying once inside, but there was a level of understanding in my primal being that knew this was more than that. It wasn't just Death I smelled, it was Human Death. Even the rotting carcass of an elk or a bear, something wildly unlikely in the state of Massachusetts, wouldn't account for what I was sensing.

It wasn't until I was approaching the broad foyer that I remembered the trouble I had gone through trying to open the front doors. If there weren't locks to throw, it was unlikely I would have any more luck on this side of them, and I had just wasted valuable time bumbling through the halls to get here. It was a more direct route, leaving out the front, but that was only if I could actually make it through.

The wall to my right sloped away as I walked, revealing a once great staircase that rolled upward to the eastern and western wings of the building. My heart stopped, sure that something would be waiting for me on those steps. But they were empty. I gazed up each wooden stair and craned my neck to take in the landing above me. Nothing. But I felt no safer.

The foyer was dominated by the stairway and the huge windows of colored panes of glass that lined the top half of the entry. A podium sat in the middle of the room, whatever bust or statue it held covered by a sheet. I skirted around it, my stomach a gummy soup at the sight of its ghostly shape. My mouth was bone dry, my breath paining my chest. I set the books on the floor reluctantly, loathe to part with my prizes, and began worrying at the rusted iron bolts that clasped the doors together. They were, of course, immobile. Like they had been welded in place.

A cry of dismay escaped my throat. I clamped down any further exclamations. Unsure how to continue, I worked harder, fingertips burning painfully as they pushed against metal.

The bolt slid—a shaking, squealing, tiny slide, but a slide nonetheless. An ember of hope surged, starting, just starting, to light a path that seemed to show a way out of here.

Then I felt a scraping, a spiky touch on my back, a cold sensation that seemed to reach through the cloth of my shirt.

I froze, rooted in place, hands glued to their grip on the lock. I swallowed loudly, throat ragged. The touch traveled up and down my back, multiplying and leaving bright burning sensations in their wake. The tracks mounted in intensity, shouting and boiling so egregiously I was sure my skin was bubbling and dripping from my body.

My legs failed first, melting into a warm and wobbly numbness that could not support my strength. I don't even know if it was my ankles or my knees that buckled first because I couldn't feel them. By the time they crumbled under me and sent me toppling, my hips and forearms no longer felt a part of me. It was the way the floor crashed against my ribs and shoulders that told me how extreme the impact was. I was quickly losing sensation there as well, however.

Ropes of ivy and holly, alien breeds with bone white stems and mahogany leaves that dripped pungent green and viscous, were snaking from the fabric that had been draped over the podium. Strange glowing eyes peered from where the cloth had lifted. Dark where the whites should be, light at the pupils, and iridescent green at the irises. A few pairs.

Behind me I heard a rustle and, with the last of my control of my own body, I turned my neck to look over my shoulder.

In my haste to escape, I had failed to note the carved leaves that ringed the door in looping figure eights. They were detaching themselves, pulling away and straining toward me. Another pair of eyes blinked at me with the impassive hunger of a carnivore.

The Ilexiataent. The Winsington's gods. Or at least the result of them.

It was such an obvious realization, it seemed a waste of my final thoughts.

I had never wished away my time with August, not for all of the pain and all of the regret and all of the sorrow. But I did now.

I wanted to tell Henry goodbye. Then I remembered the gift that had been sent to Henry's hospital room, the strange hue of the foliage and the way it smelled like nothing of this world, and I realized that it wouldn't be too much longer before l saw my husband again.

Services for **DOCTOR SCOTT RANDALL (BAKER) THORNTON** will be held on September 20th, 2010, at the United Methodist Church in Brookline, NH. He was preceded in death by his husband, Doctor Henry Carter Thornton. He leaves behind his father and mother, Peter and Dierdre Baker of Brookline. Scott was born in Brookline February 24, 1978. A quiet child who always enjoyed education, he was accepted by Miskatonic University in 1997. Scott went missing shortly before his husband died and his former associate, Mr. August Winsington, was reported missing last year. His family decided to honor his memory though his body has not been recovered.

JENNA M. PITMAN's first work was published in a monthly zine local to Seattle where it ran for nearly a year, garnering a fair amount of popularity. Since then she has had a number of stories and articles published in a variety of locations. Before moving to Los Angeles, CA, in 2012, she was a well-known member of the Pacific Northwest convention community. Currently she is a happy resident of sunny Southern California where she hikes, dances, and practices yoga daily in addition to working as a full time writer.

THE RESERVOIR

AN ACCOUNT BY JAMES DAVENPORT
as provided by Brian Hamilton

"I wouldn't drink that."

I paused, the rim of the pint glass frozen only a microscopic distance from my lips. My friend, Stan Rawlings, stared at me from across the booth. He was in his accustomed place at the old hardwood table, stacks of paper and small, old looking booklets scattered in front of him. "Wouldn't drink what?" I asked, sloshing the water around in the glass. "You see something on the news? Something wrong with the water?"

My friend shook his head. "Not on the news, no." He tapped at the papers strewn across the table. "But it's all in here. Christ, James, I can't believe no one's ever talked about this."

Whatever "this" was, it was a part of Stan's big research project for his doctoral degree. The two of us had met at Miskatonic University—I had pursued a history degree with a little help from a small scholarship, and Stan had graduated with a degree in microbiology, thanks in large part to the full ride he had gained based on old family connections. After graduating, I got a job at Arkham's city archives, but Stan had gone right back to school for a doctorate.

He'd been on this project for a year now, and apparently had spent most of his time disseminating the information in the Dutchman's Breeches, a bar we had found early in our college years. It was one of those little places you found in the back alleys and side streets of Arkham—all dark wood and even darker lighting, half filled with old regulars and whoever else might turn up over the course of the night. Stan and I may have been the youngest regulars there by a decade, but the beer was local, cheap, and better tasting than anything you could find on campus.

I'd already downed a few pints and felt a little fuzzy. I'd asked for some water to steady me out—I was going to be working the next morning, and didn't relish the idea of spending a day in those dusty old halls and shelves with a hangover. I noticed Stan hadn't ordered a drink. In fact, he'd gone and brought a plastic water bottle, something from one of the local convenience stores. Its label assured that it had been bottled on some remote island where the water was extracted from pure underground springs.

I decided to humor my friend and set the glass back down. "Alright, Stan, what's 'this' and what does it have to do with the water?"

Stan pulled his glasses off and rubbed the bridge of his nose. "You know how I had to do that research project for Professor Barnes?"

I thought for a moment. "The one about bacteria in the drinking water? The one you got removed from because you got sick?"

Stan nodded. "He wanted to help prove that Arkham had some of the better drinking water in the New England area."

"Didn't he get a big grant from that?"

"More than a grant. It was a big hit for some of the water bottling companies that pull their water from the reservoir. The same one that Arkham and the surrounding areas pull their tap water from."

"So what does that have to do with what you've got now?"

Stan put his glasses back on and leaned towards me, as if sharing some secret to a fellow conspirator. "The report Barnes used was…

altered. Slightly."

That wasn't a shock. I remembered Barnes as a pompous, over-bearing bastard who lauded his own intellectual prowess to anyone that might listen to him on campus. "I'm not surprised," I said. "I'd honestly been more unsettled if you told me Barnes had published the honest truth. So what did he find? Arsenic? Feces?" I began to raise the glass of water again, wiggling my fingers of my free hand in the air. "Some sort of flesh-eating bacteria?"

Normally introverted and clumsy, Stan surprised me as he whipped his hand out and stopped the glass's progress. His grip was vice-like on my wrist. We locked eyes, and I could see my own worried expression reflected in his thick glasses. "Worse," he whispered. "Much worse. So, please—don't drink."

He let go of my hand and sat back in the booth, his shoulders slouching as he relaxed. For my part, I set the glass back down and slid it to the far side of the table, away from the wall that I leaned against. I swallowed, my throat ironically dry, and asked, "What's in the water, Stan?"

My friend looked down at his papers and began to riffle through them. "Barnes—we, I mean, the research group—found something in the water. No bacteria, or anything that could cause sickness." He paused to look up at me. "Or, maybe not. There were particulates so small that we only detected them in one of the tests. Barnes and the other undergraduate researchers dismissed the results, but I was curious enough to take a second look.

"What I found was, well—I don't know what it was. It was almost like tiny pieces of something in the water, like flakes, only much, much smaller. When I decided to take a closer look with one of the more powerful microscopes, I saw—I saw colors, James." He choked a little at this point. "Only, they weren't colors, you know?" I didn't. "I mean, they looked sort of something like, I don't know..." He trailed off at this point and stayed silent for a few moments. I was about to say something when Stan started again.

"I was sort of, I guess, blinded for a little while. Like I couldn't process what I was seeing and just kind of shut down. I woke up in the campus infirmary. Barnes apparently found me collapsed on the floor. The sample I had taken was spilled. I guess I knocked it over when I collapsed."

"Hold on," I interrupted. "You told me you came down with a, a bug or something."

"Barnes asked me if I could keep quiet about the whole thing. He promised a little of the grant money in return, but I turned it down." No surprise there—the Rawlings were an Old Money family in Arkham. Stan paid for most of the rent on the apartment we shared in the city's downtown area. I would've bet that he'd never have to work a day in his life if he didn't want to. "Then Barnes threatened to have me removed from the school if I told anyone."

"Alright," I said, "so you saw something and passed out. What's the connection to what you're doing now? And why are you telling me?"

Stan nodded. "After I recovered a little, I went back to the lab to find out where the water sample I had looked at came from. It was pulled directly from the reservoir. And so I decided to do a little more research." He pulled out a couple sheets of paper, browned and brittle with age. I recognized them as something I had found for Stan from the archives a week ago. Had he actually stolen something?

I forgot the break from his normal character as he went on. "These papers are from the city archives, which I—"

"Got from me, yeah, and apparently stole them. Shit, Stan, do you know how much trouble we could get into if you're—"

He cut me off again. "That's not important right now, dammit! Listen—these papers list the name of the surveyor who went out into the area that would eventually become the reservoir." His finger rested next to the name of the surveyor and the year in which the document had been filed in: Mr. Howard Phillips, 1927. "I couldn't find anything else in the Arkham archives, so I took a trip to Boston to try my luck. It took them some time to find anything, but eventually they found this."

He held up a small bundle of papers that looked just as old as the survey records. The yellow-brown bundle was thick, and each page was covered with typewritten words, the old ink flaking off in places. "And that is?" I asked.

"It's something Phillips wrote after completing the survey for the reservoir. Turns out he up and quit right after completing the job, and this," he shook the bundle at this point, "is his account of why he did so. He tried publishing it, but the manuscript got lost in the process. Somehow it turned up at Boston's archives, and they went and mis-filed it under someone else's name."

He slid the old account towards me. "There's something in the reservoir, James. Phillips' story is a little rambling, and seemingly unbelievable, but it explains what I saw in the sample. What might be," he pointed at the glass of water at the end of the table, "in the water everyone in this city is drinking. If Phillips is right, something came down from the sky and *infected* an area in the hills outside Arkham—an area that was covered, eventually, by the reservoir. The people of Arkham at the time called it 'evil,' named it the 'blasted heath.' Phillips got the story from some senile old man, but he saw the area himself, all gray and crumbling and dead. Something caused that area to die, James, and if I'm right then it's still there, under all that water."

With that final proclamation, Stan stopped to breathe and sat back again. I realized I had stopped breathing, and started sucking in air from the now too-stuffy atmosphere of the Breeches. My stomach felt like it was twisting itself into a knot. I willed myself back to calmness, and wiped the thin layer of sweat from my forehead. "Do you have any actual proof, though?" I asked. "Apart from a destroyed sample and a story from a dead man, what do you have to show for it?"

"Nothing," Stan admitted, but I could see the bright spark of something in his eyes. "Nothing yet."

"Yet?" I dreaded the answer.

"I'm going to go out there," Stan told me. "I'm going to go to the reservoir this weekend, find this 'heath' and see if it isn't the source of what I saw in the sample."

I couldn't believe him. "Do you even know how to, what, scuba dive? To use any of that equipment?"

Stan nodded. "Clara's been showing me."

I rolled my eyes. Clara was Stan's self-styled "ladyfriend" and was probably the closest thing he'd ever had to a significant other in his whole life. If anything proved the cliché of opposites attracting, it was Stan and Clara. Where Stan was bookish and predictable, Clara was adventurous and spontaneous. Having spoken to her in the past, I'd found that she was also rather intelligent, so it was no wonder why Stan was able to put up with her. And it didn't surprise me that Clara would know how to go diving with all that equipment.

"She's not going with you, is she?" I was worried Stan might try to rope her into this mad plot.

"No," Stan admitted. "She's heading back to Seattle to see her folks for the weekend, but I managed to keep a set of diving gear from our last practice session. The tank's filled with air." He looked up from the table, straight at me. "But I still need someone to come with me, just in case."

I raised an eyebrow. "Just in case what?"

"Just in case anything happens." Stan kept looking at me. "If the tank goes bad, or if I get stuck down there, or if… if anything else happens."

I couldn't say no. I wanted to, but this was the guy who, despite his diminutive size, knocked out a drunken jock from one of Miskatonic's fraternities when he and his buddies jumped me in the middle of the night. Even more, I probably owed Stan just for all the money he'd loaned me since we met. So I agreed. I'd drive him out to the reservoir that weekend and help him conduct this investigation.

ל

The weather for that weekend couldn't have been better. Sparse clouds were scattered in a rich blue sky, and the sun was rising as I drove Stan up into the hills where the Arkham Reservoir lay. It was in that time right between spring and summer, right before New England became hot but after it had thrown off winter's embrace. We drove with the windows down, taking in the sights, smells, and sounds of that beautiful morning.

"So," I started after an hour's drive in silence, "do you really want to go through with this?"

Stan stopped going over the air tank he had been cradling for the ride. "We have to, right? Who else is going to go down there?"

"The cops, or the EPA? Someone whose job it is to worry about this?"

"No one's looked into this for nearly a hundred years, James. All this time and no one's noticed a thing."

I waited at an intersection for another car that had the right of way to move. "Ok, alright, then maybe nothing's wrong with the water. If it's been this long, and no one's said anything, or there's been no, I don't know, outbreaks or something, maybe it isn't bad?"

"Or maybe it just hasn't been long enough," Stan said, hugging the air tank close to his chest. Our conversation lapsed into an awkward silence that lasted until we reached our destination.

The reservoir was just as picturesque as the drive had been, the spring sun causing the dark water to sparkle and dazzle our eyes. I parked the car and helped Stan lug the diving equipment over to the small pier from which we could rent a boat. The man operating the pier wasn't trusting at first, but a quick flash of our school ID's turned him around—apparently he was an alumnus of the school's folklore track.

We picked one of the small tin boats, dumped the diving gear into it, and roared off into the middle of the reservoir, the little engine sputtering and spitting out smoke. Stan had figured out the location of this "heath" from the surveyor's report, somewhere out in the middle of the water. The bottom of the reservoir quickly dropped off, the clear water becoming a dark blue that eventually sunk down to a pitch black. When the little GPS beeped, signaling that we had reached our destination, I stopped the motor and we drifted for a little while. I helped Stan get the diving gear on, hooking up the various gauges that would feed him the compressed oxygen and allow him to see how much air he had left.

As Stan was testing out the light on his mask, I asked, "How are you going to talk to me up here? In case anything happens."

He pointed to a small box that resembled an old radio. "I've got a setup in this mask that'll allow me to speak to you with that radio transmitter. Just flip the button on when you want to talk."

"Oh, like one of those walkie-talkies I had when I was a kid." I bent down to the box and flipped the switch. "Testing, testing." I could hear my voice coming from Stan's mask, tinny and fuzzy sounding. "Looks like it works."

"Let me get in the water first. Don't want you jinxing me," Stan said as he placed the mask over his head. He saddled up to the side of the boat, gave me a thumbs up, and went over the side, splashing me in the process. I looked down to see Stan floating about a meter below the surface. "How do I look?" his voice asked from the radio.

I flipped the switch and replied, "Like something out of the black lagoon."

I could hear him laugh, and saw him flip the mask's headlight on before he turned over and started descending. In few moments he was gone, swallowed up by the dark depths. I checked my phone.

Mercifully dry, but this far into the hills it wasn't getting any signal whatsoever. The lack of connection to the internet made me wish I had brought a paperback with me, or something to waste time with.

There was another problem—Stan's, really. His rough entry into the water had soaked the GPS, which had shut off. I spent a few minutes trying to shake the water out of it. Maybe it would dry out in the sun?

I nearly jumped out of the boat when the radio crackled into life with something that sounded like Stan's voice. I grabbed at the receiver and asked if everything was alright. Stan must have started saying something, since he came on mid-sentence when I took my finger off the button. "-king fish! Goddammit! Scared me all to hell and back. Did you know that there were fish in here?"

"I didn't, no. How far down are you?"

"I just reached the bottom. I'm going to look around for a bit."

He was silent for a little while longer. I started to regret not bringing sunscreen when I heard Stan's voice again. It was strange—he sounded... shaky? Nervous? "You can still hear me, right?"

"Yeah," I replied. "Something wrong down there?"

"I don't really know. Maybe? Does grass normally grow underwater?"

I thought for a moment. "No? Is it actual grass?"

There was a pause. "It's... gray. And brittle. It's coming apart as I touch it."

I wondered if that could be what Stan saw in the sample—flakes of gray grass. But would that explain the colors? Stan cut back in as I was thinking.

"And there are bushes and, and trees down here. I don't get it. My depth gauge is going crazy here. Oh, no."

I clicked the radio on. "You should come up, Stan. If your gear isn't working right, get back up."

He must have been talking. "-ving, James, they're moving, the trees. Going back and forth and back an—is there a current here? I can't feel anything, and the grass isn't moving but the trees are, and—"

His voice cut out in a squeal of static. I sat there, staring at the radio. It must have been some sort of stupid joke. Except Stan wasn't the kind of guy to do that sort of stuff.

The radio clicked again. "Bones. Bones, so many bones down here. Fish, I think? They're so small. And others—not dogs. Raccoons? Possums? That's a dog skull, they're all around this, is it a well? It looks like, like, a ring of stones, waist high. There are more bones around it, and, and that's," he laughed—*laughed*. It was high and cracking. "Human, there are human bones down here, James, how many people go swimming here?"

Not two years back, a couple of kids from Dunwich had come down with their families to the reservoir for a day. They went missing, never found. Had they gone out into the water?

"It's dark down here," Stan continued. "Like my light's failing, it's so dark. But there's light? Light. Down in the well, the deep, down there. Colors. Colors, I've seen them before! The same, it's the same! Colors that aren't colors, bleeding out, from the sky! They're beautiful, James, you should see this, you should come down here."

I looked down into the water and saw—what did I see? Something was flashing down there, like a strobe light. But it made me feel sick to look at it, like my stomach and heart were trying to claw past each other as one tried to rise as the other fell. I jerked back from the side of the boat, listening to the radio squeal with static and what sounded like laughter. Stan's laughter. Then he spoke again.

"It's weak, so weak. It can't do anything from down here in the dark with the water crushing it down, down, down. It can't feed, can't get out, can't go like it did so long ago, back to where it came from. It's been sitting, waiting, spreading. It's in the water, James, it's here and it's in the water." More laughter.

And then silence. For what seemed like hours, Stan stayed silent.

There was only the sound of the wind-pushed waves of the reservoir gently lapping at the metal side of the boat, and the cries of some far off birds. I checked my phone—still no signal—and saw he had only been down there for thirty minutes. Had something gone wrong with the air in the tank? Was Stan down there, hallucinating all of this? Was he remembering the details of that surveyor's story?

"I'm going into the well."

The statement came with such clarity. No touch of madness, no static, even—it sounded like Stan was beside me in the boat. I turned the radio on, yelling at him, telling, ordering Stan to come back up, that something was wrong, that he was in danger if he didn't come up now. I don't think he ever heard me.

I waited. What else could I have done? Stan had taken all the diving equipment with him—there wasn't even a snorkel for me to use. He had never told me how far down he was. Even if I could have gone down there, would I have had enough air to bring us both back up? And what if he was right, if he wasn't seeing things, and something was down there waiting in the dark at the bottom of an old, forgotten well?

I waited another half hour. Stan's tank had only been filled with enough air to last an hour—if he didn't come up soon, he wouldn't be coming up at all. I stood up in the boat, hands cupped against my face to cut down on the blinding glare of the sun against the reservoir's water. I had nearly given up when I saw something, bright yellow and reflecting in the sunlight, bob to the surface some distance away. Keeping my bearings, I turned the little engine on and moved to where I had seen the object come up. When I reached it, I bent down into the water and scooped it up. I stared at it for a long, long time.

It was Stan's diving mask. The light had gone out.

ᛣ

The police were on the case, for a little while at least. I told the police that Stan had wanted to test out his diving skills in the reservoir and hadn't come back up. They suspected that I had done something to him, something to his equipment, but nothing stuck, of course. There was no motive, no reason.

I still felt guilty for not telling Stan to come up earlier, or for not dismissing the whole idea of diving in the reservoir in the first place. Maybe my inaction had killed him, in a sense.

They searched the reservoir, and found nothing. Nothing but mud and stone and fish. No gray grass, or moving trees, or bones. Not even a little mound of stones that could have once been a well on a farmer's blighted land.

I sent the surveyor's story back to Boston, and brought the files Stan had stolen back to Arkham's archives. I moved out of the apartment Stan and I had shared—without his wealth, I had no chance of making rent. I saw Clara once, at the funeral. She stood over Stan's closed casket, tears on her face. I didn't say anything to her.

What else could I have done? I wasn't going to go down there, in the darkness, where that thing might be. Where the not-colors flashed in lightless depths. Where I might find the bones of Stan Rawlings at the bottom of a well.

I don't drink the water in Arkham anymore.

JAMES DAVENPORT is a resident of Arkham, Massachusetts, and is currently employed in the city's historic archives. He would prefer not to be contacted about recent discoveries in the Miskatonic Valley's water supply.

BRIAN HAMILTON is from Philadelphia, Pennsylvania, and is a recent college graduate, freelance writer, and fan of horror literature—especially anything Lovecraftian. "The Reservoir" is one of his first published short stories. His other works have been published in ebooks and emagazines, including *The Asylum Within* (Miskatonic Press, 2014).

HOSTEL NIGHT

A MEMOIR BY JAMES CALLOWAY
as told by Brandon Barrows

The near-freezing rain of a late-October storm had already soaked through both the wool of my coat and the cotton of my shirt and was working its way through my very skin when the thin light from my buggy-lanterns momentarily won the battle against night and storm to catch the edge of a road sign half-obscured by sticker-bushes. I called Nelly—the finest equine companion for which any mortal soul could ask—to a halt in order to get a better view of the thing, warmed by a spark of hope that I might not have to spend the *entire* night out in the nor'easter. The words I read, however, extinguished that spark and filled my heart with a chill colder than any downpour ever could.

ARKHAM 2 MILES—>

I sat in the buggy, pounded by rain and chilled to the bone, and stared at the sign in disbelief. How had I gotten so turned around? I'd left Bolton around 4 p.m. headed east for Essex—a journey of two hours, at most—intending to spend the night, then continue on to Gloucester in the morning for a heavily-discounted shipment of fine cutlery fresh off the boat and waiting for my pick up. I checked my watch and found that it was nearly 9 p.m.! I couldn't explain how I'd ended up nearly twenty miles south of where I'd aimed for or what had happened to the previous five hours and, as a seasoned traveler, that bothered me a great deal.

Traveling, as much as anything, is my business, if I haven't already mentioned. James Calloway, at your service—seller of cutlery, combs, and all your assorted household needs, the right wares at the right price, brought straight to your door with a smile on my lips and a song in my heart.

Now, I'm a civilized man, but I am also a New Englander, born and bred, and my grandmother, Rebecca—a hard-handed, mean-spirited old Yankee who took great pride in the fact that her family had called New England home for six generations—made sure that my sisters, cousins, and I knew exactly what that meant. To grandmother, that meant going through life with eyes wide open to what the world truly was—what it was by her estimation, at any rate. Beneath the gambrel roof of her tumbledown old house, sitting in front of the hearth on more nights than I can count, she told us children of the strange and fearsome things that share this world with us, lurking just out of sight: the fish-men of Innsmouth; the ghouls that roam beneath the streets of Boston; the north-woods cults that dance to insane piping and sacrifice themselves to their awful and indifferent god; Keziah Mason, the witch of Arkham and her devilish familiar who went by many names; the invisible beast that made Dunwich its home; and many, many more horrors and mysteries besides. How she knew all of these things was a mystery in and of itself, explained by our superstitious neighbors and schoolmates with the obvious answer that she must be a witch. I asked her once, when I was old enough to be aware of such things, if what folks said was true. She laughed and gave me a mischievous smile, which I took to mean that she was just my strange old granny.

Regardless of how she came by her information, however, if grandmother had told it true—and those soberly-repeated stories held details even the most imaginative would be hard-pressed to fabricate so convincingly—there was no corner of this fair land that didn't hold some hidden monstrosity or horror. And there was no place as dark or foreboding as Arkham; even grandmother's voice once or twice held a tremor during the telling of its tales.

Had I been alone, I might have indulged in a little superstition and just crawled under the wagon to "rough it" for a night—as I've done before on less-inclement occasions—but even in the dim light, I could see poor Nelly shaking and shivering at the rapidly falling temperature. I could never ignore an animal's suffering, especially one so dear to me, and I wasn't about to let some silly children's stories frighten me away from safety in that storm.

I sighed, leaned forward to give Nelly's rump a pat, and asked her, "What are a man and his lady supposed to do when hopelessly lost in the most fearsome squall of the season, old girl?"

Her snickering snort told me what I already knew and a couple of tugs on the reins turned us towards the direction indicated by the sign.

ಠ

It was dark as pitch in Arkham, the blackness only minimally pierced by my buggy lanterns and the flickering gas lamps placed at irregular intervals along the crazily winding streets. And it was quiet; not simply the after-dark quiet of a small town, but a nearly *oppressive* lack of sound that forced everything else into submission. The narrow streets were devoid of inhabitants, but even so, the clip-clop of Nelly's iron-shod hooves and the patter of the driving rain were noises barely loud enough to register in my ears. The darkness and the near silence made it seem as if the entire world had been smothered by a huge, sodden blanket. I shivered fiercely and began to wonder if perhaps I'd been wrong to dismiss grandmother's tales. *Something* was surely off about this place. Too late to turn back, though, I decided, and tried to convince myself that cold and weariness were simply gnawing at my rationality.

Nelly and I continued along the streets, past darkened homes and businesses, searching for some shelter from the storm and growing—at least on my part—more hopeless by the moment. There appeared to be no life—not a lit window to be seen nor even a stray dog, as is found in almost every city on Earth—in this creepy old town, and the weather was quickly sapping what life remained within my frame.

It wasn't my first visit to Arkham—an itinerant businessman such as myself cannot afford the leisure of being picky about whose money he takes—but my first past dark. On previous stopovers, I made sure that all transactions occurred in the wholesome light of day and that I was well on my way before noon. The legacy of grandmother's tales was that I've always felt were I somehow caught after sunset in Arkham, I'd live to regret it. Foolishness, of course, but best not to take chances, all the same.

On those other trips, I'd seen Arkham as nothing more than a broken-down old New England town—one without visible industry other than the university, and supported minimally by even that. It had given some credence to my dismissal of an old New Englander's dark fables. Without the warming sunshine to dispel the shadows that lurked at every turn and could seemingly hold just about anything one might imagine, though, I was ready to believe every odd or horrific thing I'd ever heard about this lonesome place and my irrational fear of Arkham grew stronger still.

Working my last shred of optimism, we crossed into an intersection somewhere near what I guessed to be the south side of town and I pulled Nelly to a stop. Down a side street, little more than an alley, I saw a light brighter than any I'd seen since the sun set, beckoning me like a siren does a hapless sailor. I rejoiced for a moment—a glimmer of life, at last!—but paused in consideration. I didn't know this part of town—up to that point, our wanderings in Arkham had been just that and more or less random as I searched the place—and had no idea what to expect. A church, welcoming all and sundry on a dreary night? A den of thieves, waiting in the darkness to cut throats and purses? With the choices limited to investigating, and perhaps finding a spot in which to dry my sodden bones and shelter Nelly, or continuing to wander the rain-drenched night, I did the obvious and climbed off the wagon, unhitched Nelly—for the "street" was far too narrow to continue on otherwise—and headed through the too-close confines leading towards the light.

We emerged into a wider avenue and saw the light was coming from an old colonial house—run-down but still solid-looking—with a wide set of double doors, raised a few steps above the cobbled street, and hung with a pair of large, brightly burning lanterns. A sign, painted in script far too ornate for its purpose, read "Arkham Men's Hostel." I couldn't believe my luck! This place was buried in a section of the city I'd never visited and didn't know existed, and yet every turn we'd made through those darkened streets had somehow lead us exactly there.

We approached quickly—I, for my part, feeling better than I had since we entered town—but halfway to the beckoning shelter, Nelly dug in her heels and tried to turn back. I tugged at her reins, murmured soothing words into her ear, but she wasn't having it. Something had spooked her, but for the life of me I couldn't figure what—we were entirely alone so far as I could tell—and I was growing irritable, so I fell upon the last resort of all males stymied by females.

"Come on now, girl," I whined. "This was *your* idea, comin' into town. I'm sure it ain't half so bad as it looks." She snickered derisively in response and tried once more to turn around, but I gave the reins a harder-than-usual tug and she finally relented, following me slowly and reluctantly onwards.

On arrival, I noted that off to one side of the building was a little canvas-covered alcove with a bench and bulletin board, currently unadorned, and just enough space for my poor, drenched Nelly to turn sideways and stand comfortably out of the rain. I tied her reins to one of the support posts and whispered more words of comfort to her, promising to return as soon as possible. To her inestimable credit, despite whatever had unnerved her before, my gal settled in as well as she could and made the best of things, silently acknowledging my efforts on both our behalves.

Nelly secure, I trudged up the steps into the building, pausing in the doorway to wring out my coat a bit, and approached the small check-in desk, at which dozed a shapeless creature so disheveled and aged that I am still unsure as to its gender. I rang the desk bell, jolting the clerk awake with a start, and inquired about a room for the night. In response, it gave a sort of croaking grunt, pointed at a sign on the counter indicating the cost of a quarter per night, and shoved the guest registry towards me. I suppose I couldn't expect much hospitality for the price and, though a bit insulted, I plunked down my two bits and signed my name, receiving in exchange a key and a candle for my room, set in a little brass holder.

I made my way through a short hallway, off to the left of the reception area, and up a narrow flight of stairs that creaked its protest of my every step, searching for the guest rooms. My key was engraved with the numbers "3-2," which I took to mean the second room of the third floor. At the top of the stairs, I found the room easily enough down a dismal, dusty corridor lit by a single wall sconce midway down the hall.

Lighting my candle from the one in the hall, I entered the room and saw it was as dreary as the rest of the building, and that it showed no signs of having recently hosted any life of a higher order than dust mites. It was good sized, but irregularly shaped, the ceiling sloping downward on both the north and south sides, owing to being directly underneath the roof, I supposed. Its furnishings consisted of an iron bedframe supporting a bare, sagging mattress beneath a single, grimy window. Dust and cobwebs were the main decorations, although I imagined that the peeling, flower-print wallpaper must have been lovely at some point, and I appreciated the unknown decorator's attempt at brightening the place.

The only other object in the room seemed as out of place as myself. On the floor, in the corner opposite the bed, hunched a tiny grotesquerie which I noticed only when it briefly caught the candle's light. A hunk of black stone, a foot or so in height, carved roughly in the outline of a man, and wrapped about the middle with a bit of dark argyle cloth, like might be torn from a piece of clothing. I turned the thing over in my hands, wondering at who would leave such a thing here. Cold fingers ran up my spine as I held it, and I got the strangest feeling that I'd seen it before, though that was clearly impossible. In fact, something about this entire room seemed eerily familiar—something from one of grandmother's tales come to life, a frightful thought I immediately wished I hadn't had. I was glad to be out of the cold and rain, but even so, wondered if perhaps I wouldn't be better off outside with Nelly in that little vestibule. I'd been cold and tired before, and this place seemed less like a better option by the minute.

I rubbed my tired eyes with my free hand, trying to dislodge such thoughts, then stooped to replace the weird little statue, turning it around so that it faced the wall rather than the bed. In so doing, I noticed that it had been placed directly in front of what I guessed to be a rat hole, making for a mighty strange way to plug the gap in the baseboard, rather than just patching it with a bit of spare wood. It was larger than any rat hole I'd seen and, despite my love of animals, I hoped not to meet the beasty that had made it.

One final time, I considered leaving. As I removed my

still-wet clothes, I suddenly realized that I was completely, bone-deep exhausted—perhaps by the atmosphere as much as by my strange evening—and so flopped myself down onto the sad old bed, and fell almost immediately to sleep.

ᛰ

Not long after, however—at least I believe little time had passed—I awoke to a skittering noise as something moved about the wooden floor. *Rat*, I thought, jumping to the logical conclusion. Irritated at the interruption to my sleep, I reached down to the floor, grabbed one of my shoes, and hurled it in the general direction the sound was coming from. My efforts were rewarded with a little shriek—of surprise, more than pain I hoped; I didn't truly want to hurt it—followed by the "thunk" of the shoe hitting the floor and then blessed silence.

I fell asleep again, feeling rather satisfied with myself for having resolved that little dilemma so handily. Perhaps that sin of pride is why I dreamt what I did.

Within my dream, I awoke slowly as if fighting my way through a dark mist that tried to keep me within its embrace. When I finally broke free, I found that the understandable shapes of the things around me and the very walls of that miserable place itself were vanishing— melting away like wax left too close to a flame—to be replaced by lines and angles that approximated the forms of both space and objects. Heart pounding, I leapt to my feet as the bed disappeared, but realized there was nothing to do but watch as, after seconds or hours, those new shapes, too, disappeared to fall away like leaves shed by an oak in autumn, leaving nothing but a return of the deep, impenetrable blackness I'd fought my way to consciousness through. It was reality itself, I knew instinctively—sane, wholesome, known New England—that I'd left behind.

Into this new world came the sound of a voice, jabbering madly in something I hesitate to even call a language, carried to my ears by a sharply cold wind that came up out of nowhere to rip through my body like some black zephyr straight out of an icy hell. I wrapped my arms around myself, for what little good it could do, and fought against the tug that I'd swear was pulling at my very soul.

Distracted by my discomfort, I was surprised to realize how loud that crazily chittering voice had become, and that I was no longer alone. Standing before me at knee height was a sight such as I'd never before seen, whether waking or dreaming. It had the shape and fur of a rat but, monstrously, the tiny, bearded face of a man! Had I seen it running on all four limbs, I would have been hard pressed to tell it from any other rat—save for its immense size—but as it perched on its hindquarters, looking me straight in the eye as might one man to another, the thing had an unmistakably human countenance. Even its paws looked like tiny human hands!

For a moment, neither of us moved—I, frozen in shock and it, studying me keenly, its head tilted and its naked, pink tail twitching like a true animal's. Then I shuddered and began to back away, lifting my own hands up—perhaps to defend myself or perhaps in prayer, I don't know. In response, the sharp-toothed little face let out a high-pitched titter, then split into the cruelest sneer you can imagine. Whether the cackling or the evil grin, something jogged my memory and I realized that I knew this creature—this house—from grandmother's stories. This was Keziah Mason's sorcerous consort and I was in the Witch-House of Arkham itself! Before I knew it, the words escaped in a whisper: "Brown Jenkin."

At the sound of its name, Keziah Mason's devil rat dropped to all fours and lunged at me. I tried to break away, to dodge the attack, but I was not fast enough and its jagged teeth sank into the meat of my thigh. I screamed in pain and thrashed violently, trying to dislodge the beast from my leg, only to open my eyes and find myself back in reality, back in the room, but still engaged in battle with the little brown-furred demon!

Light struggled to find its way through the grime-caked window of the room, and I knew it must be nearly sunrise. Despite the filthy glass, there was just enough light to definitely make out the form atop me as that from my dream. With effort born of fear and pain, I wrenched the creature from my leg, tearing out a chunk of flesh and ripping a scream from my lungs, then rolled over and hurled the wriggling, biting mass across the room, where it struck solidly against the door. In an instant, Brown Jenkin righted himself and, sides heaving, growled something frighteningly similar to words, glaring at me with black, hate-filled eyes.

Ignoring the agony in my leg and the sickly sweet, iron-laced tang of blood in the air, I jumped from the bed and dove in the opposite direction I'd thrown my opponent, grasping desperately for the statue, the best possible weapon in the room. The creature was faster than I, however, and leapt onto my back—heavy enough to knock me to the floor on my belly—scratching and tearing at my flesh with strength those tiny hands shouldn't rightly have possessed. I screamed wordlessly, but the pain couldn't divert me from my goal as my fingers closed around the little sculpture. At its touch, I suddenly knew that it had somehow kept Brown Jenkin at bay and that I'd released this terror upon myself by my ignorance.

I flopped onto my side and rammed my back against the wall, trying to crush my enemy, but the creature was too cagey for that and released his grip just before impact, dancing away with the agility of the animal it pretended to be. I twisted into a half-kneeling position and brandished my makeshift weapon before me, its heft somehow comforting in my hand. For his part, Brown Jenkin squatted a few feet away, head cocked slightly with a look that spoke of surprise. Perhaps he was used to victims who couldn't—or didn't care to—defend themselves in this run-down hole that passed itself off as lodgings, but I was not such a one.

Gritting my teeth, swinging the statue awkwardly before me, I taunted him. "Well, come on then."

The creature's whiskers twitched, his eyes flashed, and his paws worked the air, knotting and unknotting as if they ached to rend and tear me.

"Come on!" I shouted, long past caring if I disturbed anyone else's slumber, and perhaps hopeful someone *would* be awakened and come investigate.

Brown Jenkin hissed through jagged, yellow fangs, making a sound like a flame suddenly drowned, and launched himself into the air directly into the path of my swinging stone cudgel. It was a solid blow, and under the weight of my weapon, I felt a satisfying crunch as something in the little monster broke. It was the creature's turn to howl as he crumpled into a heap on the floor, panting and making disturbingly-human sounds of pain. A part of me winced at the violence I'd done; the greater part of me wasn't as foolish—this was no animal, but hell spawn. I pressed the attack, swinging downward with all the strength I possessed, but narrowly missed as Brown Jenkin twirled away at the last instant, apparently less injured than he wanted me to believe.

Seemingly deciding on the better part of valor, the rat-thing made a run for its hole and I let him go. I was bleeding from a dozen small wounds, as well as the large one on my leg, and more exhausted than when I had fallen asleep the night before. As the long, pink tail disappeared into the wall, I stooped and rammed the head of the statue I held after it.

After that, I grabbed up my clothes—not even bothering to dress in my haste—ran down the stairs and from the building. As I left, I noted the absence of the ancient clerk, and decided they wouldn't care that I'd not bothered to check out as I hopped onto my girl Nelly's back and blazed a short trail back to the wagon, where we hitched up lickety-split—despite the strange looks and jeers from a couple ear-ly-rising passersby—and made like the devil himself was on our tail as we left Arkham behind.

When we were a goodly distance away, heading east on the road towards Essex—through what promised to be a lovely, clear day—and I'd taken the time to bind my wounds and dress in fresh clothing, I got to thinking and it finally, truly settled in that I'd met the realization of one of grandmother's stories. More than that, I felt a sense of shame at having thought my grandmother just a crazy old woman spreading myth and fear. Those stories spanned the length and breadth of my beautiful New England, the only home I'd ever known. Still, if one story was true…

"Nelly girl," I called out, tugging on the reins to bring us to a stop. "Weren't you saying just the other day how you've always wanted to see the wonders of the west? There's surely opportunities out California way for those who aren't afraid to work."

My girl just snorted as I turned us away from the still-rising sun and we headed off to find some place about which I'd heard no tales.

JAMES CALLOWAY is a traveling salesman of fine household goods, last seen in the San Fernando Valley, accompanied by his "best gal," Nelly the horse. Born in Peabody, Massachusetts, in the year 1864, he was raised in the tradition of level-headed, hard-working New Englanders after a fashion older than even his Granny Rebecca. Before his last visit to Arkham, he would have told you there is no such thing as boogiemen or monsters.

BRANDON BARROWS lives in the shadow-haunted hills of Vermont, the last bastion of Lovecraft's New England, with his wife and a pair of elder-spawn cats.

Best known for his detective comic book series *Jack Hammer* (Action Lab Comics), he's also written several graphic novels and, as part of a team, won the Ghastly Award for horror comics.

His prose has appeared in such venues as *Fantasy Scroll*, *Voluted Tales*, and the anthology *Whispers from the Abyss*. Over thirty of his poems have been published, including being chosen featured poet of the February 2014 issue of *Scifaikuest*.

THE PULL OF THE SEA

AN ACCOUNT BY MAY ELSBETH WIND
as provided by Sean Frost

I lived in Jeffrey's Creek all my life, but in death it turned out to have really been Manchester-by-the-Sea. A few years after my burial, the town name officially changed. It had been a formality, really. Everybody had called it Manchester-by-the-Sea since the trains came over a hundred years ago. Sometimes it just takes a while to make the past understand it's done.

My final day as a breathing person had been unpleasantly cold. A wind had come in from the sea, bringing the scent of diesel engines and burned fish filet. The summer residents are little more than tourists, taking over the town and shore for a few months each year before retreating to their real homes and earning the livings that allowed them to return every summer.

It was one of them who killed me. Clouds rode in atop the wind, dark clouds that promised a long and heavy rain. From the headphones that lay beside me, Cyndi Lauper told her daddy dear that she wanted to have fun. The air whipped past so quickly now that I could barely breathe. Coffee cups bounced and skated across the road. Bursts of sirens broke through the wind gusts. Above it all, there was the smell of my blood. I didn't realize what it was at first. I thought it might have been from the minivan, that somehow a piece of it had stuck to my face as it had rolled over my body.

I thought that ghosts were supposed to be angry. I'm not, really. Everyone always said that school was the best part of life, and I really hadn't been enjoying it. The classes hadn't been all that bad, although I'd wished the English teacher had better taste. I'd just never had the unforgettable times promised by the movies. I'd gone to class and come home. There'd been no Judd Nelson to see the real me, no madcap parties that focused my life, and certainly no surprising romantic declarations on my bland sixteen.

All I'd had were books, and they weren't even mine. My mom had earned a BA in English from Misk U. She'd been the first woman in her family to go to college, and she'd leveraged the degree to work in the bank where she'd met my dad. She kept her old books on a shelf in the parlor to let our guests know we were literate. When she'd found out I was reading *Middlemarch*, she'd gotten really excited about explaining it all to me. It was nice to see that she could be so passionate about something, but I really didn't want to think that much about reading. I just wanted to sink into the world that the author created and lose myself in the flow of words.

I liked my mom, and sometimes we'd watch "Masterpiece Theater," which always drove Dad crazy, but I made sure that she never knew when I was reading her books again. I'd read only after school and write the page I was on in a tiny notepad so there wouldn't even be a bookmark. She'd asked hopefully a few times if I was ready to work on another novel together, but I'd told her that school was keeping me too busy. I didn't like lying to her, but it was kinder than telling her she ruined the experience for me.

I missed her, and my dad as well, but I really didn't mind being dead. It wasn't what I'd expected from church. You try to imagine what Heaven will be like, and you try not to think about Hell because surely you're not bad enough to go there. Sure, there are ghosts in books and movies. Restless souls who seek vengeance, or gloppy slimers—it's just for entertainment, not to prepare you for the hereafter.

Yet here I stand, as I have for nearly three decades, on a stretch of Shore Road that overlooks the harbor. I wished at first that I'd died closer to Saddle Rock. I'd always been drawn to the Atlantic. Mom had told me once that the lengthy descriptions in Gothic literature were meant to evoke the sublime, a feeling of awe inspired by the scale or grandeur of the natural wonder. She said that's what she felt at the seaside. I'd felt that she was overthinking it. What I'd loved had been the sense of hidden secrets. The ocean was so vast and constantly moving. There just had to be things we didn't know about lurking in it. My cousin Janet always talked about the wonders awaiting us in space, but there's still so much we haven't learned about our own deep waters.

It wasn't the best view, but at least I could see the ocean and the people in their boats. I had fresh salt air and cool breezes that sometimes became winds that made me pull my baggy white jean jacket tight. My beach bag still held my Walkman (with my summer mix tape and seemingly immortal double As) and my favorite novel, Ann Radcliffe's *The Mysteries of Udolpho*. For a few weeks after my death, people from Jeffrey's Creek left flowers and crosses and teddy bears, which was nice even if I couldn't reach them.

The heavy traffic through the area taught me quickly that people and their things passed right through me. It took longer for me to learn that cars also had no effect. At first it was unnerving to have vehicles move through my body, but eventually I grew so used to it that I'd lie in the road and read as they roared about their business. Even wind and rain swept on without me. Aside from the ground and the temperature, I was seemingly untouchable.

It was a pothole that brought me full understanding of how I now interacted with the world. Shortly after the pavement wore away, I noticed that I felt no dip as I walked over the spot. Curious, I bent down and poked at it. My fingers stopped where the road surface had been. I even felt the rough grain of the pavement as though it was still there. As the weeks passed, I continued to test the hole, and I found that eventually my body's sense of the road matched what I saw. The opposite process occurred when the road was repaired, with my body passing through the new surface for weeks before being stopped by it.

I began to wish the village would move the benches closer to the road so I could sit and watch the sea.

For nearly ten years, I had company. His name was Johnny Nils, and while he wasn't exactly my friend, we got along okay. He'd died about twenty feet away, back in the 1930s. Another road casualty, he'd been hit by an ice truck. He was only a little kid, a 9 year old from Gloucester who had watched the world age around him for decades. Johnny asked me about my Walkman once, and when I'd explained home recording to him, the doubt on his face told me I'd better not mention the Mario brothers.

Whenever we saw each other, we'd talk about the people who went past or just watch the waves crash on the beach. A short stone wall rose to the side of Shore Road, only a few inches high from our side but much taller along the beach. We could see all of the western part of the harbor, which was the nicer side anyway. Most of the seaweed grew to the east, where we stood. There was a small boy over there that I saw so often—and always in the same swimsuit—that I assumed he was like us. We couldn't move more than eight feet from where we'd died, so I couldn't reach him to find out. I passed some time theorizing how we could extend our range to the beach, but Johnny didn't want to talk about that. I dropped the matter and asked him about his favorite candies. We only saw each other a few times a year, so I didn't want to spend the time with him being sullen.

I've never been certain what rules govern our appearance. Mornings and evenings seem to be the most frequent times of day for me, although cloudy afternoons aren't uncommon. Autumn and spring are my seasons, but I've had cold days in summer and warm ones in winter as well. Johnny tended to be around on sunny afternoons, no matter the season. Neither of us came out at night or stayed long after dark.

I asked him about that, suggesting that darkness seemed more natural for us. He looked stricken and, after he'd recovered, he stated that we should be thankful for our good fortune. Reasoning that he was scared of the dark, I indulged him in his favorite distraction.

"I spy, with my little eye, something... orange!"

He was right to be scared of the night, as it happened. The last time I ever saw Johnny Nils he was being dragged over the wall under the cover of a new moon.

ᚱ

We had just seen each other recently, perhaps a month before that horrible night. It had been a rare afternoon for me, sunny but with a salty breeze. From the general quiet and lack of children, I supposed it was a weekday in late September or early October. Johnny had been more anxious than I'd seen him before, turning always to the sea and watching the waves. I rarely saw him in this weather, so I supposed that autumn unnerved him. He certainly preferred having plenty of people in sight.

In the aftermath of what came next, I understood his disquiet. Even with what assistance he'd given me, it had been a miracle that I'd survived; now that I'm alone, I have little hope of escaping his fate. Surely his grim mood came from similar calculations as the signs foretold their coming. Don't ask what they are. I only encountered them once, and they were like nothing I'd seen before. Nor do I know their purpose. They have a language of sorts, I think. At least they produce sounds to which others respond, despite having no visible ears. In this way, they coordinate their attacks. The one thing I know for certain is that they prey on the dead.

That night, I saw them crawl out of the sea. All of us were out, every soul I'd ever seen and a few that I was seeing for the first time. Some stood pensively along the shore. One sat on the lawn of a beachfront home. There were some farther down the road. One watched through a haunted window. There were less than a dozen of us, all told. Before the dawn arrived, we would number only two.

Uneasily, I asked Johnny what was happening. Why had all of us appeared at such a time? He said nothing but peered intently at the surf. Those on the beach began to make the best of it, playing in the sand. They couldn't dig or build castles—none of us could actually move physical matter—but that never discouraged the children from having fun.

Johnny tensed beside me as his searching gaze found its target. I looked where he was facing and tried to see what he'd picked out. Dark waves crept up the shore and withdrew coyly. Sticks and other debris lay along this contested ground, and the water pawed at them like an idle cat. With a start, I realized that one object moved on its own after the water had abandoned it.

It twisted and skated across the wet sand, racing toward the boy who poked ineffectually at a nearby clump of seaweed. I told myself that the creature could not interact with the child. After all, it had been nearly a decade since a living being touched, let alone noticed, me. Yet the thing slid directly toward him, knowing the boy was there. And then it emitted a shrill, trilling cry. He turned now, alerted at last to his attacker.

More of the creatures emerged from the dark waves, slithering toward the baffled youth. Instinct took over as the first one drew near, and the boy scrambled to his feet and backed away from the glissading mob. Against these adversaries though, there was no escape. While he was limited to movement within a few feet of his place of passing, the shrieking eels were seemingly free in their range. And they were so very many.

By the time they had cornered their incredulous victim, they formed a single writhing mass. With no route to escape, he stood help-lessly as they began to wrap him in their ebon coils. At last he bent to pry them loose, but that only brought his arms within range for their assault. The unearthly cries changed now, becoming a gurgling drone. As part of the crowd dragged the struggling boy back to the sea, the remaining cluster broke into fragments to seek further prey.

And still more crawled onto the shore under the blotted moon! An adult on the beach tried to push the creatures back, pulling them from his body and smashing them together. I recognized him as Jesse Heindl, a visitor from Arkham who'd drowned the year before I'd been struck by a car. The local news had talked about him for a full week. Soon it was impossible to determine what parts of Jesse were covered by the throng and which by their inky blood. All along the sand, the shrieks of discovery drowned those of the found, and body upon body was towed into the sea.

I stared in appalled fascination, wanting to help, to run—know-ing that neither was possible. Beside me, Johnny Nils heaved futilely, his stomach offering nothing on which to blame his nausea. He had been my mentor for a decade, and now he was just a scared child. I wanted to find out what was happening, what he knew about it. I wanted reassurance from him and also for him, but I did not know what form it might take.

"How?" I stammered. "They're going out of bounds."

It was a stupid observation, but true. Under the escort of the ser-pentine creatures, our fellows along the shore were passing beyond their normal limits. For years we'd seen them move only within their bounds, confined as were we within the vicinity of death. These barricades did nothing to prevent them from being taken to the sea. One by one, the souls of the sands disappeared beneath the waves, and still more of the things emerged from the water.

Johnny clutched at the air near my left hand. At our closest, we could get no nearer than a couple of feet away from each other. I crouched and pressed my hands against the edge of my confinement. The air pushed back, more strongly the farther I reached. He called my name, and I cried that I was there. In bursts he told me all he knew about the sea slangers. "That's what Hugo called them," he told me. Hugo had been the eldest spirit along this stretch of road when Johnny had died back in the 1930s. He'd been around since the railway came through and had been the unofficial leader of the battles against the creatures until the slangers finally dragged him to the sea in the 1970s.

What Johnny Nils told me was all the more chilling for its brevity. Every generation, the slangers came under the absent moon, and they reaped the spirits of Jeffrey's Creek. None knew what came to pass beneath the waves, but those taken were never seen again. Nor could anyone explain why we all appeared on the night of their coming.

The creatures themselves were hideous. Their dominant form was of a water snake or eel, as I could see for myself from our vantage. They were three feet long on average and bore two arm-like appendages, small but able to scratch and grasp. And their heads…

Our number had decreased in recent years, due to enhanced safety and swift paramedic response. It used to be possible to aid each other in avoiding capture, prying the slangers off of bodies and crushing them against the road. They were not sturdy, merely numerous. I wondered if the things would go so far inland as the hospitals, and what resistance they must face there if they did. But we had died here by the harbor, and it was here that we would face the slangers.

The beach had been emptied of spirits, and from everywhere came the sound of the hunt. The slangers emitted a querulous noise, a bouncing gulp that might be amusing in a cartoon but that honed my fear as I heard it draw nearer. They were on the other side of our wall. I whispered urgently to Johnny. "What can we do? How can we fight them?"

He shook his head, already settled in defeat. "Stay upright as long as you can. Keep stomping. Don't use your hands unless you're killing them." He rattled off the advice as a memorized list, with no interest in what he was saying. Perhaps Hugo had drilled the instructions into him.

I rose as the first sea slanger came over the edge, its hands hoisting it up. "Come on, Johnny! Get up!" I turned to face the slithering things, and now I could see them clearly as they clambered over the wall. They came with their heads slanted downward, with bulbous onyx eyes that almost met at their tops. Their jaws hung open—not slack, but flexing as though anticipating the opportunity to bite. From between their fangs darted pale yellow tongues. These were not forked as a snake's but fleshy and wide. I would soon discover that these appendages were rasps, capable of shredding skin or locking onto scales.

Yet of it all, the hands were the worst. They looked too large for their sinewy limbs. Their arms were no longer than half a foot and thinner than a human finger at their widest. From the end of these delicate stalks sprouted palms the size of a 50-cent piece. Three slender fingers curved upward into savage claws, and gnarled thumbs flanked either side of the wrist. These savage digits allowed the slangers to attach themselves firmly to their victim, piercing through layers of muscle and flesh from multiple directions.

I started to stomp on them as soon as they crossed into my area. The road became slick with their crushed bodies. Singly they were painful nuisances, small monstrosities that were easily slain. Yet in the time one could be killed, at least two more had taken its place. Their "target located" screeches, unnerving at a distance, were deafening up close. I reeled, my sense of balance shaken by the din. My steps killed two, three at a time now, and still they came. Slangers hung from my bare legs, and I kicked at them as best I could. I used my left foot to scrape one off of my right shin. One of its arms separated from its body and dangled from me by a clenched fist.

Johnny Nils struggled a little at first, reflexively. He cried, but if there were words I couldn't make them out over the noise of the slangers. They quickly overcame him and wrapped him within their bodies. Their claws dug into each other when his flesh was unavailable, and their tongues secured them to their living shroud. Unable to assist him, barely able to help myself, I could only gape as they took his face from view. It was an impersonal black mass that writhed back over the wall, taking my friend away toward the sea. One knot of slangers parted from the bulk as though to grab onto the edge, and then they were gone. Johnny Nils had left for the shore.

By that time, I had slangers hanging from my shorts, and they'd covered me from the knees down. It had grown difficult to move my feet. They tightly encircled me, binding torn muscles so they could not flex. Once the slangers had accomplished that, they'd begun lashing my legs together. I'd rapidly been reduced to hopping, a dangerous way to move on the slick and wriggling footing. If I fell, they'd finish wrapping me in moments. I needed to keep moving or I'd be overwhelmed anyway.

I held my hands outstretched, against my every instinct to pull at the creatures attached to my body. Not that I could keep the slangers from taking me for much longer; they'd already begun pulling at my encased legs to topple me. I took measured hops, balancing myself by flailing, crushing a few of my attackers as I went. As they began to reach my stomach and bite through the top of my swimsuit, I subjected them to darting jabs, hoping to pull my fists away before they could be ensnared.

It merely delayed the inevitable. At length they caught my left hand, after which they surged up that side of me. No longer able to keep my balance, the slangers brought me down on top of themselves. My satisfaction at how many my fall had killed was swept away as their fellows rushed forward to envelop me. Now completely engulfed, I felt lurching motion as my body was dragged toward the wall. Their cries, still thundering despite being muffled, now switched to the announcement of victory.

Still I struggled against my fate. I pulled and I twisted, but the slangers held firm. Even in death, their claws and tongues kept their bodies in place. They clung tightly to me and to each other, and I could not dislodge them. I could only barely move, and every time I did another restraint was added. My efforts only served to restrict me further.

I'd lost track of time in the struggle, and the tugging and rolling stretched out considerably, yet it was all too soon that I bumped into something. I froze at first, thinking that I'd reached the wall. One good pull would drop me on the beach, and then I'd be as lost as Johnny Nils. Then I realized that what had hit the small of my back was a pole. It had to be a support for the bench. As the slangers began to pull me around the obstruction, my mind seized on a desperate plan.

I rocked and thrashed until I could twist my body to face the metal pole. My right arm had not been completely bound to my body, although it was wrapped in eely coils. I could move it almost all the way up to the elbow. And I did so now, grasping at the pole. With my hand being encased, it took some flailing about to connect, but at last I felt my wrist bang against the metal. The slangers weren't idle through this. They'd been reaching for my loose hand, and now they finally had it. They lashed my fingers to my forearm, accidentally securing me to the bar. Their grip tightened, and my fingers snapped under the pressure. I screamed into the bodies that covered my mouth.

Having quelled my struggles, the slangers began to pull me toward the wall again. Very quickly my feet started moving further, and my hand spun painfully on the bar. My feet were dragged over the wall and then drawn downward.

They pulled, and my wrist strained against the metal. Ligaments tore, and I feared that my hand would break off. The slangers held it on, keeping me in one piece even as their fellows tried to pull me apart. It was good that they held on for me, as I'd have let go from the agony. Mercifully, I soon lost feeling in the limb. All that remained was the constant pull toward the sea.

How long this continued, I can't say. Aside from the passing of seasons, I'd long since lost the ability to track time. I believe it was my longest period of awareness since dying, but that may be just the effect of feeling so much so intensely. At first I didn't even notice the dizzy sensation coming over me. I'd become lost in the endless pulling. Once I noticed it, I fought hopelessly, struggling as though trying to fight off sleep. I lost, inevitably. As I faded out I hoped to never return again.

There was coldness, but little else. No pain, nor any pressure. I heard the wind. Somewhere a television played too loudly. I opened my eyes to a cloudy sky. The leaves had almost gone. Everything was damp. I rose from the pavement. I'd returned to my place along the road. All trace of the slanger attack was gone, vanished along with my friend Johnny Nils and all the others from the shore. No bodies, no blood, only the chill of early winter.

It's been many years since then. Only one person has died on the shore, a young man who spends his time leering at younger girls. None at all have died on the road. I've seen the evidence of a few accidents, but I suppose they die closer to a hospital now if they pass at all. I've worked on my balance some, trying to improve my odds. It's a foolish waste of time, but I have nothing else to spend it on.

The night has returned, and the moon is absent. I look to the support pole that once saved me, and there's little hope there. A year ago, the old benches were removed to be refurbished. They were reinstalled just last week, but unless objects outside of our range behave differently, it'll be at least another two weeks before I can touch it. The first sea slanger has emerged from the surf, and there is little chance that I will survive. I kick off my sandals, turn on my Walkman, and await their coming. The Go-Go's shout that they have the beat. I plan to keep it with them for as long as I can.

MAY ELSBETH WIND of Jeffrey's Creek died of injuries incurred in a traffic accident on Shore Road, in the village of Jeffrey's Creek, on July 22nd, 1987. A student of Manchester Essex High School, she was just 17 years old. She enjoyed learning and had been planning to attend Miskatonic University in the fall to pursue a degree in Communications. She is survived by her parents, Gabriel Bernard Wind and Elsbeth Anna Wind.

SEAN FROST is a software developer in Michigan, who has always been torn between skepticism of the paranormal and the alluring prospect of haunting people. His writing has appeared in *Mad Scientist Journal* and in the comics "Dope Fiends of the Zombie Cafe" and "Wild Women of the Kitty-Kat Galaxy." Sean lives with four demanding cats and one very understanding wife.

COME DOWN, MA EVENIN' STAR

AN ACCOUNT BY MELISSA LI
as provided by Sanford Allen

Halfway down the *Salamander Drake*'s landing ladder, the reek of Earth air hit me in a way it hadn't in years. The sweet, nauseating odor of something long dead and recently unearthed lurked just below the chemical burn of the smog.

Wincing, I pulled on my respirator mask and gulped in a deep breath. Even recycled air from the ship's storage tanks was a welcome respite.

My fares, however—a dozen artists from the InterLogic orbital—milled at the base of the landing gear, breathing in the putrescence like they were swirling fine wine. Unbelievably, they joked and laughed, pointing at the deserted city looming in the blanket of stinking ochre smog.

A pair of them panned the distant ruin with media recorders. A middle-aged woman broke off from the group to examine the rusted corpse of a passenger car on the roadside.

I touched the com button on my belt. "Clement, are you sure the atmospheric reading's acceptable? It smells like a dead dog's asshole out here, and I don't think any of these rubberneckers are going to use their masks."

"Yes, ma'am. Double checked it at landing," the navigator rang back from the bridge, his voice tinny in my earpiece. "They're safe for the rest of the day, probably even a few. Unless the sensors are falling apart, like everything else on your ship."

Touché. Something broke every time we took the *Drake* out. She needed an overhaul, but shuttling sightseers down from the orbitals wasn't exactly fattening my account.

"You and Singh pool your cash, buy me out," I said. "I'd love to stop worrying about where the money for maintenance and inspections is going to come from." I paused for effect. "Ah, but that would require you to save your money instead of flushing it away in the sensory tanks, wouldn't it?"

I clicked off my com before Clement could mount a comeback, slid the rest of the way down the ladder.

Singh, who'd also wisely pulled on his respirator, cradled a submachine gun and looked over the map he'd pulled up on his mobile pedia. A warm wind skittered a herd of bleached plastic bags across the road.

"Why the hell they want to see this place?" he asked. "There are a shit ton of cities on the East Coast with more impressive ruins."

The remains of Arkham, Massachusetts, looked plenty grim from our landing site. Leaning streetlights canopied the road into town like the protruding ribs of a decaying beast. High, rotten awnings of once-stately homes jutted through the smog like skeletal fingers tearing open a funeral shroud.

Still, Singh was right. It lacked the scale and stately decay of Boston, even Baltimore. When one had a whole dead planet to choose from, Arkham struck me as positively quaint.

"Artists." I shrugged.

One of said artists, Booth—no first name, just Booth— approached, arm around a young woman with a shark fin of orange hair and faintly luminescent tattoos of snakes twining up her pale arms. A pleased grin peeked through Booth's dense blonde beard. The rising wind whipped his shoulder-length hair, streaked gray at the temples.

"What do you think of that view?" Booth asked me. He stood close. His gray eyes reminded me of deep, icy water.

"I've seen more impressive, but it's the one you asked for," I said. "Don't any of you want to use your respirators?"

"And obscure reality?" Booth shook his head like I was the crazy one. "No, we're here to see where humanity came from. Where some of us are destined to end up."

Shark Fin smiled up at Booth and bit her lip. She played with the hem of his two-decades-out-of-date Cossack jacket.

"You'll be accompanying us, Melissa?" Booth must have picked up my first name from the shuttle contract.

"Captain Li would be fine," I said, eager to throttle back the familiarity. "And no, I'm not. Singh takes it from here. Clement and I will be on the ship in radio contact. You've got about six hours before nightfall, so enjoy your time."

Booth, a virtual-installation artist of some renown, had been my contact, paid to reserve the ship. He also clearly led the entourage. On the ride down, the other artists hung on his every pronouncement like he was some kind of religious figure. Reading the group's body language, I sensed Shark Fin wasn't the only one sleeping with him.

Too hairy and a little soft around the middle, Booth wasn't conventionally handsome, but he did possess a rugged charisma. Maybe it was his steely confidence or those gray eyes.

"Pity I couldn't talk you into letting us experience night here," he said. "Darkness is transformative."

"It's also not safe. This city's been crumbling for almost a hundred years. Not the best place to stumble around in after nightfall. Stick with Singh and be back when he says it's time."

My jaw tensed. I'd been over this with him when he chartered the ship, not to mention a couple more times on the 48-hour trip.

"What if I increase the payment?" Booth asked. He reached into his jacket. "Great art requires risk. How much to let us take a little risk?"

I took a deep breath, thinking of the *Drake*'s waiting repairs. Then I pushed them out of my mind. I'd already lost cargo certification. If I let a load of rubberneckers die, I'd lose my shuttle papers too.

"I don't gamble with passengers' lives."

"How much?" Booth asked again.

The woman who'd broken off to examine the rusted car wandered back, now wearing her respirator. Its white rubber straps crisscrossed her close-cropped silver hair. I read irritation on her creasing brow.

"Give her a break, Booth," she said. "Six hours is enough."

Booth let his hand drop. "Alright, Aria, I guess six hours will have to do. Hope that's long enough for us to collect what we came for."

"Plenty," Aria said.

At least someone in Booth's clique had sense.

I nodded to Singh. "Take them into the city, show them whatever sights they're after. See you at seventeen-hundred hours."

"Sure you won't join us, Melissa?" Booth locked eyes with me. The cold water became unfathomably deep.

Shark Fin giggled.

"Sure as I've ever been." I turned and walked to the ladder.

The group's departing footfall sounded behind me, and someone began whistling a slow, longing song. It sounded old, flowing out in a languid pace clearly not of this century.

I looked over my shoulder, watched the group follow the road into town. Booth ambled at its rear, hands behind his back. He continued the ghostly melody, finishing it in a high, raspy voice.

"I recognize ma true love, underneath the tiny orbs of light," he sang as he and the others disappeared behind a dense curtain of smog.

ᛠ

Back on the bridge, I shed the respirator and dropped it next to my station.

Clement lay reclined in his seat, head swallowed by his immersion helmet, a shiny plastic job crafted to look like a beetle head, replete with curving mandibles. The fingers of his mesh action gloves moved as if he was casting some kind of incantation.

I never asked what kind of mock life Clement lived in the tanks—Roman gladiator, high-seas buccaneer, pleasure android—and he never volunteered it. Whatever his escape, he sure couldn't get enough of it. There wasn't much down time on the *Drake*, but what there was, he spent in his helmet, lost in a surrogate world.

I stood over him for a minute then rapped on the plastic enclosure. "Can Clement come out and play?" I asked, hoping I'd spoken loud enough to cut through its internal sound system.

He slid off the helmet, blinking. His hair, charged with static electricity, was a wild thicket.

"You could have used the com," he said.

"I don't have mine turned on." I plopped into my own chair.

"Yeah, noticed that earlier."

I sunk into my chair and put my feet up on the instrument panel. "What do you know about Booth, our fare?"

"I pediaed him," Clement said. "He's pretty well-known for virtual installations. Got pieces in the Thorsten-Gage museum's online collection. I guess that's a pretty big deal."

"Ever check them out?"

"The installations? I dropped into the one linked from his pedia entry. On the ride down, he asked me if I'd visited it."

Booth had done the same to me—a couple times, in fact. It seemed odd that an artist of his stature would care what the crew of a surface shuttle thought of his work.

"So, what'd you make of it?" I asked.

Clement shrugged. "Not much. You just walk around some big stone monoliths. The audio was kind of trippy—super 360—but I kept waiting for something to happen."

"Art, in other words?"

"Art." Clement stood, grabbing his helmet in his still-gloved hands. "Since you've got things covered from here, I'll be in my cabin."

He wasn't asking permission to leave so much as informing me he was off to shirk his duties. I was as bad at managing personnel as I was at keeping a ship maintained.

The door hissed shut behind him.

Leaning over my monitor, I keyed up the ship's pedia and opened Booth's entry.

I skimmed the text, which Clement had synopsized adequately. Booth had done well for himself—accolades and impressive earnings—but he'd walked away from his career around the time he nipped at celebrity status, said he was more interested in exploring spiritual matters. He hadn't shown in five years and instead spent his energy on an artist's collective he founded on the InterLogic orbital.

The last bit explained the entourage I'd ferried to Arkham, even if it didn't explain their destination.

The entry only had a single link to a Booth installation, something called "New Blood." The rest, I guessed, were hidden behind firewalls in corporate collections. I slid my own immersion helmet from its spot beside my monitor and pulled on my gloves.

I wasn't much on virtual reality, but the helmet sometimes came in handy when steering the ship into the snug landings at older orbitals.

Flipping up my palm to activate the rig, I plummeted into Booth's creation. After a few seconds of disorienting weightlessness, I found myself standing in a thick bank of mist. A ghostly light gave it a bluish, almost metallic, cast. I couldn't pinpoint the source.

I played with the hand controls—they seemed standard—and wandered into the fog. Faint sounds teased me from the distance. Water dripped somewhere to my left and a corresponding echo, barely audible, patted deep behind me. It gave the impression I was in an immense cavern. Somewhere much farther ahead, I sensed a faint, almost imperceptible rushing sound, like water through a pipe.

Clement had been right. Booth knew how to design sound.

I ventured further into the fog, trying to hone in on the sound of the rushing water. My eyes adjusted and I made out immense dark rectangles in the mist. One loomed a few feet ahead. I touched its greenish-gray stone surface. It felt smooth and cool, gave enough resistance to my palm that it could have been real.

Looking up, I realized the top of the towering slab disappeared into the mist. I skirted the bottom, feeling my way until, ten or twelve feet later, I found its edge. My mouth grew dry and something prickled along my scalp.

My mind knew I was wandering a virtual world, but my body steeled itself for what waited around the corner. The experience was way more immersive than the ship's landing interface. Booth could design more than sound.

I peered around the edge. More giant smooth stones lay in the distance, like buildings in a jumbled, madly designed city. Some were simple monoliths or pylons, others faceted like cut gems. They all rose high enough to disappear into the blue-tinged fog. I couldn't see a road or path leading through them, and none had doors, windows, or other openings.

A chill spread down my neck and shoulders. I stepped around the slab and moved toward the rest of the stones. A sharp cracking noise sounded directly in front of me. I paused long enough to place the source—an octagonal stone a few yards ahead. At first, the sound reminded me of an eggshell splitting, but as it continued it became wet, more like the tearing of flesh.

Another sound joined it—the frenzied scuttling of a million insect legs. It grew deafening, loud enough I felt it in my teeth. I tried to cover my ears, felt my hands bang against the immersion helmet.

And I fell out of Booth's world.

Pulse surging, I pried off my helmet. I shuddered and rubbed my arms as if trying to brush away scurrying bugs. It took a few seconds of blinking my eyes to register the bridge's banks of monitors and control panels, segue back to reality.

The red com light blinked bright on my monitor. Singh had tried to contact me on the ship's channel. Odd I hadn't heard it over the com. Maybe the immersion had been so deep, I hadn't paid attention.

I peeled off my gloves and called him back.

"Damn, Li, where you been?" he asked when he picked up.

"Away from the controls."

"I was just trying to checking in."

"Everything OK?"

"Guess so," Singh said. "Apparently Booth had some kind of itinerary he didn't tell us about. Seems like he's mapped the place out, knew exactly where he wanted to go. We're in some old mansion. I've just been sitting here the past couple of hours watching him and the rest of the Bizarre Brigade go through someone's library."

A couple of hours? It couldn't have been that long. I'd only spent five, maybe ten, minutes wandering Booth's installation. I looked down at the time in the corner of my monitor and realized Singh was right.

"You there, Li?"

"Yeah," I said, snapping back to the conversation. "A library? They found terminals down there?"

"No. A library, as in books, the old paper kind." Pixels danced across the bridge's view screen as Singh switched on his respirator rig's camera. They gradually coalesced into a grainy image. His time and atmospheric readings crawled across the bottom of the screen.

"Check this out." Singh's hands turned one of the books. Its ancient leather cover cracked and peeled like diseased skin. He flipped it open, showed off its brittle brown pages. He flipped to one with a line drawing of a human nude.

The feed was weak, still cut through with pixelated starbursts. I squinted to make out the details.

The drawing depicted a hairless body split throat to genitals. Singh's finger traced something inside the opened cavity, just below the exposed ribcage. A thick, segmented thing like an enormous centipede filled the space where the gut should be.

The scuttling sound from Booth's installation tickled the base of my skull. My stomach seized.

"Some kind of twentieth century pseudo-science?" Singh asked. He flipped the camera on himself. "There's a ton of these weird books. I guess we're staying put while they look through them."

I frowned, feeling more uneasy about Booth by the second. "Just get them back before nightfall."

I reached down to switch off the feed but stopped myself.

"Singh, did you look at Booth's installation?"

"That thing he kept mentioning on the ship?" Singh asked. "Nah, why?"

"Forget it. See you at seventeen hundred, and be careful."

"Of what?"

"I don't know," I said.

ᚱ

I stayed on the bridge, punching up more atmospheric scans. They showed a higher-than-usual concentration of organic material but nothing toxic over the short term. I couldn't shake the place's odd odor. Awash in decay and pollution, most of Earth reeked, but nothing quite like what I'd smelled outside.

I pulled up the party's location on my monitor. Each respirator was equipped with a positioning chip, and their red dots clustered, unmoving, in central Arkham. Still, I gathered, checking out the library. I didn't get why Booth had paid a small fortune to drag his posse down here to look at disgusting old books.

I told myself it didn't matter.

As long as they were back by nightfall, they could be having an orgy in the ruins for all I cared. My mind flashed on an image of Booth nude, slipping Shark Fin's shirt over her head. His gray eyes were predatory, wolf-like.

I fussed with the computer again, trying to put the image out of my head.

The immersion helmet stashed next to my monitor seemed to stare at me as I worked. For some reason, it seemed enticing in a way it never had before. I knew I should be watching the monitors, but I wanted to drop back into Booth's world, see what had cracked the stone.

Just a short visit. I knew exactly where I wanted to go.

Even if I lost a couple more hours in there, I rationalized, I'd still be out well before nightfall.

I pushed up the volume slider for the com to make sure I wouldn't miss another call from Singh. My super-ego screamed warnings, but they faded as I pulled on the helmet and logged in.

This time, the immersion felt more complete. I sensed odd swirls in the mist, veins of bluish light that seemed to bend through it. The mottled color of the stones had grown more vivid. Their surfaces looked damp and unhealthy. The distant drips and rushing water also sounded more distinct, almost too clear to have been coming from the helmet's cheap speakers.

The air grew chill as I traced my path back to the octagonal stone. It even felt moist in my lungs. I'd never been in the tanks before, but knew the appeal was their full-body experience. I wondered if the realism of Booth's video and audio could cause the body to hallucinate other sensory details.

I found the stone and touched its surface. It felt smooth like the others, but colder, almost icy.

A faint vibration tickled my palm and I heard the same splitting sound as before. The tick of insect legs returned, amplified like a speaker blared inside my cortex. I ground my teeth. The clatter grew louder and more frenzied, became a burst of white noise.

A thin fault appeared in the stone at eye level and I staggered back.

The surface split along a zigzagging fault line. Spiky shards of light leaked from the fracture. They widened into blinding beams that burnished the fog with an even more vivid blue. I squeezed my eyes shut, protecting them against the light. I turned my helmeted head.

After a few seconds, my brain reminded me this was an art installation on a public pedia. It wouldn't burn out my retinas.

I looked back at the opening.

The emanating light burned like a plasma torch, harsh and metallic, making it impossible to tell exactly what I was seeing. Best as I could tell, the stone was simultaneously cracking open and turning inside out, as if two conflicting video images had been layered atop one another.

The angles that opened in front of me shouldn't have existed—at least not at the same time.

The opening vibrated, strobing the escaping light. Beams refracted as if striking hidden mirrors. They formed a crazy lattice around me.

My depth perception disappeared. I felt weightless, as if gravity had shifted and I was about to tumble into the opening. I grabbed the edges of my chair, dug fingers deep into the foam.

And, once again, Booth's world disappeared.

I lay panting. Cold sweat pasted my shirt to my skin.

I slid off the helmet and looked at the time readout on my monitor. Again, two hours had passed. There was no way the immersion had lasted that long.

Was the installation's time slip part of Booth's artistic statement? Some kind of prank? What about the way I'd been abruptly jettisoned twice? Was that a glitch or also part of the intended experience?

As disorienting as the last scene had been, I still fought the urge to put on the helmet, drop back in and look for answers. Another few seconds and I could see what lay beyond the opening.

Suddenly, I understood Clement's addiction to the tanks.

I eyed the helmet, for a second considered pulling it back on. Instead, shoved it back into its place beside my monitor and slipped off my gloves. I couldn't continue losing time in Booth's eerie diversion. I needed to check in with Singh.

I rung his channel, got no response, and attempted it a second time. I gnawed my lip and tried to reassure myself he was probably talking to the group, too busy dealing with something else.

Nothing to worry about.

I pulled up his coordinates on the view screen. The cluster of red dots hadn't moved.

"Singh," I called into the radio. "You reading me?"

A crackle of static followed, then a reply too low to make out.

"Singh?"

"No, this isn't Singh, it's Aria." She spoke in a rushed whisper. "You've got to get out of here. Take off now."

"Where's Singh?" I stood. Tightness spread through my shoulders.

"You can't help him. Just leave. Now. Booth wants you and Clement too." Her voice broke. "The books, they aren't what he said. Captain, you don't know..."

"Where are you? Still in the library?"

"The others, Jesus Christ, the others—"

The signal dropped. Silence filled the bridge and its air became cold and damp.

I rang Clement's com and got no response. Lost, no doubt, in his little play world.

I ran to the ship's equipment locker, pushed through the clutter to the small gray safe that housed the *Drake*'s weapons. It was Singh's domain. I couldn't remember the last time I'd opened the lock.

Hand shaking, I punched the code, cursing when it didn't open. I cycled numbers through my head and frantically punched buttons. I got it right on the third try.

The door clicked and a sliver of harsh silver-blue light crept along its edge. Beams radiated from it, refracting against the roof.

I stumbled backward, covering my face. A loud, mocking clatter followed. I whirled, realizing I'd bumped a grubby plastic tub of tools from its shelf. Wrench sockets splayed across the floor like segments of a chromed centipede.

I kicked them away, cursing.

When I returned my eyes to the safe, its door hung wide open. The interior no longer radiated light. I breathed deep, told myself it never had in the first place. I'd hallucinated it, either because of stress or the lingering effect of Booth's art.

I yanked a pair of auto pistols free from their foam nests, snapped a magazine into each, and ran for Clement's quarters.

I found him lying in his bed, head lost inside his plastic bug helmet. His arms splayed to his sides, gloved hands twitching.

"Take that fucking thing off," I yelled, kicking his boot.

Clement bolted out of bed. The plastic beetle on his head swiveled as he tried to figure out which reality he was in.

♉

I slid down the landing ladder, respirator in place, pistol in hand. My boots struck the hard roadway, mushrooming dust. Clement ambled down like a sloth lowering itself on branches, no apparent sense of urgency.

The temperature outside had plummeted since morning and the smog shrouding Arkham shifted restless around the city. It burned with the angry colors of the late afternoon sun. A separate light, bluish and liquid, also mingled in the haze. I'd seen the air around Earth take on countless ugly hues, but never this one.

The chill air felt slimy on my skin.

Shuddering, I checked the map on my personal pedia. The red lights blazed from the same location they had moments ago on the bridge. If Booth and his merry band of maniacs had overtaken Singh, surely they wouldn't have stayed in the library, waiting for us to come after them with guns.

No, they'd probably dropped their respirators in a pile and moved on. No telling how far they'd disappeared into the city.

"Where do we even start?" I asked myself.

Clement had no answer. He stared at the town's decrepit silhouette, now looking even more skeletal in the bizarre light. His face bore all the emotion of his plastic helmet.

I took a few steps toward Arkham and stopped.

The running water from Booth's installation whispered in time with my racing pulse. I realized for the first time that it didn't flow per se, but *surged*. Pushed along at intervals as if from some great beating heart. It sounded sticky, viscous.

The click of insect legs, the rattle of carapaces sounded around me. The respirator air became thick and swampy. I turned, dizzy, and managed a few unsteady steps back toward the ship before my legs buckled and I fell.

Clement moved into my flickering field of vision.

"You're not ready yet," he said.

I vaguely recall Clement hoisting me over his shoulder. The clank of his boots on the landing ladder punctuated the song he sang as we ascended into the *Drake*.

Search the sky from east to west
She's the brightest and the best
But she's so far above me
I know she cannot love me
Still I love her more than all the rest
Ma evenin' star, I wonder who you are

ᚱ

Unconscious, I dreamt.

In the dream, a light, tender touch brushed my cheek and I opened my eyes. I lay nude, reclined on my back on a slab of greenish gray stone.

Booth, also naked, knelt between my legs. He smiled and pushed them further open. An erection jutted from below his rounded belly. The tip of his cock looked blue and sickly in the pale light.

The skin of his abdomen twitched. Something crawled beneath the surface.

An awful thing lived inside his gut.

ᚱ

I woke up on the bridge, reclined in my chair. My head pounded like I'd been on a weeklong binge and a dull ache crawled my muscles. I tasted chalk and wondered if I'd vomited.

Holding the chair for support, I hoisted myself to my feet. Through the view screen, I realized night had settled. It nearly blotted out Arkham—all but a swath of the city center illuminated by a ghostly silver-blue glow.

Clement was nowhere to be seen. Neither was the pistol.

My immersion helmet and gloves sat neatly arranged in front of my monitor. I wondered if Clement had placed them there.

I licked my lips, felt the itch to pick up the helmet. The installation would help me understand what was happening. I knew I was close to a moment of revelation inside Booth's world. Whatever lay inside that cracked octagonal stone, the thing that radiated from the impossible angle there, would explain it.

One more visit. *One.*

I reached for the helmet with shaking hands. The plastic surface felt cool, smooth, and reassuring. The mist-shrouded world could help me forget my aching head and body, the disappearance of my crewmember.

Singh.

No! I flung the helmet back onto my station. What was I thinking?

Booth had altered me, planted something in my brain. Those visits to his installation weren't getting me closer to some great epiphany. They were eating my psyche, making me forget he'd likely killed Singh and probably had similar plans for Clement and me.

I backed away from the helmet, shaking, and buzzed open the bridge door.

Somewhere else in the ship, Clement sang in the wavering voice I'd heard earlier, the same song about the evening star. It echoed shrill off the metal walls and made my already throbbing head worse.

I followed the sound to the open engine room door. Clement stood inside, back to me, arms swallowed up to the elbows in the drive manifold. Fragments of the propulsion core lay scattered around his feet. The metal pieces dangled stripped wires. A battered blue toolbox yawned up at the ceiling a few feet away.

My stomach dropped. The son of a bitch had all but destroyed the engine, dismantled it so we couldn't take off. With the core gone, all that would work were the taxiing thrusters, and they couldn't get out of orbit. Shit, they couldn't even jet us more than a mile or two from Arkham.

Oblivious to my presence, Clement paused his song, and with

a grunt, wrenched something from the enclosure. He tossed a metal coupling onto the floor with a clank.

I watched the metal ring roll across the deck and bang into the toolbox. Both pistols, I realized, lay inside, perched atop a nest of greasy wrenches.

I slipped into the room and grabbed one of the guns. I kicked the toolbox out of his reach. Its contents scattered and the other pistol spun into the corner.

The metal-on-metal clangor made Clement look up from his work, but he didn't seem especially concerned. He peered over his shoulder, face still impassive.

"Show me your hands," I barked. "Right now."

Clement turned, dropping a miniature plasma cutter to the floor. He raised his hands. I fought the urge to cave in his head with the butt of the pistol. My hand shook.

"Are you insane?" I asked. "We can't take off now. We're stranded."

"I haven't destroyed it." Clement spoke to me like he was explaining himself to a child. "I'm merely preparing this ship for a more important mission. We must ready it for a new power source, one that will take us to beautiful places you can only begin to imagine."

"Right now, you crazy fuck, I can only imagine getting back to the orbital."

"We've been summoned to become part of something far bigger than either of us. Did you log into the installation again? It helped me understand."

What stood in front of me was something that looked like Clement, but the words weren't his. I couldn't even be sure his mouth moved in time with the words. He was an automaton.

"Go back to the bridge, put on the helmet. It takes time, but all will become clear."

An automaton I'd grown tired of listening to.

A dozen people had already died on my watch, one a member of my own crew. Hell, maybe their fate was worse than death. What was a little more blood on my hands?

I squeezed the trigger.

Clement fell against the manifold with a heavy clunk and slid down. The back of his head painted a long red smear down the metal.

The shot's echo vibrated in my ears. It looped on itself, transformed into the frenzied scurry of insect legs. The lingering smoke from the discharge hung blue in the air.

Hands clamped over my ears, I stumbled back to the bridge and closed the door behind me. The glow from the center of Arkham mocked me from the video screen. I shut my eyes, tried to blot it out, but it still beamed through the blackness.

I dropped the pistol next to my monitor and snatched the immersion helmet. I bashed it against the wall until shards of plastic, tangled wire, and shattered circuits rained across the deck. A tiny speaker bounced off my boot.

Arkham disappeared from the view screen, and Booth's face consumed nearly its entire surface. A halo of silver-blue luminescence—identical to the light in his installation, to the one streaming up from city center—shone behind him. The crawl across the bottom told me he was using Singh's camera.

"Poor Clement. You needn't shoot the messenger." Booth flashed a carnivorous smile. Each of his cold gray irises was bigger than my head. "Fortunately for you, that misstep doesn't void our deal."

"Our deal went out the airlock when you killed Singh." I walked to my terminal and tried to turn off the screen. Nothing happened. I saw a deep red gash opened along my palm, no doubt from destroying the helmet. Red droplets wept across my controls.

I tried to press the wound closed. Blood ran warm down my forearms.

"No, Melissa, we're together in this," Booth said. "You, me, all of the others, we have an opportunity to evolve. Achieve an enlightened state, a more unified state."

"Is that what your toxic installation is supposed to be? Enlightenment?"

"No, to put it crudely, it's bait—an enticement, something to show you the possibilities that lay in store. Assuming, of course, you have the right wiring." Booth smiled. "Clement took to it faster than you did. Sadly, you didn't visit it until after we'd landed. You're just beginning to understand, but it's not too late."

"It's eating my goddamned brain, making me see things."

"Join us," Booth said. "I can make the hallucinations go away, give you the new reality the installation only hinted at."

"A new reality? Is that what you gave Singh and Aria?" I pressed my wounded palm against my side, trying to staunch the flow of blood. It drenched my shirt.

"No. They stood in the way of our evolution. Casualties of progress. I assure you, though, their deaths were painless. That's more than I can say for the one you gave Clement."

"He was under your control."

Booth cocked his head, seemed to consider the statement. "No, like the rest of us, he'd simply come to understand there are multiple dimensions ready to open into ours, boundless wisdoms to explore. He was ready to join the collective mind. As many times as you've been back to this dead planet, I thought you would understand."

"All I understand is that you're bug-fuck crazy."

"Earth's current state is the best argument for evolution, why we *must* leave human thinking behind. We warred and polluted this planet out of existence then exported those same tendencies to the orbitals. Arkham's not the end destination, Melissa, but a gateway. In the Twentieth Century, a private collector amassed an astounding book collection down here, tomes once burned for their forbidden knowledge. Only a few pieces were digitized, made it off Earth, but now we have access to the rest. Treatises on pan-dimensional existence, maps to planes beyond your comprehension, instructions for rebuilding this ship so it can jump between them."

"Well, bully for you. Why drag me into your pan-dimensional psycho party?"

"Genetic lottery, Melissa. DNA. Few of us have the capacity to see beyond this reality, to reach the next evolutionary tier. You do. Your crew did. I accessed your medical data to make sure of it. Ever wonder why you're so bad at being a starship captain? Why you can barely keep the *Salamander Drake* running? It's below your aptitude, my friend. You're a visionary, a seeker. The beings that opened my eyes need us to help them pass into this dimension. Together we can create more genetically pure hosts for them. It's what the human body is good for."

"And if I don't want to be a fucking baby factory?"

I eyed the pistol next to my keyboard. I wondered how many of Booth's people I could take out before they overran me.

Booth shrugged. "It would be a shame if you refused, but we'll have your ship to remember you by as we bend space, shift between dimensions, carry our riders to the orbitals."

Booth reached toward the screen. I stumbled backward, half expecting his huge hand to extend into the bridge. He smiled at my reaction and adjusted the camera, then stepped aside, revealing the source of the light.

The door-sized portal on the wall behind him opened along angles that shouldn't occupy the same space. Like the fissure in the installation, it simultaneously opened outward and telescoped inward. It pulsated sickly light. A gray and glistening slick of organic material trailed from it. The discarded respirators lay in a loose pile nearby.

Bile stung my throat. A thousand tiny, carapace-clad legs tickled the inside of my stomach.

Booth adjusted the camera again. He now knelt beside a dark wooden box with a brass funnel extending from it. He slid a shiny black disc the size of a dinner plate onto the box and adjusted a knob. It crackled and hissed, then poured out thin, reedy music.

I recognized the song.

"The others have already stepped through, taken on their riders. It's not painful, not really. More of an orgasmic release."

Darkness swirled at the edges of my vision. The scuttle of tiny legs, the click of mandibles played along with Booth's ancient recording. Then new sounds, *wet* sounds, joined the chorus. The sounds of flesh being consumed, of organs pushed aside.

I focused on the glowing red cluster of signals onscreen—the discarded respirators—and took long deep breaths, hoping to keep the contents of my stomach down. My legs grew weak and distant.

The bridge shifted around me, became slabs of gray-green stone. They dripped moisture. Cobalt-tinged mist billowed across the deck.

Booth looked into the camera. His eyes became hypnotic. "What do you say, Melissa? Are you ready?"

I clung to the edge of my blood-slicked console, barely able to stay upright. Eyes losing focus, I gauged the distance of the clustered red dots on the map.

Best guess, less than a mile away.

Maybe Booth was right: I wasn't much at keeping a starship in business. But I could pilot one—and, when it really mattered, pilot better than most. It would never matter more than right now.

I could think of no greater satisfaction than showing him just how good I was.

"So tell me, ma evenin' star, do you come to us on your own volition?" Booth asked. "Or do we drag you off the ship?"

I flipped the plastic cover off the console's ignition button.

"I'm happy to come to you," I said, firing the taxiing thrusters. Their low rumble vibrated the deck plates. The thrusters could build up plenty of velocity over a mile. I'd just need to bring the *Drake's* nose down at the right time.

Booth cocked his head, trying to place the rumbling. His eyes widened, first with recognition, then with panic. The analog media crackled and I sang along.

She's so far above me
I know she cannot love me.

I jammed down the throttle as far as it could go.

MELISSA LI was pilot and captain of the Salamander Drake, a Rapier-class starship operating from the InterLogic orbital. The orbital lost contact with the *Salamander Drake* on April 23, 2167, and Li is missing, presumed dead. Li previously served as a pilot for the InterLogic trade fleet and as communications officer on a corporate security cruiser. She has no known family on the orbital.

SANFORD ALLEN, at various times, has worked as a newspaper reporter, a college journalism instructor, and a touring musician. He recently released his first novel, *Deadly Passage*, bound back-to-back with Joe McKinney's *Dog Days*, as part of JournalStone Books' DoubleDown series. His short fiction has appeared in magazines and anthologies including *Horror Library Vol. 5*, *Rayguns Over Texas*, and *Innsmouth Magazine*, to name a few. www.sanfordallen.com

ABOUT THE EDITORS

In addition to editing *Mad Scientist Journal*, **JEREMY ZIMMERMAN** is a teller of tales who dislikes cute euphemisms for writing like "teller of tales." His fiction has most recently appeared in *10Flash Quarterly*, *Arcane* and anthologies from Timid Pirate Publishing. His young adult superhero book, *Kensei*, was published in 2012 as part of Cobalt City Rookies. He lives in Seattle with five cats and his lovely wife (and fellow author) Dawn Vogel. You can learn more about him at http://www.bolthy.com/.

DAWN VOGEL has been published as a short fiction author and an editor of both fiction and non-fiction. Her academic background is in history, so it's not surprising that much of her fiction is set in earlier times. By day, she edits reports for historians and archaeologists. In her alleged spare time, she runs a craft business and tries to find time for writing. She lives in Seattle with her awesome husband (and fellow author), Jeremy Zimmerman, and their herd of cats. Visit her website at http://historythatneverwas.com.

ABOUT THE ARTISTS

Information about **SHANNON LEGLER** and her monsters can be found at http://shannonlegler.carbonmade.com/.

KATIE NYBORG's art, plus information regarding hiring her, can be found at http://katiedoesartthings.tumblr.com/.

Made in the USA
Charleston, SC
23 June 2016